PEOPLE
OF ILLUSION

PEOPLE
OF ILLUSION

Geoffrey Holiday

C

CENTURY PUBLISHING
LONDON

1 613463 01

Copyright © Geoffrey Holiday 1985

First published in Great Britain in 1985 by
Century Publishing Co. Ltd,
Portland House, 12–13 Greek Street,
London WIV 5LE

ISBN 0 7126 0853 2

Photoset in Great Britain by
Rowland Phototypesetting Ltd, Bury St Edmunds, Suffolk
and printed by St Edmundsbury Press
Bury St Edmunds, Suffolk
Bound by Butler & Tanner Ltd, Frome, Somerset

The Tuareg people who inhabit the central Sahara believe in evil spirits whom they call, in their own language, Kel es Souf. Anyone encountering one of these beings, they say, cannot help but be affected; either by illness or by going mad. Even though there may be a few Kel es Souf who are harmless, it is only because they cannot do harm and not because they do not wish to.

Since, however, the Kel es Souf are chimeras bent upon mischief to the human race alone, who are encountered through sensual perception and yet who exist perhaps only in the minds of those who can perceive them they are, like human beings, people of illusion.

PART ONE
EMPTY HORIZONS

CHAPTER ONE

It is inevitable, I suppose, that the life of a sergeant in sole command of a radio station in the middle of the Sahara should strike the casual observer as romantic, enviable even. Solitude is increasing in scarcity value. Certainly, travellers passing through his kingdom – those tourists who are no longer content with the glib couriers of a conducted boredom, however expensive their fees – are astonished that man can still live alone with himself. And because it is in the heart of a wilderness they must find him, they have already lost a little of their own contact with the world outside. The edges of comparison have been blunted. The noise and nervous energy of their sprawling cities are remote and the thunder of machinery loses itself in the distance beyond his horizons.

Yet, if they were to remain, these travellers, they would set about refashioning this solitude, making its soil acceptable to the transplantation of their own loneliness. Little by little the world would creep in – for it is only the pioneers who have been able to stand on the verge of their discoveries so blinded by emotion or thought that, not until it is too late, have they seen the men and machines, the disease and misery and hatred already springing up around the statues to be raised by a bewildered posterity. Only the desert, the last refuge of man, remains: vast, inhospitable, magnificent. But already scarred with towns. On maps (which, until recently, showed only clusters of palms, a well) hotels and airfields, even swimming-pools are appearing. The desert will resist and, while it does,

3

there is time left: time to be alone and to own a little of the sky.

On the terrace of a hotel people are sitting in groups round ugly metal tables from which the paint has long ago faded to a drab, dirty pink with the combined action of the sun and alcohol. They loll in the attitude of those who are departing, who have not yet embarked upon any future and for whom the present holds only regret. Yesterday, they still existed – however briefly – in the midst of their adventure: they belonged, perhaps superficially, but always honestly, to the world they are leaving. Yesterday, they strolled down the dusty, tamarind-lined street in the *djellabas* and *serouals* that their short vacation to the Sahara had earned them the right to wear. For one crowded lifetime of a week they had forgotten that in another world they would sit at office desks, at typewriters, in noisy factories, or belong to the secure and familiar existence of an insecure Europe.

Today, the *djellabas* and *serouals* are packed safely away in the suitcases piled in readiness at the entrance to the hotel. The younger people are dressed in jeans and shirts; the older – for age is no barrier to this week of adventure – look awkward and embarrassed in smartly-cut suits and fashionable dresses. A woman fingers a small silver cross she wears at her breast, dangling on a ribbon of black silk. It is the Cross of Agades; symbol of the desert, of the veiled Tuareg, of mystery and adventure. She fingers it and thinks of the strange loneliness of the sand and the barbaric mountains; of the sudden beauty and breathtaking ugliness that is the Sahara. She remembers, perhaps, the Mass held in the long, bare chapel in the *bordj* of Père de Foucauld and the filigree shadows of the trees on the Laperrine memorial as the sun begins its descent and the mountains of the Hoggar change colour and fade towards night. She remembers the *mechoui* of the evening of departure, the taste of roasted sheep served whole and eaten with the fingers; the rough warmth of the rugs spread on the sand where she reclined and believed she

4

belonged. She is sad. But do not pity her and her companions. And above all do not laugh and say scornfully: tourist! You are never really a tourist in the Sahara: at least not in the popular, the contemptuous sense of the word.

A man comes from the bar; huge, weather-beaten, a beret set jauntily on his close-cropped bullet head. He pauses to light a cigarette and then nods briefly to the waiting people. High up and to the north a faint drone of engines is heard. The woman with the cross looks up at the pale, glinting sky. She sighs and gets up. The others also are rising to follow the man in the beret to the ancient bus that waits beyond the mud wall in front of the hotel. Two Arabs bring the suitcases and fling them carelessly into the back, behind the dusty, worn leather seats. The passengers wave to a small group of soldiers who have come out of the bar to break the monotony of standing at the long, drink-wet counter. One of them waves back. Then, with a roar, the bus moves off down the sandy street, past the tiny Arab shops, closed for the siesta; past the dull red mud houses of the poorer quarter and away through the two pillars that mark the entrance to the town. It leaves in its wake a cloud of fine, yellow dust. As the noise of the bus recedes in the distance the drone of the aeroplane reasserts itself, nearer, louder. Then it is overhead. The sun catches its wings and flashes against the silver fuselage as the Dakota banks and turns far out over the mountains, reducing height to come in on its course to the airfield fifteen kilometres north of the town. And again the sound of engines dies away and the afternoon is still and peaceful.

It is quiet with the breathless hush of the hour that follows noon. The tamarind trees give no shade at this hour; the sun is too high. The street is empty. Even the ragged Arab children have disappeared. From the bar a diffused murmur of voices – the soldiers who eat at the hotel – drifts on to the terrace. A lone figure, a man, is seated at one of the grubby pink tables. He has been there all the time, but concealed behind those who were departing and so, for a while, invisible. He is young, neither goodlooking nor ugly: just nondescript. He bends over a map spread out on the table in front of him and pushes his fingers through his thick, rather untidy, hair. He is dressed with similar carelessness in slacks that were once black, a coat-style shirt once white, and broad, desert sandals. He is called Robert Lestrange.

He does not look up as the stillness is again shattered. A dark blue, purposeful-looking truck of the type known as Power-Wagon has stopped in front of the hotel. The driver gets down.

'*Hola*, Robert,' he cries. '*Ça va?* Let us drink an aperitif together.'

Robert at last looks up. He smiles in greeting but shakes his head. The driver, a Spaniard working for one of the mineral research companies, shrugs good-humouredly and goes on into the bar. An hour passes, calm in the heat and the silence. And then the roar of the bus returns. In a moment the terrace swarms with eager, excited people. The silence is loud with the brittle voices of Paris, Marseilles, Algiers. The newcomers stand in twos and threes, questioning, calling to each other; anxiously searching for their luggage. They are smartly dressed and appear a little lost, perhaps a little apprehensive. But the cool foyer of the hotel is reassuring. It will, perhaps, not be so very different after all, the Sahara.

Robert folds up his map. He gets up resignedly and makes for the bar. A girl, young, not beautiful, asks him when she will get her luggage. He smiles apologetically and disappears through the side entrance towards the hum of voices.

The road begins to disappear now beneath drifted expanses of sand. The wheels of a small, cream-coloured saloon spin and then grip as the driver changes down to a low gear. Sand grates against the sump and the underside of the chassis, but the car thrusts its way slowly through and jumps forward, engine racing and heating, as the wheels find a purchase. The countryside is changing too. The savannah becomes sparser, the trees more thorny and stunted. The Fulani herds of long-horned cattle give way to attenuated strings of laden, long-stepping camels. Under the trees near a well they huddle together chewing interminably and belching, oblivious of the little naked boys who cut at their legs with pliant sticks, dodging like flies among them, rounding them up, heading off the rebels and introducing a confusion of noise into the peace of the somnolent afternoon. The ground is white with salt. Vultures, their small ugly heads tucked under ragged wings, sleep patiently perched on the mud ruins of a hut. The car drives on. A white cloud of dust follows it into the distance.

The road begins to descend. It winds between sloping hills of rock. There are no longer any trees. Tufts of coarse grass sprout heroically between cracks in the surface of the stone hills. A cloud of locusts envelops the car. The hard, scaly bodies strike the windscreen and lie stunned on the hot bonnet. The car enters a narrow defile. A boulder, balanced on a high, conical spur of rock appears on the right. The driver shifts into low gear as the road dips suddenly. There in front of him is the desert, flat, barren, silent. It stretches away as though to infinity.

On the rock-strewn plain the car stops. When the driver cuts the ignition silence rushes in through the open windows. For a moment there is absolute stillness. Then, one by one, the front doors creak open and a man and a woman get out. They stand hesitating, their hands still grasping the edges of the doors. They look in awe at the endless desolation around them and then behind to the hills of stone and the curious pinnacle with the boulder balanced on its peak. And further, in their minds, to the known world of Northern Nigeria which they have left. By a common impulse they move round their overloaded car – its roofrack piled high with campbeds and boxes, tyres and saucepans, and the long, narrow board proclaiming in letters of red the devious route by which, one day, they will reach London – to stand in front of it. The woman is perhaps thirty and looks younger. She is not tall, but big-boned; and beautiful with the vital sexuality of a woman who is loved and has not held back. Her husband is tall with long, awkward arms. He stoops slightly. He is older and his face betrays a nature introspective and inclined to moodiness. They lean against the wings of the car and talk in whispers. It is a habit they will never lose when they are alone like this in the desert; as though they are afraid their words will be swallowed up by the listening wilderness and even the meaning stolen from them. They are English. Their name is Johnson – Patricia and Jimmie.

It is possible he has invented these people – Patricia and Jimmie and Robert. And the girl who has lost her suitcase, whom Robert does not yet know. But not the others, not the Tuareg. They at least are real, real as the desert that surrounds his kingdom; more real than the kingdom itself – for that is illusion. And this kingdom and his illusion concerning it of necessity impose a limitation upon him. His world is circumscribed by the vast plains of the *tanezrouft*. All that happens outside it is foreign to him. So that these people, real or imagined, who penetrate into the isolation of his existence must have an external reality at which he can only guess; which precedes his knowledge of them and, finally, transcends it. It is of little importance.

One thing he would make quite clear: it would be wrong to create a legend about him – such as he has seen in the eyes of more than one traveller who has come to share or disrupt his solitude. He is not here to escape the grief of an insupportable world, to forget an impossible love. To the contrary, his presence is determined solely by the exigencies of compulsory military service and by his distaste for soldiering in peace-time France. True, a tendency to romanticise himself may have led him to volunteer for the *Corps Saharien*. But that is as far as it goes. He had already been called up and was in barracks at Algiers when he met Lisette. He was already posted to the southern territories when he knew she was pregnant. And he was already here when he received the first picture of his son and the letter informing him – oh, so casually, so carefully, phrased – that she loved him but refused to be tied; that she had her own life to live and if he cared to contribute to the boy's keep so much the better, but that, in any case, she had a good job as a stenographer and would send him photographs as time and developments merited. In a hastily scrawled postscript she mentioned that she had christened the boy René.

He was both flattered and curious to know whether it had been simply an association of ideas. More out of hope to convince her of his desire for marriage and responsibility than from the dictates of conscience he set aside a portion of his pay to help towards the child's keep and education. But the long, passionate letters he wrote her – the scrupulously remembered details of her exquisite body, of their flights of rapture, their shared, almost obsessive adoration of Rilke and the sonnets of Apollinaire – she never answered. Regularly, twice a year, a photograph arrives accompanied by a terse catalogue of unimportant events of the preceding six months which culminates in a distant, conventional letter-ending of love that means nothing. It tells him the boy is healthy, sturdy and rather plain-looking. He is also, now, seven years old. It is this last fact which seems to him extraordinary, for his military service should have ended five years ago. Yet he is still here. Or rather, he has kept returning; for there have, of course, been periods of leave.

Cut off from the world, he has often wondered what conception the average person forms of life at a lonely outpost of some colonial territory. Does he imagine a solitary white man upholding the flag of European civilisation among teeming hordes of natives – fetish worship, ritual murder and tribal warfare – a picture the popular novelist has turned to good account? For all he knows this may be true of his compatriots serving in the Sudan, in Equatorial Africa or the Cameroun territory. But here he has nothing to uphold except himself and the trans-desert radio link. There are, of course, the caravans of the nomadic Tuareg which cross his horizons at certain times in their cycle of migrations. Their freedom he envies, for he is a prisoner here. From October, when he is delivered by military truck, until May, when he is again collected, it is here that his world begins and ends. He has no transport, not even a camel, and nowhere to escape to.

For seven months his contacts with the world outside are the radio, the irregular appearance of trans-Saharan lorries with their Arab crews plying trade between Zinder, Niamey and Algiers, and a few tourists – British, German, American and French. And the Tuareg.

Yet his world, insignificant in the face of the desolation surrounding it, is beautiful. It is so exclusively his world – his kingdom – that he loves it. It stands midway between two Saharan towns roughly 900 kilometres apart, a pin-point of hope on an otherwise waterless map: the well of In Itaou – of forgetfulness, oblivion. Or so the writings of Père de Foucauld tell us. It is aptly named. There are trees here – casuarinas – and the well of exquisite, clear water around which the fort has been built, for France learned early during the pacification of the Sahara that whoever controls the water wins. Outside the fort the yellow-gold sands and black rock outcrops of the *tanezrouft* reach in every direction to mauve, blurred mountains which rise, not in chains, but barrenly separate against the encircling frame of a pale sky. Against the northern wall sand has drifted during the summers when his world is abandoned to the heat and storms and to the crazy Sudanese guardian who protects the precious well and sets the seal on his insanity with the remaining stock of *vin ordinaire* he has left stacked against the wall in the mess-room, beneath the almost obliterated and scrawled protest of some unknown predecessor. One word remains – *Jamais!* – gouged into the lime-washed mud wall with a sharp tool like the point of a bayonet. No one remembers who carved it, or why.

In a sense, he lives in a palace; for the fort was built to hold a small garrison. He has made his headquarters on one side of the inner courtyard, next to the mess-room. Beyond are the kitchen, a store-room and the radio room with the engine-house where he charges the batteries. Opposite, and running the length of the fort, is a succession of identical bedrooms with identical, army-issue, iron bedsteads painted a hideous red, and an assortment of broken tables and chairs. Naturally, there are no windows on the outer walls, only narrow slits high up near the ceiling; so his world is continually looking in on itself. But where the palm trunks came from that are laid close together to form the ceilings and support the dried mud roof which, being flat, acts also as battlements, he does not know. They must have been transported a good many hundred kilometres from one of the oases to the north. Certainly there is no evidence here of anything other than the casuarinas. And it is these trees which are the true delight of his kingdom. They grow, as one would suppose, near to the well (for the water-table is only a metre or so below the surface of the sand) and several have been imprisoned by the walls of the fort and provide continuous shade during the heat of the day; a shade which serves also to permit a patch of more or less fertile soil to flourish in the sandy floor of the courtyard: enough to support a few green vegetables to vary his diet of canned food and gazelle meat.

It is surprising also how busy his existence keeps him. He has often heard older, more disillusioned men speak of *le cafard* but has never been able to understand it. Yet his duties are not particularly arduous. There is only the radio link at dawn and dusk and occasionally a visit from the officer commanding the territory, or perhaps a patrol passing through. Then a certain amount of spit-and-polish, and observance of military etiquette is necessary. On the other hand, he is continually amazed at his scrupulousness in appearing daily for his solitary duties correctly dressed. At other times a pair of shorts or, in the evenings, shirt and *seroual* suffice. At night he wanders naked out over the cool sands, following his fantastic, moon-cast shadow until he finds himself alone between the immensity of the desert and the heavens without even the puny protection of his kingdom to stand between him and the infinite.

It is here when the moon is setting and the stars reassert themselves he seems closest to Takkest, remembering the warmth of her body against him, the sand cool to the touch the night he lay with her in a sheltered declivity not far from where he stands. He remembers also all that Amaias has told him of the marriage of Tebbilel to Ehem, of the living dunes and the dead, of the beauty of Tehit: Amaias, the leopard, always alone, travelling north to reach Tamanrasset, to become Robert's guide. Perhaps what is to happen has happened already: Time's sunstride travels a cyclical path, guiding the seasons in their migrations.

A sudden breeze ruffles his hair, caresses his skin. He shivers, remembering other caresses. Away across the desert a faint drumming begins. He closes his eyes and sees, further away to the south, a black waste of sand and abrupt mountains, a scattering of tents crouched beneath a sky bleached by afternoon heat. A darker speck moves slowly across the bleak landscape. He follows it with his thoughts, unable to determine whether he is remembering or imagining, but aware suddenly of solitude, of isolation, and opens his eyes again to shatter the vision. When he turns to walk quickly back to the protection of his kingdom the noise of the drumming becomes louder. The breeze has died away . . .

I must leave him now. In future – or the past, if time has any meaning – when his life at In Itaou intrudes, as it is bound to, then someone else can speak for him. It's all here, written down; a few grains of sand in amongst all the rest. Perhaps there will be something for me to add at the very end. I don't know. But now, as he walks away across the night-chilled sand; as an old woman far to the south at Ti-n-Afara raises her eyes to see the vision he has conjured up and the past begins to act out its histories, I shall return to the refuge of my cell until it is time for me to go with Frère Jean-Pierre on a journey to far off Djanet. Perhaps I shall pray. Or try to. Prayer is a habit I have lately acquired, and with difficulty. I know I shall miss the peace of the hermitage, the solitude and splendour of Assekrem. The world of men, the world outside, begins to encroach once more. It frightens me.

CHAPTER TWO

THE OLD woman, Abakout, looked up and saw the small, dark spot moving far away across the black waste of sand. She paused at her task and set the *agiouir*, a leather bottle in which she was churning butter, safely down in the shadow of the tent. The day had begun to die and the shadows slanted across the flat, unbroken surface of the desert. The evening wind was already stirring and the sand, beneath its black, stony crust, was cooling rapidly. Abakout rose and shaded her eyes against the glare from the reddening sun. She watched in silence for a few moments, her bent and withered body inclined in the direction of her gaze. When she was certain her eyes had not deceived her she turned and hobbled slowly towards the centre of the camp. In front of the tent belonging to the chief, the head of her small faction of the Kel Eoui, she stopped.

'*Eo*, Abba ou-Sidi,' she cried. '*Eia ouet egganid*. Come quickly. Someone is approaching.'

She stood, trembling with the excitement of her news and began to call all the camp; men, women and children.

'*Eia ouet agganid. Eia Kmet, tididin. Eo d-i-rer*. Come here everyone. Someone is coming. I tell you, someone comes.'

The children clustered around her, the little ones naked and dusty with pot-bellies and thin buttocks; the older ones reserved, curious, fear and contempt for the old woman mingled on their faces. From the tents the women began to appear, chattering with excitement. And soon the news reached the ears of the men clustered in groups near the camels that something was happening. When Abba ou-Sidi, woken from sleep, pushed aside the flap at the entrance to his tent almost all the camp was congregated around Abakout.

The old chief made a way for himself through the crowd and confronted her. At his appearance a hush fell on the gathering, punctuated by the cries of a baby frightened by the noise and people. Abba ou-Sidi, dignified and erect in spite of his years, looked sternly around him. The old slave-woman went down on her knees.

'Abba ou-Sidi, whom Allah has blessed,' she said, frightened of the attention she commanded, 'it is I, Abakout, your servant. In the shadow of the tent of Keddeka, daughter of Mekiia agg-Ali, I was preparing butter . . .'

'Yes, yes,' interrupted Abba ou-Sidi. 'Speak, woman.'

'. . . and Allah, Who is all powerful, directed my eyes to the distance from whence we are come. At first, my lord – you will know that I am an old woman and my eyes have no longer the keenness of youth – at first I doubted myself. And then . . .'

'What did you see, old woman?' demanded the chief, angry at being roused from his sleep.

'Someone comes,' Abakout said, simply.

Abba ou-Sidi was silent for a moment. Then he turned to a young man standing a little behind him.

'Akmadu,' he commanded, 'prepare your camel and ride out to escort the stranger to me. Women, go to your tents.'

The gathering dispersed as the chief returned to his tent accompanied by Tebbilel, his daughter. The men stood discussing the news and its implications for a short while; then drifted away to await further developments. Abakout found herself alone again, her moment of importance over. Sadly, she went back to the tent of Keddeka and her unfinished task: but she walked strongly and erect. Akmadu, his camel saddled, and armed with lance and *takouba* was already galloping away towards the lone figure riding in at a good pace towards the camp.

Some twenty minutes later Akmadu and the stranger dismounted before the chief's tent. The newcomer appeared to be of middle age, tall – even for a Targui – and powerfully built. His clothes were travel-stained and dusty, as though he had come from a great distance. He saluted Abba ou-Sidi gravely.

'*Salem aleikoum.*'

'The blessing of Allah upon you also,' the chief replied.

'*Ma n eouen n eouen?*' the stranger asked, enquiring after the welfare of his host.

'Well, thanks be to Allah,' the chief answered. He looked keenly at the stranger, trying to place him. '*Ma temousen?*'

'I am Hingou, warrior of the Kel Ahnet. I bring greetings from Ehem oua-n-Agouda who salutes you as his father.'

The chief nodded.

'It is well, Hingou. Tell me, what is your news?'

'My news is good, Abba ou-Sidi. Allah has been merciful to us. Our camels and sheep have multiplied and we have found good pastures. Ehem, too, is wealthy and in good health.'

'It is well,' the old man said again. 'And what does Ehem propose that he should send you away from your people across the desert to my tent?'

Hingou coughed discreetly behind his veil.

'Leave us,' Abba ou-Sidi commanded briefly of Akmadu. 'Now let us sit and discuss this matter,' he said to Hingou when they were alone.

The two men sat down in the sand outside the tent, cross-legged in the Tuareg manner, facing each other. Hingou leaned towards the older man.

'Ehem is rich in camels,' he said.

'Allah be praised,' Abba ou-Sidi murmured. 'He is like a son to me.'

'He desires to marry Tebbilel. I am here to ask on his behalf.'

'It is honourable for you to come seeking Ehem's happiness,' Abba ou-Sidi replied, 'since his parents are dead and no man of God inhabits this accursed wilderness. Soon, if Allah wills, we shall reach the pastures of Ti-n-Afara. But what is it that Ehem proposes?'

15

'He wishes the *taggalt* to be seven camels,' Hingou said casually.

The old man adjusted his veil slightly, so that the bridge of his nose became visible above the dark blue cloth.

'It is a generous dowry,' he agreed, judiciously, after a moment's pause, 'for these times. It is difficult nowadays to find wealth, for the heathen soldiers have eyes like an eagle and seem almost to read our thoughts. But it is not more than I should have wished for Tebbilel,' he added, hastily. 'She will bring much pleasure to Ehem's bed and many sons. And does he propose that the *taggalt* should be given all at once?'

Hingou nodded.

'And the marriage?' the chief continued. 'It should take place when this fast of Ramadan is finished?'

Hingou nodded again.

'Tebbilel is old enough,' he said. 'She is practising the freedom of our customs for she has attended the *ahal*. She is no longer a child.'

'Ei, it is true,' Abba ou-Sidi remarked, sorrowfully. 'She is a woman now. How quickly our children speed us to the grave!'

'Allah be praised,' Hingou said, fervently. 'You are yet in the noonday of life.'

The hour of *aser* passed in magnificent splendour: a red, inflamed sun, softened by the haze of evening, irradiated the last of the day with russets and gold. Even the bleak *tanezrouft* seemed less unfriendly and the little camp drew in upon itself as the light faded from the sky and the first stars pricked holes in the fabric of night.

The men, Hingou amongst them, were seated around a meagre fire, drinking tea and talking. As the night deepened the darker blue of their robes faded until only Ebeggi, wearing a white *gandoura*, remained visible. Silently, the women came and sat behind the men, excited at the news of the impending marriage and by the thought of the *ahal* to be held the next evening in honour of their guest. Tebbilel drew close to

Hingou as though his presence could compensate for Ehem's physical absence. In spite of her approaching marriage she was angry. Why had Ehem not come with Hingou? The customs permitted them to be together during the hours after sunset, even though they might not see each other in the daytime. And it was the hours of darkness that counted. Who would sing in praise of her beauty at the *ahal* now she was to be married? Who would dare make an assignation with her and fulfil the craving of her body which Ehem's proposal had roused? Yet I am still in *asri*, she thought, and free to follow the customs. And the thought was accompanied by a feeling of physical loss. I would have said to him: *Enker, Ehem. Irhal innek, kai enbi i*, Ehem. And he would come to me and take me. In the darkness her breath quickened and her lips parted. Suddenly she was frightened by the flood of desire, no longer directed by her thoughts of Ehem, that spread through her limbs, making her body tingle. She strove within herself to silence her body, to direct her thoughts to the conversation round the fire.

'. . . I had ridden near to the *guelta* Idjef-Mellen,' Ebeggi was boasting, 'for at Hirafok I was seeking Ahar oua-n-Alleli who was in my debt.'

'Can a lion be in the debt of a jackal?' Hingou muttered, contemptuously: for this is the meaning of the names in Tamahak. The thought of Ebeggi, a vassal, seeking recompense from Ahar oua-n-Alleli, a noble, was intolerable.

Ebeggi's eyes glinted in the fire-light, but he ignored the stranger's insult.

'It was the hour of *aser*,' he continued, 'and it is well-known that the *guelta* of Idjef-Mellen is favoured by the Kel es Souf . . .'

'Allah,' muttered several of the men, looking uneasily behind them.

'. . . I was leading my camel to the water,' Ebeggi went on, but he also had looked quickly behind him, 'when I heard, some distance away, feet crunching over the loose stones. I stopped and listened. Distinctly, I could hear the noise of a camel being led towards me. Then there was silence. But my

17

camel could smell the water and cried angrily. And out of the night came the answering cry of another camel. Had I not been wearing the amulet of iron or had failed to consult the stones before setting out I should have been petrified with fear: for I knew I was in the presence of a Kel es Souf. As I stood there a figure appeared out of the half-light, terrible to look upon. It was tall as a mountain and breathing fire, like Amamellen seeking to destroy his nephew Elias.'

Ebeggi paused to let the portent of his words sink home. The women broke out into excited chattering, frightened and enthralled. Tebbilel shivered violently. Ebeggi, proud of the interest he had aroused in himself, watched Hingou from the corner of his eye.

'I have heard tell of this giant of Idjef-Mellen,' Sekefi agg-Ali said. 'But how is it that you escaped? For it is said that to look at him will render a man mad or bring about his death.'

'Yes, tell us the rest of the story, Ebeggi,' several cried. 'Tell us what happened.'

Ebeggi was silent for a moment, prolonging the suspense.

'I do not know what happened,' he said at last. 'My senses were overpowered and when I came to myself it was morning and I was lying in the sand of the Oued Timedouine, my camel standing beside me.'

'Allah,' Sekefi said, wonderingly.

Hingou rose and walked away. Ebeggi was lying to obtain notoriety and Hingou was angry that grown men should listen to nonsense. So he walked away lest he should insult Ebeggi again and abuse Abba ou-Sidi's hospitality.

He strode slowly out into the night. He loved the sense of aloneness the desert held for him, and hated being too long in an encampment where he felt shut in and no longer free. The sky was black against the bright stars and moonless so he did not see the slight figure steal up to him out of the darkness. The touch of a hand on his arm made him start back, afraid.

'It is I, Hingou agg-Ahnet,' a voice said softly at his shoulder. 'Tebbilel. Is there no message for me from Ehem?'

Hingou peered down at the dark figure by his side. He

could see only her outline, slender, insubstantial; and a pale glimmer of teeth as she smiled.

'Are you really Tebbilel?' he asked. 'For you come out of the night like a Kel es Souf.' And he laughed.

'Allah,' Tebbilel said, fearfully. 'Do not speak of such things. Tell me news of Ehem.'

'Ehem is well, *iegoudei Iallah*. As for a message – What message could you have wished for but the one I brought to your father, Abba ou-Sidi?'

'Yet why has Ehem not come himself?' Tebbilel persisted.

'It is right that he has not come,' Hingou said, indifferently. 'But you know well, Tebbilel oult-Abba, that the duty of the *abedreh* should be fulfilled by the parents of Ehem. Since they are dead it fell upon me, his mother's brother, to make the demand of marriage to your father. Ehem is an honourable man and will claim you with the dignity befitting his people. If he had come with me he would appear like a puppy scenting its first bitch.'

Tebbilel spat angrily at the sand.

'Or is he sniffing at Takkest?' she asked, contemptuously. 'At the *ilougan* for the marriage of Koudda he leaned from his camel and snatched the headscarf of Takkest who played the *tindé*. She has breasts like a slave who suckles our children. She is fit only for puppies.'

'The tents of Elralem are pitched beyond the well of In Itaou,' Hingou said, patiently. 'Ehem is at Tounin Akourin. Besides, it is said that Takkest is preparing the *borbor* for the mad heathen who can talk with ghosts from the Hoggar. I have heard them calling him at the hour of *aser*. They do not even speak in his tongue, but with the screech of night-birds. And it is thus that he answers them, not with his mouth, but with a noise he taps out with his hand. He is truly mad.'

But Tebbilel would not be placated.

'Does Ehem choose you for my teacher as well?' she sneered. 'Perhaps he intends you should take his place at the *ahal*? I am still in *asri*, Hingou agg-Ahnet. Until I am married I may live my freedom.'

Hingou felt the girl's presence close to him. He was troubled by her proximity and by the knowledge of her beauty he had not yet seen. He sensed her young body with its passion that was part anger, part frustrated desire; as though the cool night wind touching their clothes was the embodiment of intimate caresses. Anger mounted in him and, because of it, desire also. He remembered asking earlier of the men, when the *ahal* had been discussed, which of the women were practising the freedom of the customs. Sekefi had mentioned several names; but Ebeggi, sniggering, said: Tebbilel. And now it seemed possible. In spite of his words, Hingou wished Ehem had come with him. If Tebbilel chose she could still take advantage of *asri* and none would reproach her. To Hingou the state of *asri* now seemed no less than adultery. During the past months, while Ehem had been away, there would have been other *ahals*: how many men had Tebbilel given herself to? Tomorrow, would she make an assignation and stretch herself out on the sand, feeling the weight of a man's body that was not Ehem's, because Ehem had not come? Who? Sekefi, perhaps? Himself? No, she would want a younger man. He felt her hand, small and warm on his wrist.

'Do not be angry, Hingou,' she said. She was very close and her body rubbed gently against him. 'When I am married I shall make a good wife to Ehem. He has chosen you. Ehem has sent you to me in his place. It is through you that I can feel him close to me.'

The nearness of her intoxicated him, the lilt of her voice made him powerless to resist. Her body drooped against him and he felt her drawing him down on to the cold sand. As he bent beneath her weight a noise behind him startled his throbbing senses, made him straighten up and turn, fear and guilt flashing across his mind. Tebbilel sank to her knees, breathing hard as Hingou leapt away into the darkness. She heard a cry and then the sound of feet running swiftly across the hard sand. Then she was dragged roughly to her feet.

'It was Ebeggi,' Hingou said, furiously. 'Spying on us. That jackal.'

'He is jealous of me,' Tebbilel cried. 'He desires me and I scorn him. He is a coward.'

'He is a jackal,' Hingou raged. 'Treacherous, cowardly, a liar. He will say I have lain with you.'

'But you will lie with me? Won't you, Hingou?'

His anger turned towards her and against himself. Thrusting her from him he strode away towards the camp without a word.

Carol Maillé felt bored. Almost she wished she had gone with the others to Assekrem and Idélès on the five-day conducted tour of the Hoggar. But she had not come to the Sahara as a member of that party. She was here because Paris bored her, because Europe bored her: even her own existence seemed slightly distasteful. On an impulse she had purchased a single air ticket without much thought as to where she was going or what she would do when she got there. A poster in the travel bureau had caught her eye. It depicted a veiled warrior, lance and shield in hand, mounted on a huge white camel against a background of bleak, red mountains, flat-topped and faintly menacing. Splashed across the top of the poster, she read the single word: HOGGAR. The clerk had suggested, of course, that she could, at very little cost make the round trip of a week with a tour of the mountains thrown in. Carol declined. Even at the risk of exchanging her present boredom for another in Africa she firmly demanded a single ticket. The rest could look after itself for, having independent means, she could afford to let it. But now she had arrived and already began to feel bored.

Early in the morning the two four-wheel-drive cars had departed on the first stage of the long climb to the Hermitage of Père de Foucauld at Assekrem in the Atakor-n-Ahaggar. Once again the hotel was empty. There was only the unceasing murmur of voices from the bar to disturb the quiet heat of the day. The prospectors and geologists had all returned to their camps with the commencement of the new week. The vendors of Tuareg daggers and intricate, ornamented padlocks had disappeared with the departure of the tourists. And as the day grew hotter even the murmur of voices ceased in the bar. Complete silence descended on the town.

Carol slept fitfully during the afternoon. At five o'clock she awoke and went into the bathroom. The shower was cool and invigorating. She let the water cascade over her body, turning her face into the spray and soaking her fine golden hair that was cut short with almost masculine severity. Her body appeared immature, almost virginal, with narrow hips and the small, pointed breasts of an adolescent girl. Yet Carol was nearly twenty-three. She accepted her body without giving it much thought and it made few demands on her. Once, she had slept with a man – since it had necessitated the line of least resistance – but the experience had been neither distasteful nor stimulating: it simply had not touched her. It had merely become an extension of her normal state of boredom and, as such, of little interest.

She dried herself with a rough towel and put on shirt and jeans and sandals. Then she went out. She wandered idly towards the Laperrine memorial and stopped for a moment to read the inscriptions on the graves of Père de Foucauld and the Tuareg servants who had been murdered with him. Two officers stood at the entrance to the Annexe, chatting. They took no notice of her. Hands in pockets she strolled round the *bordj* where Père de Foucauld had been killed. A slight breeze had sprung up, increasing her restlessness. She debated with herself for a moment whether to go inside and look at the *bordj*, but a countering inertia held her. She turned and began to wander back towards the hotel. The noise of the evening gun startled her and she stood waiting as the Tricolor was lowered slowly from the flagpole above the Annexe. A distant hum indicated that the town generating plant had been started up and, high above her, the red lights at the top of the latticed-steel wireless masts glowed softly against the deepening sky. The evening was clear and away in the distance she saw the great massif of Hadrien fade in the changing light of approaching dusk. The effect was so startling that, for an instant, she was moved by admiration as the mountains turned from golden-pink to blue, darkening and becoming indistinct and unreal. A deep golden light enveloped her. The shadows tilted and grew and in turn faded as the sun disappeared. A violet twilight, chill and brief, stole across the town. Carol shivered as the night touched her body through the thin shirt. She walked quickly back to the hotel and into the bar.

It was as yet too early for the evening drinkers. Except for Monsieur Jacques, Rabelaisian and jovial behind the counter and the young man who had smiled and gone away without answering her question about her luggage, the bar was empty. She ordered a Cinzano and took it to a table by the door. Robert was standing at the bar, staring into his glass of anis. Monsieur Jacques leaned over the counter.

'*Et alors,*' he said. '*Ça va?*'

Robert shook his head.

'No,' he replied. 'It doesn't.'

Monsieur Jacques clicked his tongue in sympathy and poured another shot of anis into Robert's glass, adding water.

'It's not the actual expedition,' Robert said, gloomily. 'I have enough still for that. It's the fact that I shall have to fly back from Niamey. The museum, of course, didn't take that into account. And now they have cabled me that I must do the best I can on what money I've got. But it's useless.' His voice deepened with disgust. 'Putting aside enough to get me home, anyway as far as Algiers, I can get as far south as In Itaou, but by then the Kel Eoui will have moved to the pastures of Ti-n-Afara. Besides, I want to get right into the Ténéré itself. In Paris they will never understand that it costs money. Why should they? The directors are businessmen with an eye to the balance sheet.'

Robert looked bitterly at his glass before continuing.

'No, *mon ami*, the ribbon of the *Légion d'Honneur* is not earned by sanctioning unprofitable ventures by unknown ethnologists. Oh, they're right in a way, I suppose. But it's so bloody galling.'

'*Eh, bien,*' Monsieur Jacques murmured. '*C'est la vie.*'

Robert shifted the weight of his body on to the other foot.

'*Merde,*' he said. 'Listen. I was talking to my guide today, Amaias. He tells me he has met a member of the Kel Ahnet who is riding south to ask for Abba ou-Sidi's daughter for his nephew. Abba ou-Sidi's a lesser chief among the Kel Eoui –

23

not important. But it's a chance to observe and record the marriage feast of the southern Tuareg. So much has been done here in the Hoggar. The Tuareg of the Hoggar! I want to get away from this conception of the purity of the race. I want to study them where they have been corrupted and changed by rubbing shoulders with the Sudan – where Tuareg and Hausa and Sonrhai have intermingled. Do you realise that Caillé wrote that the Tuareg of Timbuktu have four wives, fattened for beauty like the Efik girls of Nigeria? Equate that with the proverbial monogamy of the Hogg . . . *Pardon, mademoiselle.*'

He broke off and moved aside as Carol brought her empty glass and placed it on the bar for Monsieur Jacques to refill.

'Relax, Robert,' the latter said, his eyes laughing invisibly behind his inevitable dark glasses. 'You should invite mademoiselle here to see the mouflon at the *guelta* Imlaoulaouen. She is bored and you are brooding. It is an excellent combination.'

And he laughed silently as he filled Carol's glass.

People were now drifting into the bar; the military and civil residents of the French community. The schoolmaster nodded to Robert and looked curiously at Carol before launching his evening attack on the state of French politics. The two gendarmes who policed the town, one tall and fat, the other tall and thin, entered. They constituted for themselves a little universe, isolated and entire. Each night at the habitual hour they sat down at the same table, always with identical drinks to those that had preceded them on previous evenings, neither weaker nor stronger – and probably served in the same glasses. Later, the time prescribed by ritual, they would rise simultaneously from their chairs without a word and walk solemnly to the dining-room to their accustomed table and invariable food. Nobody paid them any attention.

'What is a mouflon?' Carol asked without much interest.

'What? Oh . . . It's the barbary sheep,' Robert said. He felt disinclined for bright conversation.

'What is it like?' Carol asked with the insistence of boredom.

24

'Bigger than our sheep, with great, curved horns. It's becoming extinct. The Tuareg hunted them with spears and dogs.'

'And there are some at this . . . what is the name?'

'Guelta Imlaoulaouen. No. It is a joke of Monsieur Jacques. There is an English couple, tourists, who come here. They are quite popular. When they are here they go to the *guelta* to swim – in the nude. Monsieur Jacques calls them the Mouflons.'

'Why?'

'It's a joke, I tell you. You'd better ask Monsieur Jacques.'

'And they are here now?' Carol asked, a hint of curiosity affecting her boredom.

'No. They've gone back to Nigeria.'

'Then why does he say you should take me to see these – these mouflons?'

'It is another of his jokes,' Robert said, wearily. 'He means that I should take you swimming.'

'But I have no costume. I did not think in . . .'

'Exactly,' said Robert.

Carol looked at him dispassionately.

'But I think that would be amusing,' she murmured. 'I have never been swimming in the nude.'

Robert cast a furious eye at Monsieur Jacques, who pretended not to notice.

'The *gueltas* are fifteen kilometres away,' Robert said nastily. 'Unless you've got a car . . .'

'We can go by camel,' Carol said, calmly. 'I have not ridden a camel yet. You will teach me.'

Robert swallowed.

'I can't,' he said. 'I'm leaving tomorrow.'

'That is a lie, because I heard you tell Monsieur Jacques you have no money. I have plenty of money.' Carol smiled, coaxingly. 'And I'm bored. You will take me?'

They set out next morning on two of Robert's camels. Carol looked apprehensively at the tall beast with its hard, uncomfortable-looking Tuareg saddle. Monsieur Jacques stood watching the departure, silently laughing. Eventually, Carol was persuaded to mount. With great glee Monsieur

Jacques smacked the beast's rump and Carol gave a shriek and clung desperately to the cruciform pommel as the camel lurched to its feet.

They left town by the track leading past the meteorological station and for a little way rode parallel to the massif of Hadrien, towering up on their right, away across the Oued Tamanrasset. After a while Carol felt more secure and tucked her feet comfortably behind the camel's neck. At a leisurely pace they passed the Pic Laperrine and began to descend towards the *gueltas*.

'But this is fun!' Carol cried.

Robert smiled and was silent.

Soon they crossed a small, dry *oued* and turned their camels into the mouth of the narrow gorge leading to the *gueltas*. There are five distinct basins of water, mounting to the top of the gorge at Imlaoulaouen and Carol gave a cry of pleasure when she saw the little beach of golden sand and the clear, still water of the first basin like a miniature lido.

'How do I get down?' she cried, impatiently.

Robert made his camel kneel and dismounted. Then he did the same for Carol. She slid out of the saddle and stood rubbing the backs of her thighs.

'You have to get used to it,' Robert grinned at her.

Carol ignored him and ran down to the edge of the water, kicking off her sandals.

'It's so cold,' she cried, withdrawing her foot from the pool. 'It is like ice.'

She stripped off her shirt and stepped out of her jeans and ran naked with little cries into the water. Then, with a splash she struck out strongly with a graceful crawl for the bar of rock that separated the two lowermost basins. Robert stood watching as she turned and swam back. She came running out of the shallows, shivering and holding her breasts. He threw her a towel.

'Rub yourself down,' he said.

With the sun warming her Carol threw down the towel on to the sand.

'Come on,' she cried. 'It's wonderful.' Robert hesitated.

'Come on. What are you waiting for?'

She dashed back into the water. Robert took off his slacks and shirt and stood in his underpants.

'Oh, don't be silly,' Carol called from the pool. 'There's no one to see you.'

A little embarrassed, Robert slipped off his pants and ran into the water.

'Mouflon!' Carol jeered. She swam quickly across the pool and climbed up among the rocks, the sun warm against her body.

'Bring the towels and some cigarettes, Robert,' she called down to him. 'It is good here.'

They spread the towels on the warm, smooth rock and lighted cigarettes. The sun was not yet too hot and they basked in its enveloping warmth, Carol's head pillowed on Robert's chest. Across the water the kneeling camels regarded them superciliously.

'Now I am not bored,' Carol said, sleepily.

Robert put his arm around her and enclosed one of her small, pink nipples between his finger and thumb. Carol twisted away from him.

'That is stupid,' she said, angrily. 'I do not want that. It is tiresome and ridiculous and means nothing.'

The anger died quickly out of her eyes. She knelt over him naked and unembarrassed.

'Robert,' she said. 'I have been thinking. I have money and I am always bored. And you, you cannot do what you want because you do not have enough money. That is stupid also. I will give you the money and you will take me with you. Then I shall not be bored. It is a good idea?'

She sat back on her heels, waiting for his answer.

'It's impossible,' Robert said.

'Why, impossible?'

'Well, your parents for one thing. What would they say?'

'I have no parents. Only money.'

Robert raised himself on one arm and looked at her. She was not beautiful, but her body was slender and straight. He felt indifference towards her, if anything. The caress he had bestowed had merely been a passing whim: her apparent lack of modesty had startled him and he had assumed she wanted him to make love to her. But evidently, she considered that it was no more extraordinary to ask a man whom she had met scarcely twenty-four hours ago to take her alone into the remote regions of the desert than it had been to take off her clothes before asking. Besides offering him money.

'Do you realise quite what you're suggesting?' he asked. 'My intention is to travel by camel and on foot for over a thousand kilometres in country where every drop of water needed has to be carried. It means going day after day, in intense heat, and never being free of thirst. It means living off what food can be carried also – unless one is lucky enough to kill a gazelle or adax. Mostly, the diet is rice and noodles and dates. There'll be no water for washing. You live and sleep in the clothes you wear. There will be no such thing as privacy. Have you thought of that? You will have to sleep with me in the tent and perform your bodily functions in the open. And there will be the monotony – such as you've never experienced. You talk of boredom! This will not be a picnic like swimming naked in a *guelta*.'

'I realise all that,' Carol said, simply. 'I realise that I shall be in the way and, perhaps, a nuisance at first. I am not afraid of the discomfort. But I believe, if you will take me with you, you won't regret it.'

'It's impossible.'

'It's not impossible, Robert. You need money. Unless you have money you cannot go where you want. I'm offering you that chance. But on condition, Robert, I will not be touched. Never, never! I need you, Robert, because I am bored. And you need me because I have money. But we do not need each other. Is it a bargain?'

Robert studied her imploring, determined face. Her slim almost boyish nakedness was the nakedness of innocence. She did not really understand. But the money was tempting, so opportune. He felt a sudden misgiving for what he knew he was going to do.

'I don't know,' he said – and knew it for a lie.

CHAPTER THREE

THE OLD commandant was holding out a tall, square bottle. Behind him the setting sun toned the ancient red mud walls to a deep russet. It blazed suddenly against the bottle in his hand and just as suddenly died away. From the foot of the minaret across the town came the savage chanting of a crazy Tuareg woman, hymning the approach of night like a dog crying to the moon. Darkness followed almost immediately. It brought with it, etched in sudden silences, the infinite murmuring of the Sahara night. A cry broke the stillness; meaningless, unimportant. And the vague throbbing of drums began to feel the pulse of the dying day. Nearer at hand the thin melody of an *imzhad* suddenly broke off while the unseen player moistened with her tongue the bowstring made from her long, black hair. Almost at once it began again; louder, more resonant: seeking, perhaps, to draw from the presence of night some echo of the harsh beauty of a love song it could accompany.

In the tiny courtyard of the old commandant's house they sat, waiting for the last heat of the day to evaporate, to temper the cold which presently would steal out of the increasing night. Around them there was sadness and peace; and, over everything, the incredible stars. Soon above their heads, half concealed in Orion's Belt, would appear the Cross of Agades by which the Tuareg navigate the sea of sand. On just such a night a hundred years ago, perhaps, the great explorer Heinrich Barth had looked westward across the desert towards

Timbuktu, his thoughts full of René Caillé's epic journey and of his own still to be undertaken.

As though divining and approving their mood the old commandant smiled, his heavy Breton's features illumined by the laughter in his eyes.

'Come,' he said, 'we will drink. We will drink to the great desert, to "*la vie saharienne*". And –' he arched his great, bushy brows and, half rising, bowed towards Patricia – 'to the beautiful women who come to disturb our solitude.'

He was a tall man and powerfully built – in spite of his seventy years. He looked exactly what he was: a dedicated soldier and coloniser who, after forty-five years in the Sahara, living among and loving her nomadic tribes, would never desert the enduring passion of his life. Although it was many years since he had retired he was known everywhere still as '*Monsieur le Commandant*'. '*Bonjour, mon commandant*,' the young soldiers would say respectfully when he appeared on rare occasions at the bar of the hotel. '*Bonjour, mon commandant*.' And politicians and heads of important missions visiting the town never failed to accord their first courtesies to the old veteran. And this was as it should be – for he had administered the territory for nearly thirty years with the reputation of a just and wise man. There was something of the patriarch about him, in spite of his clean-shaven features, and the years of solitude and the beautiful Tuareg girls had bequeathed him countless blue-eyed, fair-skinned children – or so it was rumoured.

'So,' he said, as he tasted the cool, milky anis, 'you will leave tomorrow for Tamanrasset? And then you will go to Spain?'

'Yes,' Jimmie replied. 'But we want to stay in Tamanrasset for a while and go up into the mountains, to Assekrem. To the hermitage of Père de Foucauld.'

'Ah, I envy you. I never knew le Père. He was a good man, a great man. He was killed soon after I came to the desert. It is beautiful, the Hoggar. What mountains! Before the sunset, the colours, the transformations – *incroyable*! You paint, perhaps, madame?' he asked, turning towards Patricia.

'Why, no? What made you think of it?'

'Oh, for no reason,' he replied, but he chuckled at some memory.

'It is a pity you are not coming back here,' he said, a moment later. 'It is difficult, you know, to buy anis here nowadays. In Tamanrasset there is plenty.'

He sighed and chuckled again.

'Your pardon, madame,' he said to Patricia, 'but you must forgive the memories and deceits of an old man. When I asked you if you paint it is because I am reminded of something that happened a long time ago. Wait.'

He rose and disappeared into the house, his broad desert sandals flapping against the dry mud floors. A moment later he returned, carrying an oil lamp and in his other hand a crudely framed picture.

'*Voilà,*' he said and handed it to Jimmie, holding up the lamp so that the light fell on to the canvas.

The portrait was a remarkable likeness, even though it must have been painted when he was in his forties. He appeared as a mature and just man, the dignity of his bearing softened and yet enhanced by the suggestion of romance inseparable from a uniform: the white tunic with the insignia of the desert, the Cross of Agades, at his breast, the black *seroual* richly embroidered with silver motifs down each leg to where the material was gathered tightly at the ankles; the trim, blue kepi that is the colour of pale sky set jauntily on his head. As now he wore the same broad Tuareg sandals.

Patricia and Jimmie gazed at the portrait, lost in admiration.

'Ah, yes,' the old man murmured, 'I was younger then.'

'Who painted it?' Patricia asked. 'Was it done here?'

'But certainly it was painted here,' he cried. 'It is now thirty years since I am in France. Who painted it? An Englishwoman, madame – but that is, perhaps, a story which will not interest you.'

Patricia flashed him an indignant look.

'You'll have to tell us now that you've aroused our curiosity,' Jimmie said, mildly.

The old commandant turned his deep-set eyes, serious now,

on the younger man and looked at him intently, as though trying to place him in some relationship to his memories. Then he shrugged and looked away.

The night breeze rose suddenly and a gust of wind caught the lamp. The flame burned up brightly, throwing their faces sharply into relief, then flickered and went out. The darkness wrapped itself gently round them, relaxing and satisfying.

'Before the war,' the old commandant began, 'before the desert attracted the number of tourists who try to cross it nowadays, a few people used to come through here – mostly French officials from the Tchad going on leave, but some missionaries also. In those days there was a bus which ran from Fort Lamy to Kano and another one north to Ghardaia. Very rarely was the crossing attempted in automobiles. Then one year two English – a man and his wife – arrived from Kano and reported to the Bureau. I was away at the time with a detachment of *meharists* on a visit to the Amenokal – the Tuareg king – who was camped near the old town of Audoghast. Since they wished to cross the desert they were told they must await my return. In consequence, three days later, the Englishman presented himself at my office with his papers. They were in order, the automobile was in good condition and equipped to carry enough water and petrol and the many other things which you know are necessary for the sand. Also, they had a letter of introduction to the Chef d'Annexe at Tamanrasset from a high official in Paris. What could I do? I did not like the idea of tourists in the desert. I could perhaps only persuade them to travel in convoy with a military lorry.

'They had taken a room at the hotel and were in no hurry. The month was January, there was still much *harmattan* in the air and they wished to wait for the brilliantly clear days when the haze should lift. There was plenty of time for them to reach Algiers before the sandstorms and the heat of summer commenced.

'One evening I was sitting at the hotel bar taking an aperitif. The Englishman and his wife were at a table in the corner – in fact the same place you were sitting at when we met the other night – and I noticed she was drawing on a small

32

sketching-block. She was very beautiful – petite and fair – and the focus of interested eyes of the soldiers at the bar. Eh, well – and of mine also!'

He broke off, chuckling and reached across the table to refill their glasses. The night was cooling rapidly and the pulse of the distant drums had quickened. Jimmie offered cigarettes and the sudden flame of a match momentarily extinguished the darkness.

'As I gazed at her, trying to see what she was drawing,' the old man continued, 'she looked up and said something to her husband. His eyes met mine and I bowed as though it were an accident I should be looking in their direction. Almost immediately he rose to his feet and came over to me. This monsieur was not looking too amiable but as he greeted me he contrived a smile.

'"*Bonsoir, Monsieur le Commandant,*" he said. "My wife wishes that you should join us."

'Aha, I said to myself, as I followed him over to their table, madame chooses to be imperious as well as beautiful. But this is, perhaps, interesting.

'"*Enchanté,* madame," I said as I seated myself next to her. She gave me a charming smile, but I noticed that the drawing had been quickly put away. It was in her lap, half concealed under the table.

'"You are an artist?" – indicating the sketching-block. She blushed charmingly.

'"Oh, it's nothing much. An amusement. I paint a little, yes."

'"An amusement that has found its way into several exhibitions, monsieur," her husband said, overhearing the last remark as he came up with the drinks.

'"So," I said. "You permit me, madame?" And before she could object I had taken the sketching-block from her lap. It was, perhaps, impertinent of me, but my impertinence was well rewarded a moment later when I found myself staring at my own face.

'"That's what comes of drawing people without their per-mission," her husband said, angrily. "Please excuse her, monsieur. It is a failing of hers."

'I looked at him over the top of the sketch. He seemed a pleasant enough young man, but a little stupid. Certainly I was not angry. I was flattered and said so.

'"You honour me, madame" – and my smile was meant for her alone – "but I do not think your subject does justice to your art."

'She considered me seriously for a moment.

'"No," she said, "I don't agree. Your features are extremely interesting. Even in repose they reveal something of the endurance and strength which you must need to live the life of the desert. I would like to do a portrait of you. Yes, a portrait of you in uniform."

'If I had been twenty years younger I might have blushed. Certainly, I wished monsieur a hundred kilometres away; though, to my immediate relief, he changed the subject.

'"How much longer do you think the harmattan will last?" he asked, rather curtly.

'I shrugged. My thoughts were still on his wife.

'"Perhaps two days, perhaps a week. One morning you will wake up and it is gone. Then you will see the desert in all its beauty."

'"Do you ever think of the Sahara as a woman?" she asked. Again those beautiful eyes were fixed intently on me.

'"The Sahara would make a dangerous mistress," I said, gruffly.

'"I think we should plan to leave in a week's time," the Englishman said. "We can allow three days to reach In Itaou and still be at Tamanrasset before February."

'"*Insh'Allah,*" I murmured.

'"What does that mean?" she asked.

'"It means if God wills," I replied. "And, frankly, madame, I shall be happier if you are travelling in convoy. There is a military lorry leaving in two weeks. Wait and go with it."

'"We appreciate your concern," the Englishman said, "but we are well equipped and we've paid the deposit should we have to be rescued. Besides . . ."

'"Besides," his wife cut in, "I want to know what it's like

34

to be alone in the desert, to be dependent only on ourselves."

'They were right in their way and I had no reason to forbid them to go alone. But it was getting late and I rose to leave. As we shook hands the girl said:

'"I will call tomorrow at your office, if I may?"

'I bowed and wished her goodnight. She was so very beautiful.'

He sighed and refilled the glasses. The moon had risen and the courtyard was full of pale light.

'Next morning,' he resumed, 'I was at my desk busy with the results of the annual census that had just been completed when Mousa, my orderly, announced that she wished to see me. She was just as beautiful in the daytime but I was busy and perhaps a little brusque as I drew up a chair for her.

'"And now, madame," I said, reseating myself behind the littered desk, "what may I do for you?"

'"Your portrait," she said, looking up at me. "When may I begin?"

'Was I entirely taken aback? Perhaps not, though I had not taken her seriously the previous evening. At first I refused, but in the end I gave in – not unwillingly. It would be amusing and I would have been stupid to deny myself the pleasure of her company. And, as it happened, her husband refused to sit quietly while she was painting. In the end it was arranged he would drive her to my house and return later when the sitting was over.

'She worked fast and talked little, eager to have the portrait finished before her departure. Each day she took the canvas away with her and refused to let me look at it until it should be completed. But it was still unfinished on her last evening. And she had seemed depressed and somehow disappointed at the previous sitting. As I heard them drive up on this last evening I went out to meet them and was surprised to see she was alone. She looked pale and nervous.

'"Tonight we have to finish it," she said. "My husband isn't coming. I told him we should be late. He is checking the stores. We leave before dawn."

'I carried her brushes and paints into the house.

' "You don't mind do you?" she asked as I led the way into the living-room.

'No, I didn't mind that she would be alone with me that evening. But the thought that tomorrow she would be gone was a different matter. I didn't dare speak. She worked silently for a while. At nine o'clock I told my servant to bring sandwiches and wine. Immediately we had finished eating she set to work again. But suddenly she seemed to relax. Smiling at me over the top of the canvas she at last broke the silence.

' "Are the Tuareg women very beautiful?" she asked.

' "I believe so," I replied, guardedly. "Why?"

' "Because I believe that, in spite of all the years you have lived out here, you are still human."

'I shrugged.

' "What do you expect?"

'She laughed, mockingly.

' "That you have children."

' "It is possible, but . . ."

' "It is possible," she mimicked. "Or – probable?"

'Suddenly angry, I shouted:

' "And if I have? What concern is it of yours?"

'But, stepping back from the canvas, she cried:

' "There! It's finished." And, turning towards me, she repeated: "It's finished. Come and see."

'She held out her hand to me and I went over and took it. She was trembling slightly. Side by side we gazed at the finished portrait. I recognised myself as I had so often seen myself in imagination or vanity. I don't know which. She was very proud of it.

' "Now," she said. "I feel I know something about you."

'I stood for a while, still gazing at the painting. At last I looked at her.

' "Do you?" I said.

'She didn't answer, suddenly withdrawn. I drew her to me and kissed her. Then there was nothing more to say.

'It was late, very late when she returned to the hotel. The next morning she was gone.'

Lost in his thoughts, the old commandant paused. Jimmie

glanced sideways at his wife. Her face showed up pale in the moonlight. A deep silence enveloped them. The old man stirred uneasily.

'They had given themselves three days to reach In Itaou,' he continued. 'It was reasonable. But I couldn't help thinking of the great basins of sand they would have to cross beyond Ti-n-Afara. Here the sand is treacherous and beneath the thin, black crust it is fine and powdery. It is easy to become stuck where the sand is black but, with an automobile such as theirs, it is difficult to get free. I consoled myself with the thought that, if they did not arrive after four days I should be informed by the radio at In Itaou. A few days out in the desert, it does not matter: my soldiers would find them easily if they kept to the marked route. But I was uneasy. In the evening, in my house, I could not forget her. In the living-room the portrait was leaning against the wall. As I looked at it again I realised she had given me to myself as she saw me. But I wanted her.

'And then, on the fifth morning, the radio message came.

'My servant woke me. It was just before daybreak. I struggled into my clothes and drove quickly to the Bureau de Cercle. Within an hour two military lorries left the town, manned by Sudanese soldiers with a French sergeant and corporal in command. They had orders to search along the route and to report by radio from In Itaou. I could do nothing but wait. It is nearly five hundred kilometres to In Itaou. With luck the heavy lorries could be there the same night. But if they found nothing they would have to return the next day to refuel. If they found nothing! Then it would mean a real search to find where they had left the marked route. They could be only a few hundred metres away, hidden behind sand-dunes, within a stone's throw of help and yet not be found until it was too late.

'All these fears were unreasonable. I knew the desert. I knew that if they did not lose their heads and abandon their automobile they would be found. But I knew also the unreasoning panic of being trapped in the sand; the fear of thirst, the helplessness. It is frightening to be out there day after day. Each morning the sun rises, the heat becomes unendurable, the very shelter the automobile gives from the sun a furnace. Each evening the sun sets, but the deceptive coolness of the night is only a short respite from the torture of the day to come. There is nothing else. And when the terrible, retching thirst begins the mirages beckon. The only reality is in the slow wings of the vultures, circling, waiting, which come out of nowhere . . . At dusk the same night the message came from In Itaou that they had not been found. I knew then I was afraid. They were now three days overdue: six days all told in the desert. And they had water for seven, perhaps eight days.

'I gave orders that two more lorries would set out at three o'clock next morning. I was going with them. With an early start we could be at Ti-n-Afara by sunrise. Nothing could be done except get some rest for the gruelling day ahead. The route as far as Ti-n-Afara is well defined. It is afterwards the real desert begins: empty horizons, burning, waterless sands. But if the route to Ti-n-Afara is well defined it is also slow, especially driving in the dark. The sky was already bright when we drew up beside the well. Tracks in the sand showed a herd of camels had been watered during the night. But the Tuareg had moved on and passed us, unseen in the silence. If, as I thought, they were of the Kel Rela tribe, coming from Tamanrasset, they might possibly have seen the English.

'As soon as the radiators had been checked and the tyres deflated to give a better grip in the sand we set off. As the day grew hot the sand became softer. Twice the great lorries almost stuck. Then one of the soldiers in the back shouted to attract my attention. But I had seen it too: the unmistakable tracks of their tyres. Relief surged through me, tempered by the knowledge we had still to find them. It was almost midday. For three hours we had been keeping the precious marks in sight: sometimes losing them momentarily over rocky terrain, or where the wind had swept clean the drifts of sand which pile up amongst the scant desert vegetation. The wind following us was hot and dry. As the noon temperature rose it became necessary, more and more often, to stop and turn the bonnets into the wind to cool the over-heated engines. Suddenly, the tracks disappeared. We doubled back and picked them up again between two dunes. Tired and angry I cursed the stupidity of the English in general and tourists in particular. We were now right off the route and travelling almost due west. And then the tracks disappeared completely.

'Before I could prevent him the driver brought the lorry to a standstill. Behind us, the other had to stop also. We were negotiating a narrow passage between the dunes. There was no room to pass. My driver let out the clutch but the back wheels spun and sank deep into the sand. Cursing volubly I jumped out. As the soldiers took down the sand ladders to place under the wheels I climbed to the top of the nearest dune. There was nothing to be seen: only the pale, irregular mountains of sand stretching away until they became lost in the haze and glare. I was about to descend when a shout came from my sergeant, standing on top of a dune some little distance away.

'"*Le voilà, mon commandant,*" he cried, gesticulating wildly. "Over there."

'But already he was running, stumbling in the deep sand. Suddenly, my fear evaporated: I knew they were safe. Then I saw him. The sergeant had reached him now and he was shaking him by the hand, dragging a water-bottle from his belt. Breathless, I came up to them.

'"Where's your wife?" I cried, grabbing him by the shoulder. "What has happened?"

'He was taken aback at my agitation and for the first time seemed surprised to see me and the soldiers.

'"She's there," he said, pointing back over his shoulder. "But there's no cause for alarm."

'I let go of his shoulder and ran in the direction he had indicated. Beyond the dune I came suddenly upon firm ground. And then I saw her. Near the automobile an awning had been slung between four poles and she was seated under its shadow, her easel in front of her, painting. Painting, I tell you!

'She turned at my approach and waved her brush.

'"Isn't it beautiful," she cried.'

The old commandant choked as he swallowed a mouthful of anis. When the laughter had subsided he said, reproachfully:

'Well, what would you? I ask you, what would you?'

It was Patricia who recovered first.

'And did you ever see her again?' she asked, gently.

He was silent for a while. At last:

'No,' he said. 'But she wrote to me. It must have been more than a year later.' He turned to Jimmie. 'Light the lamp,' he said.

Jimmie did so and the old man reached into the pocket of his *seroual* and brought out a faded and crumpled photograph, handing it to Patricia.

'I suppose he would be younger than you,' he said to Jimmie, 'but I always hoped he would come here one day.'

He seemed overcome with emotion and looked at Jimmie with the same intense longing in his eyes as before. Suddenly, they understood why he had stopped to speak to them in the bar of the hotel and why he had asked them round to his house.

'In England,' Jimmie said, softly, 'Johnson is almost as common a name as Smith. I'm sorry.'

The old man sighed deeply and his head sank forward on to his chest. Patricia nudged Jimmie and he rose to his feet.

'It's late,' Patricia said, 'and you must be tired.'

He looked up at them and smiled.

'It's a pity you're not coming back,' he said. 'It's difficult, you know, to get anis here nowadays.'

With whispered goodnights Patricia and Jimmie stole quietly away. At the door of the courtyard they turned. He was still sitting there, sunk in thought, the light from the lamp falling evenly on to his face and on to the portrait propped up on the chair beside him. As they hesitated his lips moved.

'*Je t'aime,*' he whispered.

They closed the door softly and the dark street enfolded them silent, inscrutable. A white figure stirred in the entrance to an alley opposite. Somewhere, a dog barked in its sleep. Patricia and Jimmie felt chilled and drew closer together. Tomorrow they would be alone. The desert felt very near.

CHAPTER FOUR

THE *ahal* was destined never to take place. In the grey light
of dawn Abakout stumbled and fell on her knees, her body,
wrapped in threadbare rags, trembling with cold and fear.
Around her the tents were dark and silent.

'Death,' she screamed. 'Death. Death. Death.'

Suddenly, dogs, as though scenting misfortune, and
wakened by the old woman's cries, set up a furious barking
which died away into high-pitched whines. The frightened
camp sprang into life. Men shouted and grasped swords and
lances, believing themselves attacked. Shrieking women ran
blindly from their tents carrying children. Beyond the camp
the camels, terrified by the commotion, struggled to their feet
and fought to break the restricting hobbles on their front legs.
One fell, crying piteously. As Abba ou-Sidi rushed from his
tent, *takouba* in hand, Abakout clutched at his arm. Suddenly,
a silence fell, embracing the whole camp. A faint wind stirred
softly. To the east a line of fire gripped the horizon and a ray
of light shot upward as the sun raised itself slowly towards a
new day. The men stood lost in uncertainty, clutching their
weapons. A baby whimpered and was immediately hushed at
its mother's breast. Almost at once it began crying again and
its tiny screams set off the other babies who, till then, had
been too frightened to cry. But all eyes were turned towards
the heap in the sand beyond Ebeggi's tent. Nobody moved.

In that instant of stillness the light grew and strengthened:
shadows fled across the desert, darting from the suddenly

41

exposed poverty of the tents towards the body; obscuring briefly the deep, spreading stain which had already been absorbed by the cold avaricious sand.

It was Sekefi who moved first. He pushed his way through the silent throng of men and women and children and knelt beside the body. One of the dogs, black-haired and mangy, followed him to sniff at the congealed blood matted into the blanket in which it lay. Sekefi thrust the beast away and turned the body over. A low cry escaped his lips.

'It's Hingou,' he said, wonderingly.

A murmur of amazement stirred through the camp.

'Hingou. Hingou agg-Ahnet, the stranger.'

Sekefi touched the hilt of the *tilek* protruding from Hingou's ribs below the heart in awe. The dead man's eyes were half-open and his features set in a surprised mask, as though he had been startled out of sleep to meet his death. Sekefi became aware of Abba ou-Sidi standing beside him.

'Who has dared to do this?' the old man said quietly, more to himself than to his people. 'He was our guest and brought the *abedreh*, the demand for my daughter's marriage. He was the uncle of my daughter's chosen husband. I do not understand.'

He turned and faced his people; pride and anger and shame reflected in his eyes. Tebbilel stepped to her father's side and the eyes above the veil softened as he gazed on her sorrowfully. Then they hardened again. He gripped his *takouba* until the skin was stretched taut over his knuckles, raising and pointing the sword like an indictment.

'Who has done this thing?' he demanded. 'No stranger could have approached the camp for the dogs were silent. Someone among us has dishonoured my tent.'

His gaze moved slowly across the silent and sullen groups facing him. A woman giggled nervously. Then Tebbilel spoke.

'My father,' she said. 'As we sat round the fire last night, listening to Ebeggi talking of the Kel es Souf I desired to question Hingou agg-Ahnet for news of Ehem. My joy at learning what was in Ehem's heart was tempered by his absence and I was unhappy he had not accompanied his uncle.

I seated myself near to Hingou, thinking to speak, but before I could ask that which I desired to know he rose and walked away. I rose also and followed him, away from the tents. When I came upon him he was standing gazing at the heavens. He seemed sad and preoccupied. I spoke to him and asked him for news of Ehem. He replied that Ehem was well and saluted me. We talked for some time alone, for he was the uncle of my husband. But suddenly there was a noise as of someone stealing up on us out of the darkness. Hingou, although he was unarmed, placed himself in front of me like a true warrior and went forward to meet the unknown. There came a cry and the sound of running feet. Soon Hingou returned. "It was Ebeggi," he said.'

Tebbilel flung out her arm accusingly.

'It was Ebeggi,' she cried, 'who followed us into the night and ran like a jackal from an unarmed man.'

In the astonished silence she turned and drew the *tilek* from the dead man's side and held it up for all to see. A trickle of blood ran down the blade. In the forefront of the gathering Ebeggi watched the red stain spreading over the engraved steel towards the hilt, a look of fear and fascination in his eyes.

'It is Ebeggi's *tilek*,' someone muttered.

'And Hingou rebuked Ebeggi,' Sekefi said, quietly, 'for speaking disrespectfully of Ahar oua-n-Alleli. Perhaps he followed Hingou away from the camp to kill him and failed, then stabbed him whilst he slept.'

Ebeggi rushed wildly forward.

'It is a lie,' he shrieked. 'It was not I, not I who killed him. Last night I saw them. I did not follow them: it was by chance. They were going to lie together. I heard her pleading: *kai enbi i*, Hingou. *Ira inn ek*. She was down on the sand. I didn't know they were there until she spoke. Her voice was like the whine of a bitch in heat. With the uncle of the man she is to marry. I ran away. I swear I didn't kill him.'

Abba ou-Sidi took the *tilek* from Tebbilel's hand.

'This is your dagger, Ebeggi,' he said slowly. 'You have wronged your people and my daughter's husband. You have betrayed the friendship of one who was my guest and brought shame to my tent. Yet now you seek to dishonour my daughter.' He turned to Sekefi. 'Kill him,' he said.

Ebeggi sprang forward as Sekefi raised his *takouba*.

'No, no,' he screamed.

The blow caught him on the neck and a gout of blood spurted as the sword bit deep. He fell without a sound, his half-severed head twisted grotesquely. A cry of horror arose from the women. But Tebbilel stood watching, unmoved, her fists clenched; a smile, almost of triumph, on her lips.

A swarm of flies hovered around the dead camel and the stench of putrefying flesh was heavy and sweet. It filled their nostrils and Carol turned away in disgust, slapping at the flies buzzing around her head. Amaias went over and looked at the mark of the brand behind the right cheek.

'It is a camel of the Ikenbiben,' he said to Robert in Tamahak. 'We shall find their tents near the Oued Tiberlerlarin. They are my friends.'

'How soon will we reach there?' Robert asked.

The guide made a gesture with his hand, indicating that it depended on the woman. Robert glanced at Carol who had sat down on a low rock a little way ahead and was nursing her feet. Unaccustomed equally to walking as to camel-riding, she found the going hard, but never complained. Robert's irritation at the slowness of their progress was changing gradually to admiration of Carol's endurance and courage. In three days they had scarcely reached the foothills of the Hoggar, but it had been an arduous journey over difficult country for a girl unused to the hardships of the desert.

They camped that afternoon in a narrow valley overhung by steep granite cliffs where there was good pasturage for the camels. A cluster of small thorn bushes, their foliage bright against the drab colours of the surrounding landscape, indicated the presence of water. Amaias went a little way up the valley and, kneeling down, began to scrape a hole in the sand with his hands. Soon, water began to seep to the surface. With a shallow bowl he scooped it out, allowing the sand to settle before pouring the water into the *guerba* he had brought with him. Later, Carol and Robert took advantage of the unexpected spring and washed themselves thoroughly. Amaias, at a distance, observed their ablutions with that mixture of superciliousness and incredulity which the Tuareg reserve for the incomprehensible customs of Europeans. Before it was dark Robert unpacked his small, battery-driven tape recorder and tested it out. He brushed away the inevitable sand which had seeped through the canvas carrying-case and into the drive mechanism. Carol watched him, curiously. She was still surprised he had agreed to take her with him. His deep reserve which, for a short while, had disappeared at the Guelta Imlaoulaouen seemed to shut him away inside himself. Outwardly, his appearance was quite ordinary; but, beneath the exterior, she sensed another being, purposeful, demanding, passionate. Her own nature, her fear of being involved, which lay behind her perpetual boredom, viewed him with mistrust. More than anything, she must maintain the relationship she had outlined that day at the *guelta*. She was not afraid of hardship, of thirst, of death, even: these things did not touch the fear of life contained in the depth of her being. But she was afraid of Robert. In bed that night in the narrow tent, their campbeds so close that she would scarcely need to raise her arm to reach out and touch him, she lay awake listening to her thoughts. Under the rough blankets her body lay warm and relaxed. Against her exposed face the night air was cold and sharp. A wind moaned softly through the valley, tugging at the canvas. Through the open end of the tent an uncertain light played over the small, visible expanse of the outside world. She felt strangely secure and isolated; as though the flimsy tent and the warm, uncomfortable bed stood between her and the world.

'Robert,' she murmured. 'Are you asleep?'

The answer came almost immediately.

'No. Not yet.'

'Will we reach the Oued Tiberlerlarin tomorrow?'

'We should do.'

'Do you think you'll get any recordings there?'

'It's possible.'
There was silence for a while.
'Robert.'
'Yes?'
'Oh, nothing. Goodnight.'
'Goodnight, Carol.'

Away across the flat desert the light of the torch seemed remote and inaccessible. Over there Patricia waited, shivering in the sudden night cold, alone and frightened amongst the debris of their belongings scattered around her. Jimmie climbed into the driver's seat of the car and started the engine. For three hours they had been battling against the desert; against the white, powdery sand which clutched at the tyres. It fell away beneath the weight of the car, shuddering it to a halt, the engine seething and boiling, with the chassis resting firmly on the sand. For three hours they had dug their way, foot by foot, with the sand spilling relentlessly, like a vast, amorphous hour-glass, under the wheels. Jimmie had made the one mistake the novice makes always. They had been told never to drive in the tracks of another car: but in the black sand there are no tracks; only the hard, corrugated surface of the route, blazoned by iron posts cemented into the desert. It winds, tortuously, through the soft sea of sand the French, with Gallic aptitude, have named '*farine*'. The route is rough, spine-shaking: it is only when you have been tempted to abandon it for the smooth, so seductively firm appearance of the black wastes lying to either side of it that you understand and admit your error. By then it is too late.

It was on this narrow ribbon of safety that Patricia stood, flashing the torch to guide Jimmie. He let out the clutch and the unladen car juddered as the engine raced in bottom gear. The wheels spun and he felt his hands grow damp with sweat against the steering-wheel. Then, slowly, the car moved forward. It gathered speed, the headlights cleaving a passage through the emptiness ahead. The needle of the water-gauge rose to boiling point. A smell of hot metal permeated the

46

inside of the car. Jimmie gritted his teeth and registered an overpowering desire to change up into second gear. The noise of the over-accelerated engine dinned into his ears. It increased as the speed of the car slackened when the sand gripped the wheels. For a second he thought he was stuck. Then the note of the engine softened and the car drew away. In front of him the light of the torch wavered and grew clearer. In the beam of the headlamps he could see Patricia standing immobile like a sentinel of safety. And, suddenly, the wheels caught at firm ground. The car skidded and bounded forward. With an unvoiced cry of triumph Jimmie pulled at the gear lever to relax the torture of the engine. He twisted the wheel and brought the car to a standstill near to one of the kilometre markers and cut the ignition, thrusting his foot savagely down on the accelerator. For a moment the engine continued firing and then, with a final judder, was silent. The radiator seethed and rumbled and a thin cloud of steam hissed into the glare of the lights. He pushed open the car door and got out. Patricia flung herself into his arms.

'Don't ever do that again,' she sobbed. 'I have never been alone till now, never known what it is to stand in the darkness and know fear. It is tangible, monstrous, like a childhood threat. I felt abandoned; utterly, finally abandoned.'

She clung to him, shivering. He ran his hands over her body, soothing her, pressing himself against her, murmuring unintelligible sounds. Blindly, she sought for his mouth and his being responded to her with the nervous release of tension. At last, calmed, reassured, Patricia disengaged herself from his arms. In the light of the car lamps she heated some soup on the primus stove and they made a sketchy meal. Soon after they stretched out on their beds which they had placed against the shelter of the car, utterly weary. Patricia reached out her hand towards her husband.

'Jimmie,' she said softly. 'I want a child.'

He did not answer at first. When he did his voice was far away and heavy with sleep.

'I want one as much as you do,' he said. 'But we've got to wait, darling. When we get to Spain. When I've got a job.'

47

She raised herself on her elbow.

'Oh, Jimmie,' she said. 'Don't you see it's not just a child that matters. Listen. My sister married a solicitor. After three years they were able to pay the deposit on a semi-detached house near Hendon. Then he was offered a junior partnership in the firm so they decided they could afford a baby. Life's not like that. We've been married three years. What does it matter if you haven't got a job, darling? We've still got the future. We've got each other. Oh, Jimmie, Jimmie. Jimmie!' she whispered, sharply.

The hand she held was limp and relaxed. She leaned over him, straining her eyes against the darkness. He was asleep.

'My darling,' she murmured. 'You don't know how proud I am of you, of what you've done today.' She bent and kissed his forehead. 'It is because of this, your strength, the desert, that it is here, in the emptiness of the sand and the wind our child must be conceived. Before it is too late.'

At the oasis of Tounin Akourin, near Abalessa, Sekefi agg-Ali found Ehem camped with a party of warriors awaiting Hingou's return.

'How is it you have journeyed so far, Sekefi?' Ehem asked when the formalities of greeting had been concluded. 'Why did Hingou not accompany you? Is there some delay? Has Abba ou-Sidi found displeasure in my demand?'

'Abba ou-Sidi speaks of you already as his son and your demand has been received with joy by his people. In this I am the messenger of your happiness. Yet it is in sorrow I come. Hingou is dead.'

Ehem revealed no sign of outward emotion. Only his eyes narrowed.

'Dead?' he asked, coldly.

Sekefi related how the body had been found and Tebbilel's accusation which had brought about the execution of Ebeggi. Ehem and his friends listened closely, not interrupting. As Sekefi described the killing of Ebeggi, Ehem nodded as though in agreement.

'It is well,' he said when Sekefi had concluded. 'Only a jackal and a coward would kill a sleeping man. Yet I am troubled. Why did not Ebeggi flee? Why did he wait for his treachery to be discovered?'

His friends assented. Sekefi felt uneasy. He had not stopped to think why Ebeggi had not run away; or at least removed his *tilek* from Hingou's body. He was puzzled.

'But no one had run away,' he said after a moment's thought, conscious of the cold, almost hostile stare of the men around him. 'No one was missing from the camp that morning.'

'Is there not some detail you have overlooked?' Ehem persisted. 'Did not Ebeggi defend himself?'

Sekefi hesitated. He had omitted Ebeggi's accusation of wantonness against Tebbilel. He did not wish to anger Ehem.

'He was like a mad dog,' he said, at last, 'foaming from the mouth, his face twisted with guilt and fear. His words made no sense. It was then Abba ou-Sidi ordered me to strike. Our tents had been dishonoured and the crime demanded swift retribution.'

A man sitting next to Ehem nodded his agreement. This was Moulei Sidi-Mekammed, a cousin.

'The affliction of madness is comprehensible only to Allah,' he said. 'How can we understand what was in Ebeggi's heart? It is well Abba ou-Sidi was swift in his judgment. Had Ebeggi escaped there would have been blood between your people and ours. Allah be praised that it is well.'

With an inward sigh of relief Sekefi felt the tension ease. Ehem alone remained withdrawn, but the hostility had faded out of his eyes. At last he spoke.

'It is Allah's will,' he said, quietly. 'Where are the tents of Abba ou-Sidi pitched?'

'They will be at the well of Ti-n-Afara, *insh'Iallah*, where Tebbilel awaits you.'

'We will leave before the day begins and travel fast,' Ehem said, rising to his feet.

There was a sudden cry from Moulei Sidi-Mekammed.

'See. See. The moon appears.'

49

They turned and followed the line of his pointing finger. Low in the afternoon sky the crescent of the moon hung faintly, a sliver of pale light, almost invisible to the naked eye. Ramadan had ended.

Even before he came to In Itaou René had begun to be interested in the history and customs of the Tuareg. In Algiers, soon after he met Lisette, he had found, in a second-hand bookshop in a dingy street near the Kasbah, a battered copy of the first edition of General Hanoteau's grammar of the Tamahak language which he published there in 1860. During that first long summer of military service, sprawled on Lisette's wide bed in her minute apartment overlooking the bay, while she prepared food in a kitchen that was little more than a curtained-off area of the bed-cum-living-room, or busied herself with household chores, he struggled with pronunciation and the phonetics of its alphabet. All too often his efforts were interrupted by Lisette. Petite and naked and brown – partly from the Algerian sun, partly from heredity – she would come and kneel beside the bed where he lay and, gazing intently up at him from eyes which betrayed her remote, Berber ancestry, would gently, insistently caress the inside of his thigh, disturb the hooded somnolence of his recumbent sex, until he put aside the general and embraced and took her and could, for a while, be free of the tyranny of their bodies.

In the intervals between love-making, during the hours when he could be with her, when she was satiated with both the sensuality of poetry and that of the flesh, she would salvage from the memory of some archetypal consciousness fragments of a Kabyle dialect that had been her grandmother's. Though it differed greatly from the Tuareg language, whose strangely geometrical alphabet may be as old as the South Arabian or even the Phoenician, which it resembles, he found, as had General Hanoteau a century earlier, sufficient similarity between the two to enable him to understand more easily its structure. The words Lisette whispered into his ear were softly guttural like her cries of pleasure. They went deeper into his understanding than the knowledge the dead general held out to him. While his mind assimilated the latter's syntactical reasoning his whole being was absorbed by Lisette's sensuous and sensual vocabulary. Out of them he devised a new language for their love-talk: part Kabyle, part Tamahak and part silence.

More to the point, and it stood René in good stead when he reached In Itaou, the general's studies had been based upon the dialect of the Hoggar region and culled from conversations he had had with the *Imouchar*, nobles taken prisoner during early raids into the interior. Perhaps also, René's own Corsican ancestors, whoever they were, had contributed something – a sympathy towards lawlessness, an affinity with forgotten histories, for remote languages – which attracted him to this strange people.

At In Itaou, unlike his colleagues at Djanet or Tamanrasset who went frequently out on patrol, his contact with the Tuareg was restricted to those times when, like Amaias, they came to visit him or camped in the vicinity of the fort. But he had the advantage then of being able to go amongst them, to mix with them without the barrier of military formality; without having to keep a certain distance. In this way he was able to study them and slowly to gain a better understanding of their language and customs.

Strange he found them indeed, but their strangeness did not lie solely in the fact that the men veiled their faces while the women went unveiled. The Arabs, who fear them, mock them secretly and say with a sneer: 'Their hearts are craven so they veil their faces and hide and send out their women to fight.' This is untrue. Indeed, their courage is fanatical as when, again and again, they charged the guns of Lieutenant Cottenest armed only with lance and shield and their two-edged, cross-hilted swords. No, their strangeness lies deeper: in the anachronism they present to our twentieth century. How can this people retain its primitive identity, even to the use of an alphabet whose source is still unknown today, in the face of a world changing and developing around them? They are not a people of barbarous tribes, isolated in the swamps of inaccessible jungles. These are, perhaps, the descendants of the Berber conquest of Spain, a people of nobility and chivalry whose women enjoy a status second only to that of our own; whose ancestors may have been among the Greeks and Phoenicians settled on the Mediterranean shores of Africa, or the invading Persians spilling out of Egypt with their god Mithras into the hinterland of Libya.

René grew to like these tall, courteous nomads who came bringing him bowls of fresh camel's milk and the hard, sun-dried dates which are their sustenance on the long journeys of migration. In their blue, enveloping robes and veils with only the eyes, cold and haughty, visible their nobility was apparent. He found their women graceful and slender, their hands especially beautiful; and soon learned that their deceptive shyness concealed natures at once both fierce and sexual.

It is they who rule finally, not the Amenokal. In them is vested the line of descent, the traditions and the folklore of their people. And not only these, but the powers of divination and magic also. How many Frenchmen are there in the Sahara today who will never escape from the bondage of exquisite pleasures these faun-like sibyls fasten about their limbs, who have lost the desire to escape? The slow poison of their domination, the *borbor*, destroys will-power as surely as their magic potions destroy the cells of the body.

In exchange for the gifts the Tuareg brought him René treated their sick – animals as well as men – and friendship grew between them. As his knowledge of Tamahak improved the barriers to understanding fell away, one by one. At first there had seemed to be an insurmountable obstacle, an aloofness which never relaxed beyond the ritual tea-drinking outside their tents. Then, little by little the aloofness became tolerance and soon he was able to wander into their camp without formality, without suspicion. And he began to form ideas about the structure of their society, about their customs and to learn of their beliefs.

Although in name they are Moslems, the Tuareg believe with almost childish superstition in a race of super-human beings, at once demoniac and mischievous in their dealings with mankind, whom they call Kel es Souf. Everything is the work of the Kel es Souf – everything, that is, except the mirage which nobody seems able to explain. One evening, after the ritual glasses of tea had passed round the circle of dark, cross-legged figures for the third time and the name Allah seemed to hover in the cool air, René tried to draw them out about the Kel es Souf. The night was clear and windless, the western horizon rimmed faintly with light, the east already dark and heavy with stars.

'How may one recognise the Kel es Souf,' he asked of Adhan who was seated next to him. 'What manner of people are they?'

Adhan, named and renowned for his strength and courage, did not answer. He looked quickly behind him and the name of Allah escaped his lips. Elralem answered for him, old and wise and perhaps on his last journey.

'Irmar,' he said, addressing René by the name the Tuareg have given him, 'we have named you thus because you are troubled within yourself. So have you come to be known by all who seek water at the well your people have stolen from us. Because of your hands which heal you are loved. Therefore do not, I beg of you, seek out the Kel es Souf. Because you are not of my people, yet close to them, your spirit cannot comprehend those things which to us are real and have followed us down the centuries from Lemtuna, our mother. The Kel es Souf are everywhere: in the voices that answer us among the mountains, in the sudden storm that strikes the quiet waters of a *guelta*. At night they walk the desert and in the silence you will hear their drums whispering out of the darkness. They take upon themselves the forms of humans, of animals – even of things – and their evil is wrought most surely at the hour of *aser*, the hour when darkness hovers in the sky.'

His voice ceased and, in the ensuing stillness, a faint drumming reached René's ears. It was a sibilance half heard, half imagined; as of the wind distantly sifting through the night-chilled sand.

'It is the wind,' he said, 'blowing the sand.'

'There is no wind, Irmar,' Adhan answered quietly.

CHAPTER FIVE

THE CAR topped the ridge of the hill, bumping over the uneven track and began to descend once more to the level plain. On the horizon ahead a cluster of trees seemed, like a mirage, to be floating in a vast lake. They had become so accustomed during their journey across the sand wastes to these illusory seas and forests which appeared suddenly and then vanished, or fled away in front of the car's approach, that, at first, they paid little attention. Yet, as the distance that separates reality from its image decreased, the trees seemed to become more substantial. The lake shrank and a long, low building seemed to rise above the surface. Then, suddenly there was no longer any illusion.

'There it is,' cried Patricia. 'We've arrived.'

Now the fort was discernible in some detail and Patricia pointed out a figure standing on the roof, waving. Jimmie beat out a tattoo on the horn button. The sudden blast of the powerful horns startled him and he jerked away his hand as though he had been bitten. He steered the car carefully between the deep drifts of sand that flanked the approach. On one side of the gateway a defunct-looking petrol pump stood like a sentry on duty; on the other a large metal sign said: IN ITAOU.

'My God!' Jimmie exclaimed, stopping the car outside the entrance. 'The wild man of Borneo.'

Patricia stared, uncertain whether to laugh or be alarmed. A man was approaching, naked except for a pair of shorts and sandals on his feet. He was of medium height. His skin was deeply bronzed and his broad chest covered with thick black hair. His face – or rather his nose and eyes, for nothing else could be seen – was framed by an immense black beard which seemed but a continuation of the mass of hair covering his head. He ambled out to the car and thrust out a large hand.

'M'sieu, 'dame,' he said, genially. 'Je suis le sergeant-chef de poste. Ça va bien?'

Jimmie got out and shook hands and introduced Patricia and himself. The sergeant bowed to Patricia and his very deep, blue eyes glinted with laughter.

'I'm afraid my appearance has startled you, madame,' he said as he held open the car door for her. 'This is a very provincial hotel, this In Itaou. We have no barber, but there is a bar. Come, let us refresh ourselves. Drive the automobile inside the *bordj*, m'sieu. I shall escort madame.'

He led Patricia through the entrance and into the courtyard of the fort. In front of them stood the well and as Patricia leaned over to look into it there was a flutter of wings and a score of tiny red-breasted love-birds flew out, chirping and agitated.

'How lovely,' Patricia cried. 'But how did they get here?'

'They were brought by a colonel who is now retired. In the day they live in the cool shadow of the well; at night they perch in the store-room where it is warm.'

'They're beautiful. Jimmie,' she called to her husband who had just brought in the car. 'Come and see. The well is full of birds.'

'The water is good also,' the sergeant remarked as Jimmie joined them.

He showed them into a long, narrow room. In one corner stood a small, dusty bar built of concrete. Above it a large poster was nailed to the wall.

'I don't believe it,' Jimmie said.

The poster depicted the empty horizon of the desert. In the foreground a man stood gazing – like Jimmie – at an immense glass of beer, so cold that beads of frost clung to the outside.

The glass seemed to hover on the horizon. Overhead, the sun blazed from a pale sky.

'I'm bloody thirsty,' Jimmie muttered, running his tongue over his dry lips.

The sergeant chuckled.

'And now, madame would like a cold beer?' he enquired.

'Don't be unkind,' Patricia said, her eyes fixed on the poster.

'It would be a cruel joke,' the sergeant said, 'but for this. Come, you are thirsty.'

They turned away from the poster and saw, for the first time, a large kerosene refrigerator at the far end of the room. The door was already open and the sergeant withdrawing three tins. He handed them to Jimmie and reclosed the fridge. 'Sit down,' he said, 'while I fetch glasses.'

Patricia and Jimmie looked at each other.

'I still can't believe it,' the latter said.

But the beer was real and cold. They sat at the long mess-table and sipped it. They couldn't even remember beer tasting so good.

'You will wish to stay tonight?' the sergeant asked. 'There are beds ready for you. I will show you how the shower-bath works. Then I will see about dinner. Let me see . . . There will be soup, a pâté, gazelle steaks, some salad, naturally, and dessert. You will excuse me for one minute, madame, while I attend to one or two things? One cannot call for "Marie" here, you understand.'

'Let me help,' Patricia offered.

'Thank you, but it's not necessary. Besides you are tired after your journey. It is my pleasure. I think also we will take some wine from the special reserve for this dinner. It will merit it.'

He went out and they heard him bustling about in the kitchen next door, whistling amid the clatter of saucepans.

'You don't suppose we could stay here for a few days?' Patricia said. 'This place is a miniature paradise.'

'I must say I would like to check one or two things on the car and change the oil, before we go any further,' Jimmie said.

56

'We can ask the sergeant tonight. Can you imagine,' he added, 'this happening to us in Nigeria?'

'And that menu,' Patricia agreed. '"Some salad, naturally" – in the middle of the desert! Only the French could do it.'

The sergeant put his head round the door.

'Come,' he said. 'I will show you the shower-bath.'

He led the way across the courtyard. All the rooms on this side of the fort appeared to be bedrooms.

'I will find you blankets and sheets afterwards,' the sergeant said in passing. 'You may choose your room. We are not crowded just now. The shower is my own invention,' he explained a moment later. 'The reservoir on the roof is filled from this drum. One has to pump.'

He gave a few vigorous strokes to the handle of a rotary pump to demonstrate his meaning, then disappeared round a corner into a short and narrow passage which ended at the outside wall of the fort.

'To the left is a toilet,' he said. 'It does not work.' He shrugged. 'One has the desert. The shower-bath is on the right.'

He turned to Patricia.

'It has no door, madame,' he said, apologetically. 'But, no matter. We are alone here. When the *bordj* is full it is better to sing.'

They entered the shower room and the sergeant indicated the rose in the ceiling made from a very large tin.

'It is necessary to pull this cord,' he explained – and pulled it. A heavy spray of water almost engulfed him. He jumped hastily back letting go the cord. The deluge ceased.

'*Oui,*' he said. '*Ça marche.*'

The dinner, after they had bathed and found clean clothes, was excellent. They sat late over coffee and a bottle of cognac which Jimmie had produced as an offering to the feast. Patricia broached the subject of their staying for a few days.

'But, certainly,' the sergeant said at once. 'It is prudent to see to the repairs to your automobile. As for me, I am alone here. It is pleasant to have someone to share my solitude.'

'We have plenty of food and things,' Patricia said. 'We must pay our way.'

'We couldn't stay and not expect to,' Jimmie added.

The sergeant smiled. He had put on his tunic and *seroual*. His beard was freshly trimmed. His eyes twinkled as he regarded the two tourists. He raised his glass.

'Cheerio,' he said in English.

They all laughed.

'Don't you find it lonely here?' Patricia asked.

'Naturally, but to be alone is not so very terrible. One must have the taste for it.'

'But why don't they put two of you here?' Jimmie said. 'Surely, it would be less strain if you had a companion, someone to talk to, to relieve the boredom.'

The sergeant lighted another cigarette and blew a cloud of smoke towards the low ceiling.

'There are places like this,' he said at length, 'where two sergeants are in garrison together. I have experienced it once. It is always the same.' He leaned forward. 'You must understand that the solitude is not inside one. It is out there: it is the desert.' He flung out his arm in a wide arc, as though to embrace the desolation beyond the rough white-washed walls and the intimacy of tobacco smoke and alcohol. 'It is out there and with that one can come to terms. Listen, there are two men. They meet, perhaps for the first time, at the bar of the hotel at Tamanrasset. They meet because they have been ordered to go together to a place such as In Itaou where they are to live for a number of months alone, just the two of them. Over their drinks at the hotel they talk and discover their common interests, their preferences and prejudices, their personalities, even. They see before them a great friendship; they plan how they will spend their time, make themselves comfortable. *Le cafard?* No, it will not be for them. And it turns out exactly as they imagine – for the next few weeks. In the end they will come to a common understanding. Rather than kill each other they will observe a rigorous discipline. Each will go his separate way within the confines of the walls which have suddenly become closer together; in their little

58

world that has unaccountably become so small it is difficult to avoid tripping over each other's feet. They will begin to take their meals separately – that is the first step. One will move his bed to the opposite end of the fort. There will be clearly defined hours for each to make use of the communal living arrangements. And, finally, a complete silence will descend; communication will be by polite notes addressed one to the other when circumstances demand. No, believe me, madame – my solitude is to be preferred.'

He smiled at Patricia and her heart went out towards him.

'Yes, I suppose you're right,' Jimmie said. 'When I was in the army I found it could get too much of a good thing just sharing a room – let alone being shut up with the fellow for months on end.'

The well of Ti-n-Afara, lying on the old caravan routes to Bornu and the Hausa states, was a watering-place of some importance. It lay in the middle of a narrow plain covered with coarse vegetation which, nevertheless, afforded good pasturage. *Ekechchekir*, the Tuareg called it. To the east the northern massif of the Mountains of Aïr rose sombrely into the sky, hiding the sterile dunes of the Ténéré which lay beyond. Westward the bleak region of Tamesna, broken only by scattered outcrops of rock, reached away to the far distant mountains of the Adrar-n-Iforas. It was here that Abba ou-Sidi had decided to await the outcome of Sekefi's mission and the arrival of Ehem and his people. Blood had been assuaged with blood and the old chief knew the way was open still for his daughter's marriage. He had instructed that the tents be pitched to the east of the well, near enough to ensure their water supply but far enough distant to provide adequate pasturage for the prolonged stay necessary while awaiting the arrival of Ehem, and for the seven days set aside for the marriage festivities. Already, around the well, the pasturage had been overgrazed by herds passing south. The period of the cool north winds was over. Each morning the sun rose high above the mountains and the noon heat increased.

At night a bitter wind blew from the east, bringing no relief.

Tebbilel kept to her tent during this period of waiting and seldom ventured out in the daytime. She was uneasy and her mind occupied with thoughts of how Ehem would take the news of Hingou's death. Would he be satisfied with the retribution dealt by Sekefi at her father's command? Or, would he demand further revenge; perhaps even withdraw from the marriage? That he would come either to claim or to repudiate her, she did not doubt. And it was this that caused her uneasiness. Three days after the end of Ramadan she decided to disclose her fears to Abakout; for the old woman was wise and could help her. The marriage must take place at all costs. But it was more important still that Ehem should accept the fact of Hingou's murder without question. There was only one way in which this could be accomplished.

That night, as soon as the camp was asleep, Tebbilel stole out among the tents to where the old woman slept, always a little distant from the others of the *iklan*, the slave caste, who feared her. It was very dark and she picked her way carefully, making no sound. She kept her *ekerhei*, the headscarf which was the symbol of her puberty, close about her face. Invisible, silent, she moved with the darkness until, at last, she stood above the dimly-sensed shape of the old woman lying on the sand. Tebbilel knelt, her heart beating loudly, and reached out with her hand to nudge Abakout gently awake. As she leaned over the old woman she was aware, suddenly, of two eyes, their pupils enlarged and smouldering, staring up at her out of the darkness. She started back, trembling, her hand clutched to her breast. A feeling of terror urged her to get up and run, but she was held motionless by the slow fire of those eyes, which should not have been visible on so dark a night. Tebbilel knelt, fascinated and afraid.

'You know,' she whispered, hoarsely. 'You know.'

'I know many things, daughter of Abba ou-Sidi,' the old woman muttered. 'I know you have come to me because you are afraid of Ehem. What is it you want of me?'

Tebbilel mastered her fear with an effort.

'Come,' she said. 'Come where we can talk without fear of being overheard.'

'With what will you buy my speech – or my silence?' Abakout demanded, malevolently.

'Here, take this. It is a token only.'

And Tebbilel thrust a ring into the old woman's hand.

'It is a trifle. For this I will hear what you have to say.'

'Yes, yes.' Tebbilel grew impatient. 'You will tell me what I must pay when you have heard me.'

Grumbling still, the old woman rose slowly to her feet. She wrapped her blanket closely round her body and followed the girl to a place safely distant from the camp where they could talk without fear of being overheard.

The night wind moaned softly. Accustomed now to the darkness Tebbilel could distinguish shapes looming out of the night, the camels over by the well, a low ridge of sand behind her and the outlines of the tents, insubstantial and distant. She experienced a return of her fear and shivered as the wind flapped at her clothes. The presence of the old woman close to her seemed menacing and evil. Suddenly, without asking any questions, Abakout began speaking, her voice intoning the words softly so they merged with the wind and it seemed to the frightened girl it was the wind that spoke. As she listened she grew pale and clutched at the old woman's arm. Abakout threw off her hand, roughly.

'No,' Tebbilel whimpered. 'No. No. I cannot do this.'

In her turn Abakout grasped the girl.

'You must,' she hissed. 'It is the only way. You will meet me here tomorrow when it is dark. The journey is not great. And, remember, you will pay me with a young goat when the thing is done. Now, go.'

She gave the girl a violent push and Tebbilel stumbled away into the darkness, half running, heedless of noise. She thought only of the safety of her tent and the terrible thing which she must do.

The next day she complained of nausea to her father and kept to her tent. When evening came she told him she was going to find Abakout to obtain medicine for her sickness as she could not eat. Thus she would not be missed and her absence at the hour of *azzouzeg* for the evening meal would go unremarked. In the darkness beyond the camp the old woman awaited her.

They set out as swiftly as Abakout's age would allow, walking in a straight line with the Cross of Agades always on their right. The sky was clear and the stars could be followed easily. For once, the bitter east wind was still and only a slight breeze ruffled the surface of the sand. The desert appeared luminous but remote in the uncertain starlight. Behind them the voices and evening noises of the encampment faded into silence and the glow from the fires in front of the tents became quenched by distance. Soon the scant pastures lost themselves beneath low, softly undulating dunes, here and there thrusting dry, brittle stalks above the enveloping sterility of the sand, as though fighting a last battle against oblivion.

Progress across the dunes was slow. The broad soled *irratimen* prevented their feet sinking into the soft, still-warm sand but, to be certain of maintaining their direction, it was necessary to clamber up each slope and down again into the trough, never deviating from the course that Abakout had determined on setting out. By the time they reached the black, endless plains beyond the dunes it seemed to Tebbilel she had been walking all night. Her head ached; her throat was dry and painful. An agony of tiredness clutched at her thighs and knees. She wanted only to sink down on to the stony ground and rest. But Abakout, with determination lending her strength, forced the girl in her wake with sneers and jibes.

'You are a child,' she taunted, 'to be fatigued before the stars have moved across the sky. Is it thus you will plead on the night Ehem will ride you across the bed of sand? You are ill-named, Tebbilel oult-Abba, for you will have nothing without courage and endurance.'

Tebbilel did not answer. The fear she felt for the old woman burned inside her with a flame of hatred. But, at last, Abakout was silent too, her breath heavy and labouring as she stumbled over the hard, uneven *tanezrouft*. Suddenly, she stopped:

motionless, listening. Tebbilel, behind her, stood still, her teeth chattering with cold and terror, eyes wide. The wind stirred her clothes and it was as if invisible hands passed over her body. She wanted to run, to experience the relief of flight; anything rather than to remain alone in the dark emptiness with this old woman who could cross the desert like a young warrior. But she could not move. Across the plain the ghostly drumming of the night pulsed gently, enveloping her, immobilising her fear. Abakout did not move. She stood rigidly, arms extended as though to embrace or ward off some unseen presence. Only her lips moved in a silent incantation as she stared at the ground. Tebbilel watched, fascinated. Then the old woman turned and, with curiously controlled movements, hobbled away. Several paces distant she stopped and again peered at the ground. At her feet a low mound of stones broke the surface of the desert. But, in the darkness, it could not have been discernible for it was not until Tebbilel, fighting down her fear, came up that she was able to see it. She gave a little cry for the mound was an ancient tumulus, an *edebni*. Abakout threw herself down on the grave and began a low chant, then placed her ear to the stones. The sound of the drumming increased, to die suddenly away. Complete silence, still and terrible, descended round the two women. As Abakout rose to her feet the glow of a fire pierced the night away to the west. And then another. Tebbilel threw herself forward at the old woman's feet.

'Kel es Souf,' she moaned in terror. 'It is the camp of the Kel es Souf. We must fly. Come, quickly. Quickly, before they suspect we are here.'

But Abakout thrust the girl away and stood looking at the distant glow of the fires.

'Do not be afraid,' she said, scornfully. 'I, Abakout, have listened to the voices of the Kel es Souf speaking to me from the *edebni*. Come. We have work to do and the place is near here.'

Without paying Tebbilel any more heed the old woman started away, walking rapidly and erect now towards the north-west, away from the fires. Tebbilel, more afraid to be alone than of Abakout, followed, her face grey with fear. Soon Abakout stopped and, as Tebbilel came up behind her, said without turning:

'This is the place.'

The girl scanned the dark ground for some sign. Was it here, she thought, that I spoke with Hingou? But she could not recognise the place. Then Abakout, with unerring instinct, walked a little distance to the left and gave a low grunt of triumph.

'Come,' she commanded, softly. 'It is here.'

Unwillingly, Tebbilel moved to her side. She knew what awaited her and shrank from the knowledge. But Abakout was already bending over the shallow grave and scratching away the loose surface with her short, broad fingers. In horror, the girl saw appear the robe and then the features of Hingou. The dead man was laid in the grave on his right side, his face turned towards the east. Impatiently, Abakout signalled to the girl to help her. Sick with terror, Tebbilel obeyed, her fingers shrinking at the contact with the cold flesh as they turned over the body. Then the old woman reached into her *gandoura* and brought out a knife and a small goatskin bag. She handed the knife to Tebbilel.

'*Iend 'ed. Isegbet 'ed aoulid,*' she commanded, her voice low, sibilant, obscene.

Tebbilel looked stupidly at the knife in her hand, then at the pale, dead face in the sand.

'*Iend 'ed,*' Abakout hissed, thrusting her face close to the girl's. She snatched the knife and ripped the clothing from the body, pointing to the exposed genitals.

'*Iend 'ed,*' she repeated, pressing the hilt again into Tebbilel's shaking hand.

'I can't,' the girl whimpered. 'I can't.'

In repugnance she looked at the almost naked corpse. But the urgency of the old woman had communicated itself to her. Without knowing exactly what she did her hand reached out and touched the cold flesh. A shudder ran through her body. As though of its own volition the knife plunged downward. The sense of unreality gripped her. She was aware of

64

Abakout close to her, kneeling above the grave and the goatskin bag in her hands, of the inert body that offered no resistance to the knife. Overcome with nausea, Tebbilel staggered to her feet, retching. Then she sank to the ground in a faint. When she came to her senses it was as though the nightmare had never happened: as though it was yet to take place. Near the grave Abakout was standing as she had been so little time ago. The knife and the bag had disappeared. The sand was smooth and undisturbed; the two, flat stones again marking the head and foot of the grave.

'Witch! Devil! Unclean thing!' the girl screamed.

Her throat, dry with fear and thirst, made no sound. In hatred she staggered to her feet. Swaying, she rushed forward, fist raised. Abakout spat contemptuously and, turning, began the long walk back to the camp.

A tiny, soot-blackened teapot simmered gently on the embers. Carol watched curiously as a Targui sprinkled leaves of green tea into another, similar pot on the sand in front of him. The flickering light of the fire lit up his veiled face, giving it a sinister quality as he peered into the teapot and retrieved between his finger and thumb a pinch of tea. Still dissatisfied, he added a few more leaves and replaced the teapot on the sand. Carol was acutely conscious of a feeling of isolation as she sat in the circle of dark-robed figures with the desert closing in on her and night hovering in the sky like a physical presence. Beside her, Robert was withdrawn into his own world, talking animatedly in Tamahak, the words now guttural, now limpid and flowing, but always sensual and alive. It seemed to Carol that behind their outward calm, their reserve, the motivating force of these Tuareg was passion. And she shrank from it. Isolated as she was she felt this breath of passion in the air around her. Because of it she could take refuge no longer in her boredom. It frightened her.

Early that afternoon they had arrived at the Oued Tiberler-larin and pitched their tent to one side of and away from those of the Ikenbiben. The valley, through which the now dry river made its way in the brief season of tornado and flood, broadened out at this point to form a basin of rock and sand several hundred metres in diameter. To the north, the mountains of the Hoggar climbed towards the sky. Low hills of black rock enclosed the lake of sand, concealing the first reaches of the *tanezrouft* spreading away, empty and toneless, towards the savannah lands south of the desert.

The tents of the Ikenbiben were neither many nor prosperous. Carol had experienced bitter disappointment. In visualising a Tuareg camp she had not exactly imagined sumptuous tents and the romantic setting of a cinema film. But she had not expected this appearance of squalor and poverty. At the time they arrived most of the men were away tending the herds, but the women and children had drifted over to indulge their curiosity. They observed Carol closely, chattering and laughing amongst themselves. When she asked Robert why she should be the centre of interest he had explained with a grin that they had taken her for a man until Amaias enlightened them as to her true sex. They were speculating, he said, why she had no children. Carol blushed angrily and sought refuge in the tent.

Her thoughts were interrupted when the teapot boiled over. The Targui reached out and took it from the embers, pouring the water adroitly into the other pot containing tea. From a pocket he produced a lump of coarse sugar which he folded into the hem of his *gandoura* and crumbled by striking with a stone. Unhurriedly, he placed the sugar into the empty teapot and poured in the tea. With elaborate ritual he transferred the steaming liquid from one pot to the other several times. Then he poured a little into a tiny glass. He raised the glass and peered at it. Daintily, he sipped and, turning his head, spat into the darkness. The remaining contents of the glass he emptied on to the sand at his feet. He fumbled again in his pocket and produced another, smaller piece of sugar which he crumbled and added to the brew. Again the ritual pouring from one pot to the other and the tasting. This time he contented himself with spitting out the tea in his mouth. He was satisfied. He filled two glasses and handed one to Carol, the other to Robert.

'We are the guests,' Robert whispered to her. 'We have to drink first, before the others. Suck the tea in noisily with relish: it's the right compliment.'

Carol tasted the sweet, mint-flavoured syrup cautiously. Reassured, she sucked noisily as Robert was doing and handed back the empty glass. Three times the tiny glasses went round the circle and, at the third time, a murmur of Allah arose.

'The first glass you drink for yourself,' Robert explained, 'the second to your host and the last to Allah.'

'I like it,' Carol said. 'Don't you ever get a fourth glass?'

Robert laughed.

'The fourth glass is reserved as an indication of very special friendship. I doubt that many Europeans have merited it.'

'Are they going to sing for you?' Carol asked.

'I don't know. There's a very good *imzhad* player here, Amaias says. A girl called Tehit, but I understand she's shy. She won't be in *asri* yet and so can't attend the *ahal*.'

'What is this *asri*?'

'It means that from puberty until marriage they can indulge in what we would call free love.'

'Then they are immoral.'

'They don't think so.'

Across the circle of the fire excited chattering had broken out. Someone cried:

'Isef, *aoui asahar*.'

A young man sitting next to Amaias raised his hands in refusal, shaking his head.

'Isef,' Amaias said, laying a hand on the younger man's arm. '*Aoui anea oua n Taouhimt*.'

A girl sitting behind Carol giggled and shouted something across to Amaias. There was a burst of laughter.

'What are they saying?' Carol asked.

'They want Isef to sing,' Robert said. 'Taouhimt – the girl who shouted out just now – is in *asri* and Isef has been

67

making eyes at her. So Amaias suggested he should sing about Taouhimt. But also, it's known that Isef has been looking at her sister, Tehit, the girl I was telling you about who's not yet in *asri*. They're pulling his leg about it.'

'Do they think of nothing but sex?' Carol said, disgustedly.

'They never think about sex – they practise it.'

'They're animals, savages,' Carol said with a shiver.

Robert shrugged.

'That's what they call us,' he said, indifferently, 'but, in their own way, they're civilised too.'

Carol was beginning to feel chilly and a little hungry.

'Are you going to record the singing?' she asked.

'No. I don't think so. If this girl, Tehit, was going to play – yes, perhaps. But I don't think we'll hear anything worthwhile tonight.'

'Why don't we go back to the tent, then? It's cold now.'

'You go back. I'll stay for a while.'

Carol rose to her feet without another word and, making a way for herself through the women seated on the fringe of the circle, walked quickly away, her hands thrust deep into the pockets of her jeans, a scowl on her face. Amaias watched her go, his dark eyes expressive of hostility and contempt.

Alone in their tent Carol threw herself on her bed. She was angry without quite understanding why; and a feeling of resentment against Robert grew in her mind. From the direction of the camp she could hear a harsh voice singing, accompanied by clapping. He treats me like a fool, she thought. And yet he himself is ridiculous the way he behaves with these people – as though they are superior. How they must despise him, a member of the race that conquered them, and laugh at him behind those stupid veils! She stretched her limbs on the narrow, uncomfortable bed, trying to relax. A moment later she sat up and lighted a cigarette. She was not bored, but a feeling of discontent was growing within her to which she could not put a name: as though it were no longer sufficient to have embarked upon this journey across the desert simply to escape from herself; as though the desert itself demanded more from her than she was able to give. She lighted another cigarette and lay back on the bed. A noise close at hand startled her and, for a moment, she thought it was Robert. Then a voice murmured out of the darkness and she recognised the unfamiliar language: it was Amaias. A woman's voice said, clearly:

'*Enker,* Amaias. *Aher i.*'

There was a silence. In the distance the singing had stopped. A confused murmur of voices remained. Carol sat up, rigid on the edge of the bed, the cigarette burning her fingers. She ground it out savagely with her heel on the canvas floor of the tent. A cry of pain, of pleasure reached her ears. She started to her feet. Outside the tent she paused, her heart pounding. She felt the wind on her face, soft and clinging, like the passion she sensed in the night, embracing her, enveloping her, subjugating her. Where was Robert? Her intuition told her, but she refused to accept its message. With a shudder she turned and almost ran towards the murmur of voices from the dying fire. Among them she would find Robert's. From the darkness behind her a whisper, sexual and demanding, followed her fleeing feet:

'Taouhimt. Taouhimt.'

The fire was almost out. The women had gone. Two old men remained. They looked at her curiously. Robert had disappeared.

'And it is near here that Hingou was killed?' asked Ehem.

'The camp was over there,' Sekefi replied, pointing to the east. 'If we set out at dawn we will reach it before the sun rises into the sky.'

The two small fires which had frightened Tebbilel cast a flickering light over the figures grouped around them. The men sat staring into the flames and talking. The camels, which had inclined to be restless, had settled peacefully at last for they knew water and pastures were near at hand.

'Before noon we should reach Ti-n-Afara,' Ehem's cousin said with authority.

'That is so, Moulei Sidi-Mekammed,' Sekefi concurred with

the respect due to an older man. 'If Ehem wishes we may pass the grave of his uncle.'

Ehem nodded gravely.

'It will be well,' he said, 'for I loved him as a father.'

'He was a lion,' one of Ehem's companions said, 'and desired by many women.'

'Allah is merciful,' Moulei Sidi-Mekammed murmured.

As the first light crept over the horizon they set out on the last short stage of the journey. As Sekefi had said they reached the scene of Hingou's murder just as the sun blazed into the new day, sending fingers of light leaping into the sky. Far off, the dunes glowed pink, then gold and paled until at last they became lost in the shimmering haze of white light reflected from the sky. Ehem remained seated on his camel, looking down at the two graves. Ebeggi had been buried hastily, the sand thrown up in a heap and there were no stones marking his grave.

'It is this one,' Sekefi said, quietly.

Ehem forced his camel to kneel and slipped out of the saddle. He stood looking down at the grave of his uncle in silence. His companions remained mounted, ranged behind him. At last Ehem looked up.

'Is there not a wind that washes the sand at this time?' he asked.

Sekefi nodded.

'But there are traces in the sand here,' Ehem continued, 'of the feet of two people. See. The imprints are still sharp and clear.'

The others dismounted and crowded round.

'Some travellers, perhaps,' Moulei Sidi-Mekammed suggested, 'who, seeing the graves were fresh, dismounted to inspect them.'

Sekefi made a tour of the graves.

'These are the tracks of our camels,' he ventured. 'There are no others. But these same footprints lead away towards Ti-n-Afara.'

'Who would come to this place without camels?' someone asked. 'One cannot travel without water and food.'

'It is strange,' muttered Sekefi. 'It is eight days now since we left this accursed place. Everything is as I remember it.'

'Who would meddle with the dead?' Ehem said, almost to himself.

The others looked round, uneasily. The sun rising at their backs reassured them.

'Perhaps we shall find where these people dismounted further on,' Moulei Sidi-Mekammed suggested, 'and came only a short distance on foot to examine the graves, before going their way.'

'Come,' said Sekefi. 'Let us leave this evil place.'

Ehem, still gazing at the footprints, placed his own foot alongside. He considered the difference in the size of the impressions in the sand.

'Who would meddle with the dead,' he repeated, 'except a jackal or a woman?'

CHAPTER SIX

EACH NIGHT the moon rises she reveals a little more of her belly, like a woman who cannot defend herself against this purposeful recurrence of darkness; who must finally give herself, naked and white, in a field of extinguished stars.

The heat of the day increases: the first sandstorms will not be long delayed. Sudden hot winds send towering demons of sand roaring across the noonday desert. The Kel es Souf are everywhere! Already sand begins to drift perceptibly into the sheltered corners of the courtyard. The heat dies slowly. When the night chill asserts itself it is as though one is experiencing an emotion as decisive as the first revelation of love. It is to the night that one returns finally from the hours of awakening.

At In Itaou the fort has become the centre of leisurely and transient activity. Underneath his motor car the Englishman lies oil-deep in the sand and searches for signs of weakness in a structure designed to withstand nothing more savage than the pot-holes of country roads. René did not understand this enthusiasm for crossing the desert in small, unsuitable vehicles. Not only did it seem to him to be uncomfortable and probably an expensive way to travel, but also dangerous.

Nevertheless, he found monsieur Jimmie – as he called him – strangely sympathetic for an Englishman, and admired him. He envied him also. For Patricia, his wife, who flits about the courtyard engrossed in a hundred trivial, necessary tasks, breathes vitality into everything she touches. Even in repose, when she sits at one of the iron tables to drink a beer, her hand shading the curve of a smile, her very stillness is the suspended motion we call life. René knew he desired her. His hand would tremble at an accidental contact. Patricia knew this also and smiled at him without a trace of coquetry. If she ever gave herself to me, René thought, she would give herself – oh, so generously! If only there were time and opportunity!

There was a feeling of departure already in the air. Tomorrow the English couple were leaving. Soon Elralem would come to tell René it was time. Migration is as much an instinct as restlessness. One morning he would awake and find the tents gone. Then he would be left to direct the steps of a few desultory travellers until May when the truck arrived to take him to Tamanrasset and his kingdom would be dismantled and closed up, like toys in a child's playbox, for the long weariness of summer.

But today he has some more visitors.

It was during the afternoon when René was about to take a shower that Lestrange walked in through the gates. He had a companion with him, a youth dressed in stained shirt and jeans, fair-haired and sullen. Then Lestrange introduced him as Mademoiselle Maillé and René realised he had been mistaken. In the gateway their guide waited, holding the camels' reins.

'It's Amaias!' René cried and went to greet him.

Later, over beer, Lestrange tells him his plans. They will stay for the night, but tomorrow they must leave for Ti-n-Afara. His companion interests René. She is very young, he thinks, but without allure. He has met Lestrange before, but has never had a chance to talk to him about his work. Now perhaps there will be an opportunity. The girl puzzles him, for she does not seem to be a student from the museum in Paris where Lestrange works. Lestrange treats her courteously but distantly, while she responds with sullen hostility. René does not think they are sleeping together and tries to satisfy his curiosity with veiled and flattering questions.

'As a matter of fact,' Lestrange says, 'it's due solely to Mademoiselle Maillé I'm here. As usual the museum hasn't given me enough money. Mademoiselle Maillé offered me the necessary financial help in return for being allowed to come with me. So you see, in every way I've the best of the bargain.'

Mademoiselle Maillé's face becomes openly hostile at his clumsy gallantry. René observes her closely. No, they are not sleeping together, he decides. This meeting with a girl who has money was simply fortuitous and explains why he has brought her. It doesn't explain, however, why she has wanted to go with him. Somehow she is out of character.

'You're very courageous, mademoiselle,' he says with a smile, 'to undertake so hazardous a journey. Lestrange is very fortunate.'

'I was bored,' she says with a shrug.

'And you are still bored?'

She hesitates. Lestrange says:

'She's wonderful the way she adapts herself. You would think she was always in the desert.'

Mademoiselle Maillé flashes him a look of anger. Lestrange seems oblivious of the effect he has on her. No, René thinks, you're not bored. And when you find this out for yourself it won't be without its compensations. It would be amusing to make this little experiment and he hoped Lestrange would appreciate what must inevitably happen.

The English couple join them; he still shaking off the sleep of his siesta, she clear-eyed and smiling. She brings into the room a sensuousness of movement so perceptible everyone is aware of it. Mademoiselle Maillé withdraws into herself. Lestrange rises to his feet and René makes the introductions. He fetches a bottle of anis and glasses. The Englishwoman leans forward in her chair. Her bare arm rests for a moment on the table. Slowly it raises itself to support her chin as she listens intently to some remark Lestrange makes. It is a movement languid and sensual, like that of a woman who has just been made love to. René looks at Mademoiselle Maillé. She also has seen it, and her eyes reflect the frightened fascination of a rabbit watching a snake.

'I've heard,' Lestrange says, 'that the *tazenkharet* is still danced by the *iklan* among these people camped outside. I've

74

seen it danced at Idélès by the *haratin*. I should like to get a recording of it.'

The Englishwoman raises her eyebrows enquiringly.

'The *iklan*,' René explains, 'are the slaves of the Tuareg. In the oases there is also a class of freed slaves, *haratin*, who tend the gardens. The singular of *haratin* – *haratani* – means "one who is free in the second generation". At Idélès, as Monsieur Lestrange says, they perform this dance which has been imported there from the region of Aïr.'

'Don't the Tuareg ever dance themselves?' she asks.

'No, madame,' Lestrange replies. 'Not the pure-blooded Tuareg.'

'In Nigeria,' the Englishman says, 'I worked in an office in a town. My clerks spoke English and wore European dress. We know so little of Africa. And now we're leaving.'

'I envy you,' his wife says to Mademoiselle Maillé. 'You're fortunate, madame, to be able to go with your husband into the heart of the desert.'

Mademoiselle Maillé scowls.

'He is not my husband.'

'Oh, pardon, of course . . . How stupid of me.'

She breaks off, confused by the girl's hostility. Lestrange says quickly, turning to René:

'Do you think it possible to arrange a *tazenkharet* for this evening? Madame Johnson would enjoy it.' He turns to her. 'It's something unique, exciting. A fusion of two natures. The negroes dance and chant in the centre of a circle and the Tuareg women sing. Between them, between their two natures, there emerges a balance and a tension that is true art. It leads up to a climax. After this the sheer endurance of the negroes, who will dance until they fall, prevails.'

'It sounds wonderful,' the Englishwoman cries.

'They're savages,' Mademoiselle Maillé says in disgust.

'Surely they're Moslems, mademoiselle?' the Englishman says. 'Like the Hausa. They can't be savages, really.'

Mademoiselle Maillé shrugs and says nothing.

'Yes, they're Moslems,' René says. 'But at heart they're

pagans. Their belief in magic is stronger than their belief in Allah.'

'It's the women,' Lestrange adds. 'And particularly the slave women. They have the power of divination. And the dead, also. When a person dies the corpse is believed to contain untold powers. Certain organs are used in magic potions and love philtres. They're taken at night from the grave by the initiates and become the active agents in the alchemy of black magic which work on the subject to be killed or dominated.'

'How horrible!'

Madame Johnson shudders and puts her hands to her breasts. Watching her, René wonders whether, if he can arrange with Elralem for the *tazenkharet* to take place, there will be a chance to slip away with her to one of the tents during the excitement of the dance. Would she come with him?

'It's not a pretty subject,' Lestrange continues, 'but an interesting one. To be effective the potion – the *borbor* – must contain something of the person to be dominated or destroyed. The usual ingredients are nail-parings, skin, hair, tears, perspiration, seminal fluid, menstrual blood and so on, depending upon the result desired. The actual preparation of the *borbor* is very important since –'

'Oh, shut up!' Mademoiselle Maillé interrupts angrily. 'Do you have to disgust as well as bore us?'

She pushes back her chair and goes out into the courtyard. René grins at Lestrange who waves his hands apologetically. The Englishman sucks at an empty pipe, pretending not to have noticed. His wife looks sad and sips slowly from her glass.

'Oh, well,' René says to Lestrange. 'You can't have everything at once. At least, not yet.'

Lestrange looks at him in surprise. Still grinning, René gets up and moves towards the door.

'I must go and see Elralem,' he says, 'to arrange for the *tazenkharet* to be danced. And then I must attend to the radio. Courage, my friend!'

*

76

Robert slung his tape recorder over his shoulder and picked up the small canvas bag containing the microphone and spare batteries and tapes. The courtyard was bathed in moonlight, so bright it would be possible to read a newspaper without straining one's eyes. He could see the English couple waiting outside the fort, talking with René whose tunic gleamed whitely in the luminous dark. Carol was still in her room. The thought of her made him suddenly uneasy and he wondered whether she were regretting her rashness in undertaking the journey. It would be cruel if she decided to withdraw from it now. He must be careful, play up to her caprices. Once they were away from In Itaou the die would be cast: she would be in his hands again. At all costs she must be prevented from giving up. He went next door to her room and knocked. There was no reply. He went in.

Carol was lying on her bed, fully dressed. She sensed Robert standing in the doorway, but gave no sign she was aware of his presence.

'Carol,' he said, quietly.

She lay utterly still, her face lost in shadow. Robert thought she had not heard.

'Carol,' he repeated. 'They're waiting for us. Are you coming?'

He saw her slight body stir.

'No,' she said at last. 'Go away.'

He went closer.

'What is it? What's the matter?'

'Go away. That's all.' Then she added, bitterly, 'Can't you see I'm sick to death of the Tuareg? You like them. All right, go to them. Make love to their women. Do anything, but leave me alone.'

A pulse of anger began to throb in Robert's temple.

'It didn't work out, did it?' he said when she had finished. 'I was a fool to suppose it would. I warned you that day at the *guelta* what it would be like. Well, now you've had your taste of it.'

'Go away,' Carol repeated, wearily.

'Let me tell you something,' Robert almost shouted. 'It

77

hasn't begun yet. The discomfort and the monotony and the hardship are yet to come. And that'll take guts, more guts than a silly, bored society girl can find. I'm here because I have something to do, to believe in – not because I've never learned to live with myself.'

Carol jumped up off the bed.

'How dare you! You talk of being here because you have something to believe in! You're here because I make it possible. I'm paying for this, understand?'

Robert, his face white with anger, threw all caution to the winds.

'In that case,' he said, icily, 'I suggest you ask the English to take you back with them tomorrow. They'll be able to squeeze you into the front seat. You were right when you said we didn't need each other. And that goes for your money, too.'

He turned abruptly on his heel and went out into the moon-filled courtyard. Now you've done it, you fool, he told himself as he went to join the others. Now you've really done it.

Between the camp of Elralem's people and the fort, not far away from the tents, the dance had begun. A large circle of onlookers had formed around the dancers and, grouped together at one point on its perimeter, some Tuareg girls stood laughing and talking, beating out a simple rhythm with their hands. Inside the circle a dozen negroes moved around with a strange, shuffling gait, their bodies leaning backwards; now bringing their feet together, grunting in time with the movements of their limbs as they jumped and shuffled. Gradually, the pace quickened, the hand-clapping became a definite rhythmic pattern and the concentration of the dancers began to turn inwards upon the movements of the dance. With one accord the negroes began to intone '*bērrr bērrr bērrr bērrr*' as they circled slowly inside the ring of watching Tuareg. Then, above the babble of talk, the grunts, the chanting and hand-clapping, a single voice rang out, pure, shrill, from the

78

group of women. It rose, savagely exultant, finding words without meaning, without sequence, to carry the fluid line of the melody:

> 'The white camel of Adhan
> stands and cries.
> In front of it is the camel of Kado.
> The lump of sugar which is broken
> you strike upwards and the pieces fly.
> The women, the boys, gather them up.
> The women have put on their headscarves:
> > that of Takkest is new.'

As the voice died away on the cadence from the throats of the women came the piercing trill of the *terelilit*, triumphant, beautiful. On the outer perimeter of the circle Patricia drew in her breath sharply.

'It's wonderful,' she whispered to the sergeant who was standing beside her. 'I didn't expect it to be like this.'

The sergeant smiled at her. Jimmie was helping Robert with the recording several paces away, where the women were singing.

'It's because you are so alive,' the sergeant said. 'You are passionate by nature and because of this life touches you deeply. These people are alive also. I would have been surprised if their music didn't stir you.'

'And you?' she said, softly. 'You feel it also.'

'Yes, I feel it. Lestrange does, too. But not in the same way. For him it is the incidence of the music in the lives of the Tuareg that is important. However much he wishes to feel with them he is separated by his research. For me, it's sufficient to be with them. We meet on a day to day basis and our only motive is to live according to the demands life makes on us. The little I've learned about them I've learned because it's necessary to me – not because it may be of interest to the rest of the world.'

'And are you happy living in the desert?'

'Happy? I don't know. Certainly, I'm happy at this moment. Tomorrow, or the day after, I may no longer be happy. But it's the expectancy that there will be other moments like this in the future that makes it possible for me to realise I'm happy now. And you?'

Patricia hesitated.

'What you say is true,' she said at last. 'And so it's difficult for me to answer. Yes, I'm happy. But I'm afraid, afraid of the future. We've given up our life in Nigeria and Jimmie hasn't a job. We're going to Spain now, for a holiday. Then he'll look around. We have to settle down sometime, I suppose. It's not because the future's unsettled that I'm afraid: it's the thought of the narrow, suburban existence that's waiting for me. I want to have children, but Jimmie feels we should be settled first. He's right, of course. But are we so helplessly enmeshed in the pattern we've been brought up to recognise? Is there no alternative?'

The dance was becoming faster, its rhythm more insistent. The dancers swayed, hypnotised by the movements of their bodies. In the centre a huge negro pirouetted slowly, his eyes rolling, foam flecking his lips. In his extended hands he grasped a *takouba*, the naked point resting against his throat. Another dancer stumbled and sank to the ground, his face distorted, in the grip of a trance. The chant which had blended, and been the counterpoint of the Tuareg girl's song, changed. Now it dominated the dancers, absorbing them into its frenetic pattern. Against its primordial metre the voice of the girl was swept away. In the moon-washed sterility of the desert black Africa cried aloud in remembrance of its lost freedom. Patricia shivered. The sergeant put his hand gently on her shoulder.

'Don't,' she whispered. 'Please don't.'

'There is no alternative,' he said.

Robert replaced the tape recorder on the rickety table near the door of his room. He was tired out with the nervous tension he always experienced when absorbed in his work. But the quarrel with Carol had been blotted out in the excitement and satisfaction of the evening. The recordings were good: far better than the previous ones he had made at

Idélès last year. With a yawn he began to strip off his shirt. Then he knew she was there. She had made no sound, no movement. He turned. She was sitting on the edge of his bed, her clasped hands showing white against the dark jeans. A wave of resentment flowed through him. He wanted to humiliate her, hurt her.

'What do you want?' he asked.

He made a gesture with his hands, signifying nothing. She got up from his bed and came and stood close to him.

'Robert, I'm sorry for what I said, for the way I behaved. Please forgive me. I want to go on. Don't make me give up now. I'm confused, Robert. For so long I haven't known how to endure my life: it's hung so heavily round my consciousness. At last I'm free of all that; free, in a sense, of myself. But I've got to have time to understand, Robert; to know what it is that's happening to me.'

He didn't answer. His limbs ached with weariness, his head throbbed. Somewhere at the back of his mind he was aware of the need to make a gesture, to concede to her humility, but he was too tired. Then, without another word, she slipped past him and was gone. He heard the door of her room close. Almost automatically, he finished undressing. With a sigh of relief he flung himself down on the narrow, hard bed. Outside, the moon was setting. Darkness and silence enfolded him.

CHAPTER SEVEN

'THEY ARE coming! They are coming!'

The cry spread through the camp and, with it, excitement: Ehem was coming, the marriage feast was beginning. Quickly, the women and girls gathered to greet the bridegroom and his friends. Young warriors mounted their camels and rode out of the camp, sending up clouds of dust. Already, the *tindé* had appeared and the women grouped themselves around the drum, clapping their hands in time with its deep rhythm.

'Where is Tebbilel?' someone shouted. And a new cry, interspersed with laughter, rose from the women.

'Tebbilel, Tebbilel! Hide yourself. Your husband approaches.'

'*Tazale, tazale,*' the young woman playing the *tindé* cried. 'Sing. Sing.'

And as the bridegroom's party approached, surrounded by Abba ou-Sidi's warriors, the voices of the women swelled into triumphant song.

'Ehē. Ehē.
Ehem is coming from the north.
Ehē. Ehē.
He rides a white camel swifter than the wind.
Ehē. Ehē.
He is strong in courage as the lion.
Ehē. Ehē.
He comes to marry Tebbilel.'

With cries the warriors swept into the camp, brandishing *takoubas* and spears. From the throats of the women came the piercing beauty of the *terelilit*, exultant, sexual, as the camels thundered past.

Alone in her tent Tebbilel listened to the noise of rejoicing. Her head ached and she shivered with a fever that was the result of strain and fatigue from the events of the preceding night. Now, for seven days, the beat of the *tindé* would fill the long hours, the pace quickening as the slaves danced the mesmeric dances of their ancestors, then changing to the rhythms of her own people: delicate lilting measures, the *aliouen, seienen* and *taré*; the music of her marriage to Ehem. For these seven days she was forbidden by custom to see him during the hours of daylight. After dark they would meet and on the seventh day she would be escorted by the women to the marriage tent. Until then she would withhold herself. With the *borbor* Abakout was preparing and the with-holding of her body she must inflame Ehem's senses and bind him to her irrevocably. Yet, she was afraid. At last, lulled by the monotonous beat of the drum she fell into an uneasy slumber.

A little before the hour of *aser*, she awoke. The drum was stilled momentarily. All the accumulated heat of the day seemed to have awaited this moment which portended the advent of night. The air was breathless and heavy. The fever had left her but Tebbilel felt herself enveloped by a lassitude that made the slightest movement of her limbs an agony of effort. The camp was quiet. Away beyond it she could see the tents of Ehem and his friends, pitched to one side in accord-ance with the ritual prohibition. A few children were playing half-heartedly near the tent of Sekefi agg-Ali. A girl, lying on her belly in the sand whilst a friend plaited her hair, looked up with only a vague flicker of interest as Tebbilel passed by. The sand was hot and rough to her bare feet. She walked quickly, almost unnoticed, across the camp to where Abakout awaited her.

'So,' grumbled the old woman, 'your husband is come. It is well. Tonight, you will bring to me his strength that I may bind him to you. Tomorrow, it will be finished and I shall be paid for my silence.'

Tebbilel shifted her feet uneasily. There was mockery in Abakout's eyes, mockery which might contain the hint of a threat.

'What if I cannot bring it tonight?'

The old woman spat in disgust.

'Are you not a woman, Tebbilel oult-Abba? Must I teach you everything, like a child? Ehem is a man. Whatever is in his mind, tonight he will recognise only the hunger of his body. Tomorrow, he will think only the thoughts which you give him.'

She shuffled away quickly as someone approached. With a start Tebbilel recognised Sekefi agg-Ali, whom she had not seen since the day of Ebeggi's death.

'I salute you, daughter of Abba ou-Sidi,' Sekefi greeted her.

'The salute on you, also, Sekefi.'

'No illness troubles you?' Sekefi asked, looking at her keenly.

'I am well,' the girl replied, ignoring the implication behind his question.

'Then, perhaps, it is for the assurance of pleasure that you consult Abakout? She is wise in these matters.'

The girl drew in her breath sharply. Was Sekefi such a fool as generally supposed?

'I consult her for nothing,' she said. 'She is a slave of my father. What is your message? Does Ehem await me?'

'He is coming to the camp to salute you. When it is dark it is his right.'

Tebbilel nodded.

'He will find me at the tent of Fenouki. It is there the *ahal* will take place.'

She watched Sekefi thoughtfully as he walked away into the gathering darkness. No, he would suspect nothing, but she would have to be careful. Tonight, it might be difficult to move about the camp unobserved.

*

Abba ou-Sidi regarded the younger man gravely.

'It is a grievous thing, Ehem oua-n-Agouda, that has be-fallen our tents. May Allah be my witness. I would give my right arm it had never happened.'

Ehem leaned forward, his hands clasped round his knees.

'When Sekefi agg-Ali came bringing the news of my uncle's murder, my heart was filled with a cold and deadly anger,' he said. 'Yet, it did not assuage my grief. That which Allah ordains is beyond our knowledge, I know, and two men have died. But I do not understand.'

'My son, when we move a stone and uncover a serpent we do not ask why the serpent strikes: we kill it.'

Ehem was silent for a moment.

'You are right, Abba ou-Sidi. Let us speak no more of it. This is not an occasion for sorrow.'

'The seeds of wisdom are strong within you, Ehem. I am proud my daughter will bear your sons. Even now she awaits you with impatience at the *ahal* of Fenouki. Aie! It seems but yesterday her mother was brought to the tent that had been raised for us. It is a fine thing to see, a tent that is new and the *adebel* waiting for the moment of joy. When I took Tebbilel's mother I swore the *adebel* would remain a whole year to testify to our happiness. I pray Allah, my son, that the bed of sand which will carry the imprint of your bodies will endure also the tempests of the years.'

The old man rose and went into his tent. Ehem remained for a while, lost in meditation. Then he too got up, brushing the sand from his *gandoura*. The sound of an *imzhad* reached thinly to his ears. He followed it and came to the tent of Fenouki. Near the entrance Tebbilel stood, looking dreamily out into the night. Moonlight fell softly on to the silver ornaments at her throat and was reflected. She was very beautiful.

Sekefi agg-Ali stood listening. The moon cast a pale light over the camp, drawing long, nocturnal shadows from the squat tents. Over by the well a troop of camels was being watered, before the herders drove them south through the cool night. Nearer at hand two people were talking in low, guarded tones and it was these voices which had caught Sekefi's attention: one of them belonged to Tebbilel.

It was late, for Sekefi had stayed talking with the men long after the *ahal* was over. Early on Tebbilel had led Ehem away into the night. Soon afterwards Fenouki had disappeared, laughing, with Moulei Sidi-Mekammed. One by one the women departed, sometimes alone, sometimes in the company of a man, until only a few of the men remained, talking and boasting of their experiences with love. The subject was not to Sekefi's liking for, in spite of his youth and courage, he seemed fated to be passed by when it came to affairs of the heart. With the sword and lance or in the game of *karé*, a kind of hockey, his speed and strength and dexterity were second to none. But, except when his body was engaged in strenuous physical action, his mind worked slowly. He was by no means a fool: it was simply that, realising the limitations of his intellect, he used it cautiously. Thus, at the *ahal*, when he had at last decided to solicit an assignation from Kana or Rati or Fatima it always happened that Mousa or Jibril or Akmadu anticipated him. Yet, he was not shy of women or afraid of being repulsed. In the last analysis, his lack of success was brought about by his inability to appreciate as quickly as his friends that subtle moment when, without any display of immodesty, a woman will indicate by a kind of sensuous telepathy that the conversation was sufficiently far advanced to permit of less circumspect allusions and of more practical suggestions concerning the true nature of love.

It was for this reason that Sekefi, troubled by the pangs of desire and little inclined for sleep, had not returned to his tent. Instead, he had walked out towards the well and circled round, re-entering the camp at the far end. He had reached the shadows of the first tents, near to where the *iklan* slept, when Tebbilel's voice came softly to his ears. Instinctively, he drew back into concealment, supposing she was with Ehem and not wishing to appear to be spying on them. A feeling of unease accompanied his involuntary movement, for he disliked stealth. A moment later his uneasiness increased: it was not Ehem with Tebbilel, it was Abakout. Fragments of their conversation reached his ears.

'. . . I will bring it to you after sunrise.'

'What must I do?' he heard Tebbilel ask.

'The powder . . . mix it with . . . food must . . . prepared . . .'

Abakout's voice finally trailed away. Although he had only been able to catch a word here and there the meaning of what he had overheard was clear. Sekefi felt a tremor of fear run along his spine. Abakout, he knew, was expert with poisons, like all the women of her race. But for whom was the poison being prepared? Surely, not Ehem? Why should Tebbilel want to poison her future husband? Then, if not him, who else? And for what reason? A dawning suspicion began to fill his mind. It was not a poison that was to be administered, but a *borbor* to dominate Ehem. Tebbilel was afraid, that was it. She was afraid of Ehem. Then he began to remember Ebeggi's accusation just before he killed him. A procession of thoughts and memories crowded into his bewildered mind and, as though the words had been spoken again, Ehem's question at the grave of Hingou.

'Who would meddle with the dead – except a jackal or a woman?'

The words seemed to fill the night. A profound silence followed. Had he spoken aloud? The cries of the herders and the grunts of the camels at the well came clearly to Sekefi's ears, but he heard without hearing. A picture, minutely detailed, flashed across his mind and he seemed almost to feel a shock run up his right arm from wrist to shoulder as the body of Ebeggi with its grotesque, half-severed head fell forward into his horrified remembrance. Gradually, his mind returned to a realisation of his situation. The camels at the well were moving off. With a start, he realised the two conspirators were still talking. Had they not heard him? Had he been so completely reliving his thoughts that they had taken the shape of sound in his mind?

'. . . tomorrow,' Tebbilel was saying, 'my father gives a feast in honour of Ehem and his people . . .'

No, he could not have spoken his thoughts aloud. Carefully, for he had no desire to hear more, he retraced his steps and re-entered the camp near his own tent. He flung himself down on to the heap of skins that was his bed and lay, eyes open, staring up into the darkness. The tent, made from tanned mouflon hides and supported on a framework of wooden hoops and poles, gave off a warm animal smell. The horror with which Sekefi had first understood how he had executed an innocent man abated. It had been the will of Allah. No blame could attach to him. Yet, it puzzled him that Tebbilel should have killed Hingou, a man whom she had never set eyes on before that night. What could have possessed her, first to kill and then to accuse another man of so senseless a crime? The uncle of her chosen husband, dead by her hand! It was indeed madness. He sighed deeply and turned over on to his side. The heavy, sensuous darkness was already stifling his thoughts with sleep. The next moment he was wide awake again. He sat up. The consciousness of what his knowledge portended cleared the fog from his brain. That he knew Tebbilel to be a murderess was one thing: now he had to decide what he must do with his knowledge. To begin with, she was the daughter of the chief: would he be believed? He remembered the calm way in which Tebbilel had contrived to throw her guilt upon Ebeggi. But why Ebeggi? That she had killed Hingou with Ebeggi's *tilek* showed that her accusation had not been thought up on the spur of the moment. Laboriously, Sekefi's mind groped for the clue he had possessed at the moment when he knew beyond all doubt that Tebbilel and not Ebeggi had killed Hingou. What had Ebeggi done? Or, what had he known? And then, for the second time, he remembered Ebeggi's accusation. But again his thoughts stumbled against irreconcilable hypotheses. Why should Tebbilel kill Hingou because Ebeggi knew they were making love? To protect herself? It was too involved. Was he certain, after all, he was right? What if Tebbilel was simply procuring a potion to ensure the satisfaction of her sexual appetite? It was well known amongst his friends that she loved with the ferocity of a lioness, that she would not be denied. He was feeling drowsy again and his body relaxed against the smooth skins upon which he lay. Gratefully, he abandoned the task of unravelling the tangled skein of Tebbilel's motives and actions. His limbs were heavy with a sensual lassitude. He thought confusedly of Tebbilel. How good it must be with someone so beautiful. No, it would serve nobody to accuse her. She would marry Ehem. But first she would give Ehem the *borbor* and he would be in her power. She was very beautiful. Sekefi's eyes closed. Just before sleep overtook him he murmured, without quite understanding why, the words of a Tuareg proverb:

'Whosoever places a rope around his neck, Allah will provide someone to pull it tight.'

The feast that Abba ou-Sidi gave in honour of his daughter's approaching marriage was lavish; perhaps because he wished to dispel any lingering stigma against his tents and to lay, finally, the ghost of Hingou. Be that as it may, by good fortune an antelope of the species addax had been caught and killed and three goats were butchered. Late in the afternoon shallow pits were dug in the sand and fires lighted in them in readiness. Then the embers were removed and the carcasses, cleaned but without the addition of fats or spices, were placed in the pits and covered with sand. On top of these 'ovens' the embers were rekindled and the meat allowed to bake slowly for several hours. At other fires the women of the *iklan* were busy preparing the national dish of the Tuareg called *esink*. They pounded corn until half was turned into flour. This they separated, the remaining grains being poured into pots of boiling water and allowed to cook slowly until they swelled. Then the flour was added and stirred into the boiling liquid so that an even consistency and firmness resulted; a kind of porridge. The *esink* would be served hot with camel's milk in bowls for, unlike the Arabs, the Tuareg eat with spoons.

The men ate first, seated cross-legged on the sand. To one

side the women were gathered, tending to the needs of their menfolk. They would eat afterwards. And, finally, the *iklan* would satisfy their hunger with the remains of the feast they had cooked for their masters.

Abba ou-Sidi had placed Ehem and Moulei Sidi-Mekammed on either side of him. The others of Ehem's party and the men of the camp, Sekefi amongst them, had seated themselves in animated confusion near the fires. There was much laughter, and jokes passed freely from mouth to mouth. But the women sat silent, keeping well into the background. Tebbilel, behind her father, waited, her heart thumping in her breast, for the moment when she must pour from the little bag concealed in her clothing some of the powder Abakout had given her into the bowl of *esink* she would hand to Ehem. She had experienced no difficulty with Ehem the previous evening, as Abakout had predicted. Indeed, she had endeavoured to direct the conversation to the subject of Hingou's murder, but Ehem had steadfastly refused to talk about it and dismissed it as an incident of the past. This refusal of his had frightened Tebbilel, who saw in it an attempt to conceal his suspicions. Not even his caresses had been able to still her fears and the fact that he seemed not to notice her unresponsiveness – she who always gave herself with such passion – caused her further uneasiness. Until he had eaten of the *borbor* she would not feel safe.

By now the carcasses had been retrieved from the 'ovens' and were being gently beaten with sticks to shake off any sand clinging to the skin. A murmur of admiration and pleasure arose at the sight of the addax.

'Allah be praised,' Moulei Sidi-Mekammed said, turning towards his host. 'It is indeed a feast, Abba ou-Sidi.'

The old man fluttered his hands benignly.

'Allah is merciful,' he replied, 'for He directed the steps of Akmadu to some rocks wherein the animal was hidden.'

'Truly, it is good fortune, now that such beasts are no longer plentiful and the heathen forbid us to hunt them, as is our custom.'

'I remember in my youth,' Abba ou-Sidi said, pensively,

'how I killed a mouflon with only my sword. It was a beast of terrifying size and its horns could have desembowelled me with one blow. I had found its spoor while climbing the mountains to command a view of the country for, at that time, we were troubled by the Tibbou and there were raiding parties in the vicinity. I soon picked up the tracks of the mouflon and I was following them along a narrow passage among the rocks when the beast jumped from above and stood menacing me, blocking my retreat. The passage in front of me ended in a sheer drop. Agile as I was in my youth, I could not have scrambled up the side of the mountain quick enough to escape those horns. And the beast had been wounded; the flesh of one shoulder was laid bare to the bone, doubtless in some contest of strength over a female. I drew my *takouba*. As the beast charged I flattened myself against the rocks and lunged for its neck. By the grace of Allah the sword entered and did not break. But the force of the charge was so great that the hilt of my sword struck me in the stomach and I collapsed across those terrible horns, completely winded. When I recovered I was able to stagger down to get help, for I could not carry the carcass alone.'

'Truly, you are a great hunter,' Moulei Sidi-Mekammed said admiringly. 'The heathen do not understand these things and I have heard they encase their meat in iron which must be removed before they can eat it. It is a strange practice.'

'They are indeed mad,' another of Ehem's friends said, 'for whenever they come near a *guelta* they throw away their clothes and jump into the water. Yet, they must find favour in the eyes of Allah for I have seen this happen three times and they do not drown.'

'Allah is all merciful,' Abba ou-Sidi said. 'His ways are inscrutable and He has created the world, even to the heathens. It is said in Kano that it is the heathen who built the mosque to His glory. This thing I do not understand for the heathen rule there as elsewhere. It is probably because they believe in nothing.'

He took the bowl of *esink* Tebbilel handed him and spooned it to his mouth, carefully inserting the spoon under his veil which he lifted away from his chin with his other hand at each mouthful. He ate rapidly and with relish and returned the bowl empty to his daughter.

'It is good,' he said, 'to sit down together like this, my people around me, near to our tents; to do honour to him who has chosen my daughter and to his friends. It is thus we invoke the peace of Allah.'

He turned towards Ehem.

'My son, to an old man departures have in them something of death. When you shall depart with my daughter to your people you will take with you my youth and my age. Yet, I would not have it otherwise. It is better the flower be plucked than it should wither on the tree.'

He nodded wisely and, losing himself in his thoughts, did not at first see Ehem rise to his knees and sway drunkenly before pitching face downward on to the sand. An exclamation of horror rose from the women. Almost at once Moulei Sidi-Mekammed and another of Ehem's friends rushed to help the stricken man. Abba ou-Sidi, when he realised something terrible was happening, sat stunned, unable to move. Men crowded round, asking what had happened. The women, frightened, cowered away. Moulei Sidi-Mekammed was the first to speak.

'It's nothing,' he cried. 'He breathes. It is but a faintness that overtakes even the strongest; a fever against which even the lion is powerless. Let us take him to his tent. He will sleep and, tomorrow, laugh at his weakness.'

Abba ou-Sidi rose, distraught. First, Hingou; and now Ehem.

'You are sure, Moulei Sidi-Mekammed?' he asked, fearfully. 'He will not die?'

'I am sure, Abba ou-Sidi. Do not be alarmed. Let us take him to his tent. See, already he regains his senses.'

Ehem stirred and groaned, supported in the arms of his cousin. With difficulty he was raised to his feet and, between two of his friends helped away towards his tent. Half curious, half fearful, the people of Abba ou-Sidi followed. The fires were dying down. The frightened slaves had fled to their quarters. Only Tebbilel and Sekefi agg-Ali remained. The girl's breast heaved with a feeling of triumph. She stood, looking into the night where Ehem had disappeared. She shivered, as though cold and, at that instant, became aware of Sekefi watching her. He began to walk slowly across the space separating them. Something about the way he moved communicated a feeling of fear to Tebbilel. Her triumph evaporated. She retreated backwards towards her tent.

'What do you want?' she asked.

Humiliated and angry, Tebbilel lay sobbing noiselessly on the floor of her tent where Sekefi had left her. The camp was silent. How much time had elapsed since Ehem had been carried away she did not know. Even while she had lain with Sekefi's weight pressing her body into the yielding sand, when her father and her people were returning to their tents she had not attempted to cry out. She had not resisted Sekefi. His sudden appearance, his assurance had terrified her. Perhaps, even, his blind, sexual strength had awakened some echo in her own animal being. And he knew. By what means he had come upon his knowledge she neither knew nor cared: it was sufficient that he had reconstructed for her, with such deadly precision, the murder of Hingou. And yet, she knew, he could never prove it. What perversity of fear, then, had made her submit? She could not answer herself; any more than she could understand the cold calculation of her fury against Hingou who had refused her. There was violence in her: bitter, sexual, which could be assuaged only in the violence of an orgasm. She groaned softly and her half-naked body twisted in an agony of revulsion. Her breasts hurt where his hands had bruised them and her thighs ached. She had been taken and broken: he had used her and thrown her aside without a thought. And it will be so always, she thought. He will come and take me and I shall not protest. And Ehem, who will be my husband, will know nothing, for he is in my power. But the other will possess me and give me nothing. And, one day, I shall kill him. Until then I shall submit. And when I lie with my husband and strain against him, crying out for fulfilment, it will not be to Ehem I cry, but to this other who will never fulfil me, who will never give me peace.

CHAPTER EIGHT

THE ENGLISH have gone. For a while René will remember them, until the tracks left by their car are obliterated. The desert has a short memory. Lestrange also, with his girl sullen and silent, has followed Amaias into the empty distance. They too will be forgotten. Their small caravan is journeying to another future. One day it will arrive, but who knows where? The English will never arrive; their destination is too vague. Their desire to escape can only deliver them into the hands of an irresponsible fate.

Once again René's kingdom is returned to him. In the silence that deepens around him he reads the letters Lestrange has brought. (He is dependent for mail so entirely upon chance travellers that letters lose their urgency long before they arrive.) Among them is one from Lisette, which surprises him as it is scarcely three months since she last wrote. The envelope is slim and he knows something must have happened. A sudden fear that it is the boy makes his hand tremble as he tears it open. The letter is brief and, behind the characters of her long, sloping hand, he can sense Lisette's distress. He sits down in the sand and rereads her letter in the hope of being able to understand. (It is a curious fact about dispossession that it occurs suddenly and can never be anticipated. Death never surprises: it is so much a part of existence that the only inconstants are time and place.) No, the boy is well – on that score he is assured. It is Lisette. Lisette is going to marry, who wished always to be free. The man is a motor salesman: a fact of little importance. What concerned René is that he accepts the boy. Would he then no longer have a son? He began to think in anger of lawyers and ways to contest this dispossession of his flesh. But could a legal ruling ever prove to him he had a son? Would he ever be anything but a stranger to him? René felt a change was taking place and no longer recognised himself as the person he had been last week or even yesterday. His anger and the feeling of dispossession that had aroused it seemed unreal, outside him. Or perhaps it is he who is outside? More and more, he tends to think of the world beyond his kingdom as a novel he has read, in which for a time he lived and moved, lending to its author a quite fictitious verisimilitude. He had never been so conscious of this as now when the English couple and Lestrange with his girl have gone their separate ways, compelling him to invent for them destinies they may never fulfil.

For a while now he has a respite. A lorry has been signalled from the north, but this will not arrive for several days. It is not one of the usual trans-desert lorries, for it has a Swedish crew. In the interim he is able to reaccustom himself to the silence. Life, a stillness of shadows beneath an incorruptible sun, began to reassert itself. And, as the afternoon light faded, the shadows, like dark ghosts, stir and stretch and slide silently away across the desert to nocturnal hiding-places where the moon would not find them.

A girl from the camp arrives with a bowl of camel's milk which she holds out between long, shapely hands. She watches as René drinks. He smiles and thanks her, but she says nothing. For almost a week now she has been bringing him milk, yet not one word passes her lips. Her name is Takkest – and that is all he knows about her. She has the delicate, pale beauty of the noble Tuareg, a purity of race that is becoming rare. It seemed to him strange he never saw her at Elralem's camp. That he had heard of her, or that her name was mentioned in the song of the *tazenkharet*, signified nothing. She seemed to slip in and out of his life so silently, so completely he could almost believe she was not real, a Kel es Souf. Her beauty disturbs him and twice she has visited him in dreams. Yet this also may be just another symptom of the change taking place within him, because it is only when she appears, when he is confronted by her existence as he is now, that he realises he has dreamed about her. It is as though she holds the key to one of the doors of his consciousness, which he may enter only through her. So it is not desire he experiences (though soon he would have to take a woman), but antipathy to it: he does not want to desire Takkest. He tells himself he is being absurd. Takkest is beautiful and her body will be exquisite. As he hands back the empty bowl he undresses her with his eyes. Her own become veiled under his scrutiny and he knows that if he wanted he could take her then and there in the sand at his feet. If she were to give a sign, in spite of his antipathy to desiring her, or perhaps because of it, he knew he must possess her. Takkest does not move. René goes to the store and takes out tea and sugar to give her in payment for the milk. Then she is gone without a word. He crosses the courtyard to the entrance to the fort, but already her slight, dark figure has disappeared into the swiftly gathering night.

'There's a lorry over there,' Patricia cried out suddenly. 'Look, someone's waving. It must be stuck.'

Jimmie swung the wheel and the car slewed round, a cloud of sand rising from its tyres. Changing gear, he headed towards the stationary lorry, searching for a patch of firm ground where he could stop without becoming stuck himself. He found one a little way behind the other vehicle and brought the car to a standstill. The man who was waving ran towards them. He arrived breathless and apparently in tears, gesticulating wildly and talking an incomprehensible language. Jimmie held out his hand and addressed him in French. The other seized it but shook his head helplessly as Jimmie asked him again what was wrong. Still grasping Jimmie's hand he began to drag him towards the lorry. There was another little man sitting on the step of the cab, his head in his hands. From the tailboard of the lorry a steady trickle of water was splashing down on to the sand. There was a large crate in the back, so large it filled the whole lorry. As they came up to it Patricia gave a little cry.

'Oh, no. This is too much!'

The man seated on the step looked up. His face brightened.

'You English? That is best,' he shouted. 'We are Swede. No one understands.'

But Jimmie and Patricia paid no attention to him. They were gazing in awe at a placard on the side of the lorry. It carried a map of Scandinavia, Europe and Africa on which a series of arrows indicated a route running from the Arctic Circle to the Equator. There was writing, also, in five languages. Patricia picked out the English.

'"This block of ice,"' she read out, '"weighing five tons and over a thousand years old is being transported from the Arctic Circle to the Equator completely insulated with glass fibres . . ."' She broke off, almost choking. 'Jimmie,' she shrieked, laughing hysterically. 'It's a block of ice, an *iceberg* in the middle of the desert! It can't be! Tell me it isn't true, Jimmie.'

The two Swedes were beginning to look alarmed.

'Madame,' said the English-speaking one. 'You must not make jokes. I beg of you, help us.'

Patricia, doubled up with laughter, leaned weakly against the side of the lorry.

'Think of the sergeant's face at In Itaou,' she gasped, 'when he sees an iceberg arriving.'

Jimmie looked critically at the water seeping from the back of the lorry.

'It'll probably just fit into his fridge by the time it gets there,' he said, unkindly.

'Oh, sir,' cried the Swede. 'What can we do? We are stuck many times. '

'You've got sand-ladders,' Jimmie said. 'Let's see if we can get you out.'

He unhooked two steel ladders from the side of the lorry and dropped them on to the sand. The back wheels had dug in deep. He looked round for a shovel.

98

'Where's the shovel?'

One of the Swedes unstrapped it and handed it to Jimmie. He began to clear away the sand from under the back axle. Patricia was watching a cloud of dust approaching from the east.

'There's someone else coming, Jimmie.'

He looked up and wiped the sweat from his face. The roar of a powerful engine could be heard and soon he was able to distinguish a dark blue truck.

'It's a Power-Wagon,' he said. 'Probably belongs to one of the oil-prospecting companies. What a bit of luck for our icemen if it'll convoy them to In Itaou.'

The driver of the Power-Wagon had seen them, for the truck changed direction and headed towards them, quite indifferent to the deep, soft sand through which it ploughed effortlessly.

'My God! That's what we need,' Jimmie said, admiringly.

The blue truck came to rest close to the lorry. Two men got out.

'*Hola,*' cried the driver. '*Vous êtes en panne?*'

'No,' Jimmie replied, in French. 'Just stuck in the sand.'

The two men came over to inspect, bowed formally to Patricia and nodded to the men. The driver, slimly built and dark-complexioned, looked like a Spaniard. His companion was tall and rather scholarly. A geologist, Jimmie thought. The driver had just seen the placard on the lorry.

'*Merde alors,*' he muttered. '*Je suis devenu tout à fait fou! Cinq tonnes de glace? Ce n'est pas possible.*'

Patricia laughed and the Spaniard screwed up his face in a grin.

'*C'est un petit glaçon, je pense, maintenant,*' she said.

The driver doubled up with laughter.

'Oh no,' he gasped, '"a little ice-cube". That's very good.'

The geologist was trying to question the Swedes.

'They don't speak French,' Jimmie told him. 'One of them speaks a little English, that's all.'

'And you are English?'

'Yes. We stopped to try and help. My wife and I are going

99

north. Apparently they've been stuck many times already.'

'It's not surprising,' the geologist observed, drily. 'But we are going now to In Itaou. They had better come with us.'

'I'll tell them,' Jimmie said.

The driver of the Power-Wagon had finished clearing the sand away from the wheels. He placed the ladders expertly in position, then turned to Jimmie.

'I shall drive it out to that patch of firm ground,' he said, pointing. 'You and the *patrón* and the Swedes will push.'

He climbed into the cab and started the engine. Jimmie explained to the Swedes what was happening. They took up their positions behind the lorry, Patricia with them. The Spaniard let out the clutch. The big, double wheels spun and then caught as the four men and Patricia pushed. The engine roared at full revs in bottom gear and slowly the great lorry moved forward, increasing speed. Suddenly, it leapt away on to firm ground. The two Swedes were dancing with joy. The Spaniard turned the bonnet into the wind to cool the engine and jumped down from the cab.

'Explain to them that they must follow me,' he said to Jimmie as he came up to him. 'But they must not drive in my tracks. If they are careful and go where I go, they will not get stuck.'

Jimmie passed on his instructions. The Swedes thanked him profusely and, shouldering the ladders and spade, set out for their lorry.

'Give our regards to the sergeant,' Jimmie said as he and Patricia shook hands with the geologist and his driver. 'I wish we could be there to see his face when he reads that placard.'

From the centre of the group of women a drum could be heard, its uncertain rhythm breaking through the noise of laughter and voices. Milling round the women more than a score of men mounted on magnificent camels added confusion to the excitement which seemed to rise with the dust and fill the air. Carol, as she followed Robert and Amaias, sensed this excitement. The scene evoked for her the feeling she had experienced in Paris when she had seen the poster of the mounted warrior against the background of mountains. Up till now the dusty poverty of the Tuareg camps had depressed her. Perhaps if she had gone with the other tourists on the week's conducted tour of the Hoggar and then returned to France she would not have lost the illusion of romance. But now, with sudden pleasure, she realised the poster had not lied after all. With admiration she gazed at the tall camels, white and grey and sand-coloured; at their veiled riders, erect and proud in their cross-pommelled saddles; at the trappings of green leather and silver and the gay saddle blankets patterned in red, black, orange, white, green and yellow. And how different the people themselves! The dusty, travel-stained robes to which Carol had become accustomed had disappeared: the desert was *en fête*. Their dark blue, indigo-stained *gandouras* gleamed with a heavy metallic sheen. Silver ornaments festooned the throats of the women. Here was no poverty: here was elegance bordering on vanity.

She pushed her way through the children who surrounded her, who tugged at her clothes and asked in curious French, their small hands outstretched, for cigarettes. Robert was already setting up his tape recorder while Amaias stood over him, talking with the women and satisfying their curiosity about the stranger and his mysterious box. Slightly breathless, she reached his side. Without looking up he handed her the microphone.

'Here, hold this,' he said. 'I'm going to take a level on the drum. It won't be much use, but it'll give me some idea. I can't expect to group the singers as I want them. In any case, it's more authentic to make these recordings exactly as they happen. I can always move around with the microphone until I find the best place. The melodic cycle is short so nothing will be lost.'

He placed headphones over his ears and switched on the recorder, setting the volume control to an approximate reading on the level meter. This would give him a reasonable safety margin against the possibility of distortion through over-recording. He preferred to have to raise the level of his recorder, if necessary, rather than have to reduce it and run the risk of distortion. After listening for a few seconds he switched off, satisfied, and took the microphone from Carol's hand. She sat down beside him.

'What happens first?' she asked, pushing her wide-brimmed straw hat back from her forehead. 'Does the marriage ceremony take place now?'

The morning sun was already hot. She looked flushed and absurdly young. Robert grinned at her. Their quarrel at In Itaou had cleared the air and, although she had been reserved in her manner – in a sense impatient over her lack of privacy during the journey to Ti-n-Afara – she seemed happier.

'Today is the final day of festivity before the marriage,' he said. 'We couldn't have timed our arrival better. First of all there will be the *ilougan*. It's like a quadrille on camel-back. It will last for hours. All day there will be singing. Then, in the evening, the bride will be conducted by the women to the tent where her husband awaits her. They will sing the marriage song, the *taré*, as they escort her. We must not intrude too much but, with luck, I'll be able to record a little of it.'

'Which is the bride? Is she among the women here?'

'No. She'll be in her tent. But the bridegroom's bound to be here among the men on camels. As soon as the *ilougan* begins we should be able to point him out, because he won't actually take part. But, look! It's beginning.'

He jumped to his feet and slung the tape recorder over his shoulder, automatically checking the connections to the microphone and headphones. The rhythm and the tone of the drum had changed. Now, as they watched, the camels were forming two lines, one at each end of the camp, like opposing armies preparing for some battle of antiquity. Momentarily, the drum ceased. Robert pressed the switch of his recorder, feeling the tension he knew so well rise up within him. Through the headphones he heard the first notes of the drum, two beats close together, the second accented, the phrase repeated and then growing into the subtly shifting, elaborate rhythm of the *ilougan*. His hand holding the microphone was damp with sweat as the voice of the singer rose above the lilt of the drum, reaching him across a gulf of centuries, tinny and insubstantial through the headphones but captured, he knew, in the full richness of its beauty by the perfection of the machine. And, as he listened, he understood that the tension of his nerves was the tension of pure happiness. Now the quadrille of the camels was beginning. From one end of the camp a warrior whipped up his mount with the free end of the rein. The beast started forward across the sand, swinging in close to the women. As it passed, another camel detached itself from the opposing line and, with great strides, covered the distance separating the two ranks. Turn and turn about the swift riding camels crossed and recrossed the camp in groups of twos and threes, drawing closer each time to the group of women, sending up spurts of sand at their feet. Suddenly, a warrior leaned from the saddle as he galloped past and, reaching down, seized the headscarf of the nearest woman. Brandishing his trophy, he rode away shouting in triumph, across the camp. As he turned and headed out into the desert the women shrieked in simulated fear and anger. The drum faltered and stopped. From each end of the camp the mounted warriors surged after him in pursuit, uttering savage cries. Startled, Carol clutched at Robert's arm as the camels thundered past, leaving a cloud of dust to settle slowly. The women clustered round the one whose scarf had been stolen were talking excitedly. The camels were almost out of sight when Carol saw them close in on the fugitive and head him off. Surrounded, he reined in his mount. Then they were returning, the captive in their midst. As they entered the camp the drum began again and the singer took up the melody as though nothing had happened. Herded by his friends, the scarf-snatcher rode up and handed the garment back to its owner. With one accord, the women burst into the *terelilit*, voicing their admiration. The piercing treble of their voices swung the needle of Robert's recorder dangerously near the distortion mark. Mingled with the pure beauty of the women's trilling the grunts of the camels and shouts from the men stood out harsh and clear and Robert experienced an emotion, part excitement, part satisfaction, at the climactic effect of the different sounds his machine was recording. The spool of tape was almost used up, but he knew he had got what he wanted. As the warriors rode back into line for the *ilougan* to begin again he switched off the recorder and turned to Carol with an expression of real achievement on his face.

'Let's get away from here,' he shouted above the noise. 'I've done all I want. Now we can relax until the afternoon. I don't know about you but, my God! I'm thirsty.'

The same evening, surrounded by his friends, Ehem waited in the nuptial tent for Tebbilel to be brought to him by the women. He did not remember his fainting fit of the night of the feast and had awakened next morning as though nothing had happened. Misunderstanding the enquiries of his friends and of Abba ou-Sidi concerning his health, he had replied that 'he would not break his lance on the night of his marriage'; and they, relieved to see him well again, forgot the incident entirely in the excitement of preparation and festivity. But Ehem, who, by custom, did not take part in the public rejoicing, found himself often alone or in the company of the older men. The days of waiting had seemed long and, at night, he could not sleep. Tebbilel, as was natural for a girl on the threshold of marriage, had become withdrawn and evasive, scarcely allowing him to touch her on those rare occasions when they were able to be alone together. Never had Ehem known such tumultuous desire, agonising because unfulfilled, which made him tremble even at the thought of Tebbilel. He was afraid of sleep, of the images it brought him of the woman he desired. But, eventually, his body rebelled and sheer fatigue forced his eyes to close. So, from time to time, he had dozed only to awake sweating with fear and certain that Tebbilel had been spirited away from him by evil forces. Now, at last, the days of waiting were over and soon he would possess her and so free himself from the torment of his flesh.

'Is it not the hour?' he muttered, rising impatiently to his feet.

'Give thanks to Allah that the moon is past, Ehem,' Moulei

Sidi-Mekammed said, complacently, 'else your ardour would serve you nothing. It is well known that women sometimes play these tricks against which we are powerless.'

'Truly we are in many ways their slaves,' a young warrior said, feelingly. 'Before we marry them they show us much kindness and love; yet, afterwards, they think nothing but evil of us and accuse us of dalliance at the *ahals* when we are away on a journey.'

'And, of course, you do not, Akelaoui?' Moulei Sidi-Mekammed enquired.

The others, except Ehem, burst out laughing.

'It is natural for a man to be a man,' Akelaoui protested. 'When we are away from our wives it is no different to exercise our right to be men than to practise with the lance and *takouba* so we can defend our tents.'

'There is, however, a difference in the choice of weapons,' Moulei Sidi-Mekammed said, pointedly.

'Are they not yet coming?' Ehem cried, gripping Akelaoui by the arm. 'Go. Go and see.'

'It seems Tebbilel has bewitched you,' Moulei Sidi-Mekammed reproached him gently. 'Such evidence of your desire is unbecoming and, to your friends, ungenerous for we shall not, saving the mercy of Allah, be so lavishly entertained this night as you, my cousin, ought to be. And, for your own sake, I beg you, be calm: the pleasures which you await with such eagerness are all too short without anticipating them through impatience.'

It was at that moment they heard the voices of the women singing. The men clustered round the entrance to the tent.

'It is the *taré*,' Akelaoui cried. 'They are bringing Tebbilel.'

Surrounded by the women, Tebbilel walked slowly across the camp to the tent where her husband awaited her. She was dressed in her finest clothes, the *takamist n'kora* a robe of fine cotton and, over her head, the *tabarikant*, a great veil or scarf of wool woven in Tripoli which fell in soft folds on each side of her face, framing her beautiful features. At her throat hung ornaments of silver and her wrists were heavy with bracelets of blue, opaque glass. She wore only two rings, on the third and fourth fingers of her right hand. Beneath her robe she clutched the new pair of sandals – the symbol of her break with her family, her childhood, her past – which she must surrender at the entrance of the tent. She would shed no blood on this night of marriage nor cry out against the first cruel penetration of her flesh, for she was a woman already. And so, in spite of an unease that she felt for the future, she walked with a dignity and assurance towards her marriage, unencumbered, as are most Tuareg women, by the fear of her virginity. But she was afraid. The presence in the camp of the two heathen had disturbed her, believing them to be spies sent from Tamanrasset. Why should they pretend to be interested in the music and customs of her people, as her father believed? It was unlikely and, therefore, suspect. Yet she could not protest against their presence for fear of arousing suspicion that she had something to hide. Sekefi, she had not seen since the night when he had come to her tent and made love to her. Although she knew beyond doubt that Ehem was in her power she was afraid. And yet, such was her nature that her fear aroused only the desire to be subjugated and possessed by man. She knew, and the knowledge intoxicated her, that Ehem, inflamed by the *borbor* she had administered on the night of the feast, would take her as she wished to be taken, panting and moaning like the animal she was. Gone, for the moment, was her fear of Sekefi and the power he could wield over her. Ehem was waiting for her. And he would fulfil her; he must fulfil her. Else, she would never be able to kill Sekefi.

Not far away now, she saw the tent where her husband awaited her. In front of it stood his friends, as though barring her path. Her heart was beating wildly and she felt faint and weak. The song of the women accompanying her came to her ears as though from a great distance.

> 'By the grace of *Iallah*
> our sister is leaving us.

Tonight she will give away her sandals
and a man will claim her.
Give to our sister those things
which are beautiful, Ehem,
as she will give to you her beauty
like a flower opening to the night.
And from the seven camels of her dowry
let her ride the most gentle,
the white that is marked with grey,
for *Iallah* is all merciful.'

And, as they came near, an old woman left the group and entered the tent. The men stood aside for her to pass. Inside, she sat down on the right of Ehem, saying nothing, and waited. Into her old body would pass any evil spirits that might be hidden in the tent, which seek to enter into the soul of the bride as she reveals herself to her husband in the abandonment of the flesh. After a few moments the old woman rose and went away. Now the bride could enter, her happiness ensured by the simple trick of exorcism.

Avoiding the eye of the old woman as she came out of the tent, Tebbilel moved towards the entrance. There she was stopped, the men still barring her progress. A cousin, the son of her mother's sister, addressed her sternly.

'Tebbilel oult-Abba, what do you seek here? You cannot pass.'

'I come to seek my husband,' she said. 'Let me pass.'

'Then give me the sandals.'

She reached inside her robe and held out the sandals. Her cousin took them and stood aside. The family ties had been cut. Without a glance behind her Tebbilel stooped and entered the tent.

PART TWO
KEL ES SOUF

CHAPTER NINE

THE MOUNTAINS drew nearer. They hung remotely against the sky, a garish backdrop softened by the faint haze surrounding them. The camels, moving slowly, almost dreamily, pushed against the heavy air, their malevolent eyes fixed unseeing on the distance. At the rear of the little caravan, Carol sat listlessly in the saddle, the rein trailing loosely over its pommel. Ahead of her Robert and Amaias led their beasts with the pack animals following behind. She, too, would have to dismount when they reached the mountains. Above them the sun burned opaquely in an ashen sky, its oven-like heat reflected mercilessly by the undulating sand. Dressed in a dark blue *gandoura* and headscarf like a Tuareg girl Carol still found the heat almost unbearable. The unbroken sea of dunes frightened her with its look of blind emptiness. Its cruel and motionless waves were a maze in which the paths could only be the crazy circumlocutions of a brain reeling against the horizon of an encircling sky. But now the mountains were closer, solid and reassuring. She fixed her eyes on them like a tired swimmer and let herself be carried gently towards the shelter of their towering cliffs. The ground began to rise and outcrops of rock pushed up through the hot sand. Overhead, three vultures circled slowly, their wings crucified against the grey sky. They appeared from nowhere and as swiftly disappeared into the haze. A little after noon the caravan entered a narrow gorge; overhanging cliffs of eroded sandstone leaving a jagged ribbon of sky above their heads. The heat in the confined space was oppressive. A few stunted tamarisk bushes hugged the base of the cliffs. In the shadow of a rock a horned viper lay coiled asleep, burrowed into the sand, a portion of its head showing. Presently, tufts of *drinn* began to appear, indicating pasture for the camels and, possibly, water. The gorge began to widen and the passage inclined, becoming strewn increasingly with boulders. Sand changed to stone and progress slowed perceptibly. Some way ahead a wall of rock rose sheer across their path, the flattened, shadowless perspective thrusting it forward so that it appeared to seal the canyon. Behind them the narrow opening through which they had come was closed by distance and the vague twistings of their path. Then, an hour later, they stood upon a gently sloping beach, gazing into the clear water of a *guelta* that had been hidden from view. Behind it the wall of rock which had threatened to bar their passage swept around in a southerly arc to form a natural basin some forty metres in width. But to the north a vista of towering rock monoliths, a dead city of geologic ages, grotesque and magnificent, spread across the plateau towards a great, central massif in the distance. The air was fresher, though there was no breeze. A silence, more profound than anything Carol had experienced in the desert, enveloped them as though they were the only living people in the midst of a petrified universe. At last Carol broke the silence.

'Do we camp here?' she asked, her voice dry and brittle from thirst, but tinged with awe.

Robert nodded.

'This is our last certain water supply until we reach Anou-Mellen. And we have to cross the dunes again when we leave the mountains.'

Carol shivered.

'I hate them,' she whispered. 'They're frightening. If a person became lost in them it would be as though all his life up to that moment was an hallucination brought about by fear and thirst. No other reality could exist in that finality of sand. I wonder if it's possible to stand further away from the idea of God, or nearer to that of death?'

Robert shrugged. He was hot and tired and metaphysics

bored him. His mind was occupied with more immediate matters.

'Once we're across the dunes,' he said, 'we shall be almost in the sahilian zone. Anou-Mellen lies on the fringe of the real desert. It's the starting point of the trans-Saharan motor route. We might even find a plane there to take us to Niamey but, in any case, there'll be plenty of lorries.'

'But what's the point of making this detour across the sand-dunes to get to Anou-Mellen?' Carol asked. 'It is a detour, I know. I've checked it on the map. There won't be any music to record. What's the point of it? Are you trying to prove something to yourself? Or, to me?'

'What the Hell should I be trying to prove?' Robert said. 'Does there have to be a reason for everything?'

He walked angrily away to help Amaias make camp. Carol went and stood at the edge of the *guelta*, staring down into the still, clear water. The trek across the burning sands had affected her nerves and now Robert's harshness upset and hurt her. She became aware of a trickle of moisture down her cheeks and, when she put a hand up to her face, was surprised to discover she was crying. It angered and humiliated her, just as she felt so often that Robert humiliated her. At the sound of his footsteps she kept her face turned away so that he wouldn't see the tearmarks where her fingers had rubbed them into the dirt on her face. But he stopped a few paces behind her and called out:

'Do you mind being alone for a while? Amaias has found some scrubwood and I'm going to help him gather it. We'll need a fire tonight, even at this altitude.'

Carol shook her head. She didn't turn round, but waited until she knew he had gone away. She heard him talking to Amaias and when at last she did turn they were already some distance away, leading two of the pack camels. She watched them until they disappeared among the strange, eroded shapes of the rocks that were like the mad architecture of an urban god. Alone, a sense of peace enveloped her, calming her nerves. She so longed for solitude, not to have to live day in and day out in close proximity to anyone but herself. That

Robert had warned her what it would be like did not lessen her resentment. Nór did the fact that Robert had kept to his part of the bargain. Would it have been better if he hadn't? she wondered. What could she have done if he had decided to take her? Cried out to Amaias for help? And what then? She knew she would not have cried out. She knew also that she had asked the impossible in the terms of her bargain, that the intimacy in which they had lived these weeks could have only one ending. She had been blind not to realise that her behaviour at In Itaou when she had turned on him in fury and contempt was caused by his indifference to her, by her knowledge that he had made love to a Tuareg girl; that she had swallowed his insults and clung to him when he gave her the chance to escape. They knew too much about each other. Only the illusion of sex could prevent them from hating each other in the end. Saddened, but no longer crying, she slipped out of her clothes and waded into the cold water. She saw her body was thinner. The bones protruded slightly at her narrow hips and her breasts, always immature, were scarcely more than two darker rings surrounding the nipples. As she ducked beneath the surface of the water she thought: I have so little to offer him. She stood up again in the shallows, rubbing the water from her eyes. When she opened them she saw him standing at the edge of the *guelta*, watching her. She covered herself with her hands, turning away from him a face suffused with anger and shame.

'Go away,' she moaned. 'Damn you, go away.'

They broke camp soon after dawn the next day and entered the first streets of the city of rock, the weird half-light accentuating the unreality of their surroundings. The paths of erosion along which they led the camels were broad and cut straight and true, forming a system of rectilinear thoroughfares between the dunes and pinnacles and mushroom shapes of rock towering fifty metres above their heads. In the shelter of an overhanging cliff Robert discovered engravings of animals – elephant, giraffe and antelope. He got out the camera and took some flash pictures. The technique of the drawings was superb and Carol commented on it.

'They're probably early neolithic,' Robert said, 'and exceptional for this region. Most of the really fine rock paintings and engravings have been found much further north, in the Tefedest and the Tassili-n-Ajjer.'

'Who did them?' Carol asked. 'What kind of people could have lived here? It must have been more habitable then, perhaps not a desert at all.'

'No one yet knows the answers to these questions,' Robert replied, thoughtfully. 'The pre-history departments of the museum are engaged in finding them and there's a team of archaeologists in the Tassili at this moment. But it will take years of research, even to establish the basis for a new theory. Certainly, the erosion preceded the engravings here. That much is obvious, but whether it argues desert conditions such as we see them today is not so certain. There's always the possibility the artists came here from a more fertile part of the continent. But, again, the number of paintings and engravings found already seems to indicate that they're the work of settled inhabitants. And the period of pre-history they cover is too great.'

'And the erosion? How did these strange rocks come to be formed?'

Robert replaced his camera in its case, carefully wrapping this in sheets of polythene and stowed the equipment safely away in his saddle-bag before answering.

'This was a plateau originally. The erosion may have started with fissures appearing in its surface, possibly due to changes in temperature of the earth's crust. I don't know. I'm not a geologist. But once fissures are formed, water action and the process of rock destruction that takes place over the ages will do the rest. Even now you can see the effect of superficial water action, particularly at the bases of the rocks where they curve inwards. And a lot of it is quite recent. This is probably a watershed during the brief period of rains. It could explain the *guelta*.'

Further on they came across a troglodyte family of Tuareg,

adding another reality to the illusion of the petrified city. An old man, his face senile and stupid, cried out to them *Baraka, Baraka* (the Blessing of God) and laughed with an inane cackle as he asked Amaias who they were and where they were going. Amaias explained and the old man laughed his dry cackle again and was silent. A woman came from the dark recess of a cave and stood staring at them, a baby held in her arm, supporting with her other hand a long, pendulous breast, wet and swollen with milk. The baby whimpered and she gave it the breast, still staring. Behind her, two naked boys, almost emaciated, edged closer on long, spindly legs, eyeing the camels. Amaias looked fiercely at them and they fled. The woman took a step backwards.

'*Enele,*' she said, without hope. '*Ekf aner enele.*'

'What's she saying?' Carol whispered.

'She wants flour,' Robert said. 'Food.'

'Tell Amaias to give them some,' Carol said. 'These children are starving.'

She pulled some glucose sweets from her pocket and held them out towards the children hiding behind their mother.

'Here,' she coaxed. 'Take them. They're good.'

The two boys eyed her warily, blinking at the sound of the strange words, but made no move. Carol unwrapped a sweet and put it into her mouth, chewing on it with obvious enjoyment. The children followed her every move and at last a flicker of interest appeared in their unnaturally bright eyes. Shyly, they came forward and took the handful of sweets, then retreated again. The old man let out another cackle. The woman had not moved, the baby still sucking noisily at her breast.

'Give them some tea and sugar and flour,' Robert said to Amaias. The woman's eyes followed the guide as he went over to one of the pack animals, but still she did not move.

'I don't think she's all there,' Robert said. 'Inbreeding and syphilis haven't helped these mountain tribes.'

Carol did not answer. She went to help Amaias who had opened a sack of provisions. The woman half turned in their direction.

'*Aoui agera*,' Robert said to her.

She understood for she went back into the cave and returned quickly with a small leather sack and two cracked, wooden bowls. As Carol filled them the woman stared stupidly at the food, bent forward, her free breast, long and heavy, swinging from her body. Then Robert told Amaias to hurry up and reload the camel. The sun was already hot and he was anxious to get started. When they were a little distance away Carol turned and waved. The Tuareg stood in a small group, watching them. The old man cried out in his thin voice *Baraka, Baraka* and the woman raised her other breast to the baby's mouth.

By afternoon the plateau and the city of rock lay behind and below them. The way now was steep and often narrow with sudden precipices as the track they were following twisted and climbed through the valleys, its loose surface of scree treacherous to the feet of the laden camels. Amaias, leading the pack animals, kept turning round to make sure that the woman and Robert, who was bringing up the rear with the three riding camels, were all right. He did not approve of Carol's presence. The place of women was in the camp. It was another peculiarity of these heathen that their women should behave like men and even resemble them. He still felt some resentment towards Robert for introducing the unnecessary complication of a woman on this journey. On the two previous occasions when he had acted as Robert's guide they had been alone and it was better thus. What else were the *ahals* for, if not to calm the hot blood of men between their journeyings? But this woman did nothing for Robert, Amaias knew, for neither the sighs nor the silences of love had reached his keen ears during the weeks of travelling. That she had given the *borbor* to Robert he did not, for one moment, doubt. Why else, then, should she have been angry that Robert had taken a woman of the Ikenbiben at Tiberlerlarin? Robert was a man with a man's body. But Amaias knew women were jealous and inconsistent in their ways, besides being beautiful. And so, dangerous. When they desired you they could bind your limbs with caresses and your mind with magic. Like Taouhimt. No, not Taouhimt for, beautiful as she was, he had mastered her. He felt a momentary shame for the way he had murmured her name in the sand of the Oued Tiberlerlarin like a youth frightened and eager in the arms of his first woman. Like Isef, love-sick and foolish, who had wanted to lie with Taouhimt that night when he took her from under the boy's nose and almost drowned in the turbulence of her flesh. A man must take, Amaias thought, grimly. The act of love is the act of possession, of war. Let those who wished surrender their manhood to the hands of a woman. He was Amaias, the leopard; his way swift and always alone. He was a noble and his father had died in battle when Amaias was young. His family had become scattered and he had grown up dependent upon no one. And now, in becoming a guide for the heathen, he had renounced, in part, the remaining ties with his people. The leopard, moving always alone. No woman would ever trap him. He was free and strong. At the *ahal* he could safely relax his freedom; satiate his strength and singing blood in the uprush of pure lust, knowing always that the next night he would lie down alone in the quiet sand, his spirit at peace with his body and sleep indifferent to the oblivious stars. But soon, desire, like a god, would demand his allegiance to the night again. It was there, already: a tightening of the scrotum, a singing in his veins. He knew, after this journey, he must return to the Oued Tiberlerlarin. Perhaps it was due to Carol's presence, to the idea of woman as the constant factor in man's relationship with himself, that made him uneasy with a presentiment of the future. That, one day, the seed, proud and heavy, the ripe fruit of his solitude, would cry out to him with the voice of a child, binding him as no woman could bind him in the moment when she, too, cries out against the loss of the man who is already diminished and drawing away from her. Before the next moon he would return to the Oued Tiberlerlarin. Of this he was certain. There might be rain in those far off mountains of the Hoggar. The earth would smell fresh and cool and fulfilled. There would be an *ahal*. Somehow, Taouhimt would know he was coming. But he would not return to Taouhimt. Let Isef learn to be a man beween her long, encircling legs. He would seek out her sister, surely in *asri* now, and say to her: 'Play me the melody of the earth drunk with water, Tehit, little wasp. Amuse us with your *imzhad*.' And, afterwards, he would take her and lay her in the cool sand and devour her innocence. He would be free of Taouhimt, of woman, of himself, even.

The going was painfully slow. At one point it was necessary to unload the camels and carry the heavy *guerbas*, the sacks of food, the tent, piece by piece, scrambling over jagged rocks, through passages so narrow the camels could not have attempted them laden. Their faces and hands were raw from the biting wind that tore through the thin material of their *gandouras*, chill against the sweat clinging to their bodies. Even the tough, mountain camels suffered horribly and the rocks were smeared with blood from the cuts in their pads. When darkness fell Robert called a halt and they made camp, too tired to bother with anything but a handful of dates and some biscuits. There was no wood for a fire and they lay down in their clothes on the cold rocks, wrapped in blankets, Carol and Robert close together to share the warmth of their bodies, Amaias proudly alone. At last they dozed fitfully and awakened, chill and cramped, as the sun climbed high into the new day. As the warm light crossed his face, Robert stirred and opened his eyes. The skin was stiff and sore beneath his beard. A constricting weight lay on his shoulder and he disengaged Carol's arm, cold and inert, from across his body. Her cheek, at once pale and feverish, was buried in the hollow of his neck. Not consciously aware of her closeness, he arose and stretched. His head ached and one shoulder was numb. Carol did not stir. There was no sign of Amaias.

Robert found himself standing on a broad shelf of rock which ended in a sheer drop. Below, and in the distance, the first dunes appeared remote and unreal. With a tremor of fear

Robert saw a vision of Amaias's body, broken and bleeding, among the rocks of the lower slopes. He took a step towards the precipice, when a voice startled him.

'I do not want that,' it whispered. 'It is tiresome and ridiculous and means nothing.'

He turned and saw Amaias standing near the camels. Then his eyes travelled to where Carol lay. She moaned in a half-sleep and her body twisted beneath the blanket, pushing it down from her chest.

'On one condition,' she said, distinctly. 'I will never be touched. Never, never, never.'

The descent to the sand-contoured plains was painful and difficult. Often the camels stumbled on steep, uneven slopes. The pack animals snarled and bit viciously at each other's legs during the long, tortuous journey down the side of the mountain. When it happened, it happened so suddenly that not even the watchful and careful Amaias could prevent it. They were negotiating a difficult passage, narrow and uncertain. To one side lay a drop of only a few metres. It was sufficient. The second camel, enraged by the attack of the one behind, turned to snap with bared, yellow teeth. In an instant it had lost its footing. It staggered on the brink, fighting hopelessly to retain its balance. Then, with a despairing cry, disappeared over the edge. In a cloud of dust, followed by an avalanche of small stones, it rolled down the slope and came to rest on its side on the ledge below, winded but unhurt. With a snort of fear and anger it staggered to its feet and stood trembling as the dust, caught in the rays of the sun, glinted and settled. From the damaged *guerbas* strapped to its back a steady stream splashed down on to the hot stone. Helplessly, Robert watched as the precious water poured over the rocks, forming rivulets amongst the sand and stone, drying away almost as soon as it touched the earth. Amaias, who had launched himself over the edge immediately, could do nothing. The *guerbas* were limp and empty in his hands. Then Carol began to laugh, helplessly, hysterically. With a savagery bordering almost on hate, Robert turned and hit her across the mouth. The laughter stopped. Carol looked at him in astonishment and her hand, caressing her bruised mouth, was wet with blood.

CHAPTER TEN

THE POWERFUL jeep pulled itself along the dry river-bed slowly and efficiently in four-wheel drive. The driver, a corporal from the Annexe, puffed dreamily at a cigarette, his blue kepi pushed rakishly to the back of his head, as he steered expertly between the holes in the sand where water lay close to the surface. Sitting beside the corporal, Jimmie and Patricia wondered how much further he would get without bogging down in the sand. A wheel wrongly placed and the heavy vehicle could sink up to its axles before the driver had a chance to act. The river-bed seemed to stretch unendingly into the distance.

'When do we begin to climb?' Patricia asked.

The corporal flicked his cigarette over the side and turned to her with a cheerful grin.

'It's hot,' he said. 'It's always hot driving through this *oued*. In half an hour, madame, we shall camp. You must wait until tomorrow. Then we shall drive to the top of the world. You'll see.'

It had been a stroke of good fortune, meeting the corporal in the hotel bar and learning he was to take supplies to a camel patrol bivouacked in the valley beneath Séouénane not far away from Assekrem. Somehow, permission had been obtained for them to go with him in the jeep. They could never have made the trip in their small car through the sand, let alone up the steep and winding escarpments which the road followed to reach the Hermitage of Père Charles de Foucauld.

At last the jeep, bouncing and swaying, left the river-bed and clambered on to firm ground. The track led now through a narrow valley. Near the entrance, but sheltered from a strong wind that had suddenly arisen, the corporal stopped. In front of them, framed in a gap between the rocks, its pure outlines hazed with violet, the Pic Ilamane soared against the sky. It seemed so close that Patricia drew in her breath.

'Why not go on?' she cried. 'And camp a little further along the road at the foot.'

'Don't be deceived, madame,' the corporal replied. 'If, tomorrow, we leave at dawn the sun will be hot before we get near to Ilamane. Further on, there are no sheltered places where we could camp near to the road.'

He gave an order to the *goumier* sitting in the back and the Arab began to unload the sleeping bags and provisions for the night's camp. The corporal placed his hand against the *guerbas* slung from the side of the jeep. They were cold.

'Good,' he said. 'We'll have an aperitif soon. When the sun goes.' He breathed deeply. 'The air is wonderful. At Assekrem, also. But there it is too cold for my taste.'

'I see you have to carry a lot of petrol,' Jimmie remarked, tapping the three jerrycans fixed in a cradle at the back of the jeep. 'Or, perhaps, they aren't full?'

The corporal laughed.

'Oh, yes, they're full all right. One for the engine, one for the radiator and the other for us. Petrol, water and wine. Indispensable to anyone in this country!'

'Have you been in the desert a long time?' Patricia asked.

'Nineteen, nearly twenty years – not counting the war, of course. I joined the army when I was scarcely more than a boy. It seemed the best thing at the time, what with the slump. I can't say I've regretted it, either.'

'Do you know the sergeant at In Itaou?' Jimmie asked. 'He's a nice chap.'

'René? Yes, he's a good sort. But he's intellectual. I'm a rough and ready sort of fellow. You have to be to live out here.'

'What will you do when you retire from the army?'

The corporal looked embarrassed.

'The fact is, madame, I think I'll stay here. I'm a mechanic by trade. The captain's promised to recommend me for the job of running the garage for the Annexe. I'd be a civilian attached to the army. What with my pension and the extra pay, I'd do nicely. You see, I've got a wife back in town, a Tuareg woman. She's not much to look at now, but ten years ago she was a real beauty. And I'm fond of her. We've got four kids, two boys and two girls, nice little things. Chekkouda Thérèse takes after her mother. She'll be beautiful, too, when she's older. Only not so dark, you understand.'

'Have you any pictures of them?' Patricia asked. 'I adore children.'

Rather diffidently, the corporal pulled out a frayed leather wallet and extracted some snapshots. There was a faded one of himself and his wife standing in front of a flat-roofed mud house, typical of the poorer quarter of the town beyond the hotel. The girl, for she was scarcely a woman at the time of the photograph, was dark. Probably from shyness, she was trying to avert her face from the camera. Even so, there could be no doubt concerning the corporal's claim regarding her beauty.

'This is my favourite,' he said, and pride and love shone in his weather-beaten face. 'That's Chekkouda. She was three when that was taken. She'll be eight just after Easter.'

The photograph showed a little girl balanced on the handle-bars of a bicycle. Her father, in the saddle with one foot on the ground, was smiling down at the upturned face of the child. It was the face of her mother, only smaller and childish and, as the corporal said, lighter in complexion.

'She's lovely,' Patricia said.

The corporal took the photographs from Jimmie and returned them to his wallet.

'Let's have that aperitif,' he said, gruffly. 'The sun's almost gone. I've got a bottle of anis and some Cinzano. Which would you like?'

They sat down on the rocks and drank anis. The *goumier* had erected a little fireplace of stones and was preparing a meal over a fire of dead wood. The light was fading and Ilamane looked ghostly and insubstantial in the brief twilight.

'It's a funny thing,' the corporal said, 'the way the Tuareg figure things out. Take that mountain, for instance. Ilamane. Near the summit there are two indentations, just as though someone had hacked out slices from the stone. According to the Tuareg, Ilamane was a fine fellow and a great one for the ladies. Well, one day he falls for a mountain to the north called Tararat — that's a woman's name in Tamahak — and starts paying his attentions to her, much to the disgust of the great massif, Amdjer, who had been enjoying Tararat's favours for a long time. Amdjer tells Ilamane very definitely where he gets off. So Ilamane takes his lance and knocks his rival down. But Amdjer, who has the reputation of being a brave warrior, seizes his sword and deals Ilamane two very discouraging blows on the neck which take all the fight out of him. To this day, Tararat and Amdjer have lived side by side in peace, joined by a ridge and you can see the wound made by Ilamane's lance.'

'What a lovely story,' Patricia said.

'But that's only half of it,' the corporal continued. 'Ilamane was a vain fellow — not that he hadn't cause to be as you've seen for yourselves — and it wasn't long before he was preening himself again and casting an eye over the girls. Soon he's in love with a mountain called Tahat, but again he has a rival, this time in Ti-Heïene. Having learned his lesson, Ilamane hastened to place himself close to Tahat and began wooing her. Soon, Ti-Heïene, furious at being jilted, decided to go off and seek his fortune in the Adrar-n-Iforas. He set out along the Oued Amded and soon came upon a mountain called Eheri. Eheri, a very brave fellow, didn't at all approve of Ti-Heïene abandoning the Hoggar for foreign parts. Quickly, he moved from his accustomed place and set himself down in the middle of the *oued*, blocking all escape. Ti-Heïene understood what was in Eheri's mind and, rebuked by the example of the other, settled himself near the wells of Tin-Dahar. You can still see the craters that mark the original locations of Ti-Heïene and Eheri.'

'I suppose one should cease to be surprised in the Sahara,' Jimmie said. 'Even at the sex life of mountains.'

'Believe me, m'sieu,' the corporal said, seriously, 'the Sahara never ceases to surprise one. Even those of us who have lived in it most of our lives. It is a serious business, living in the desert.'

They began the long, steep climb into the mountains just after dawn. It was cold, bitterly cold in the open jeep and the wind found its way even through their warmest clothes. In the remote light Ilamane appeared to be sleeping. The jeep, jolting over the stones, followed the winding valley and soon the mountain was lost behind narrow walls. As the track tilted gradually towards the sky the jeep, in low gear and four-wheel drive now, seemed to cling like a fly to the loose surfaces. At one moment a sheer drop into the valley below, made more terrifying by hairpin bends, threatened to engulf them; at the next they were roaring down from the summit of an escarpment and the peaks soared above them on every side. Startled camels, hobbled by their forelegs, stumbled up the steep track in front of them, forcing the corporal to slow down dangerously until the frightened beasts, more by chance than sense, changed direction and clambered, crying their fear, up the uneven slope of the mountain and off the road. The corporal drove with an assurance that often seemed hazardous in the extreme.

As the morning wore on, the sun's heat began to warm them. Up and up the road took them, the air becoming thin and rarefied until it seemed, as the corporal had said, they must reach the top of the world. Ilamane, sharply defined now by the clear light, rose serenely to the north enthroned in a ring of mountains like a distant and beautiful god. The track dipped and climbed again, always gaining a little more height. From the summits it could be seen, a ribbon of white dust, now stretched across the wide valleys, now twisted and buckled by the upward sweep of the hills. Soon, pasture appeared, covering the landscape with a faint sheen, overlaid with wild flowers, white and purple and red. Goats and camels browsed, tended by a few Tuareg. Then the track launched itself upward again until the bonnet seemed to be pointing at the sky. Expertly, the corporal changed down to low gear, revving his engine, to negotiate a tight hairpin bend halfway to the top. A moment later he had brought the jeep to a halt beside a small, stone hut. Across the next valley the massif of Ti-Djamaïne rose sombrely into the sky, its twin towers of black rock like a great gutted cathedral.

'*Voilà*,' the corporal said, switching off the engine. 'We have arrived.'

'Surely, this isn't the Hermitage?' Patricia voiced her dismay, taking her eyes from the grandeur of the mountains to stare at the stone hut. 'It's deserted.'

The corporal laughed and shook his head.

'Look up there, madame. There's Assekrem.'

Their eyes followed the direction of his pointing finger. High above them a flat-topped mountain rose steeply on the other side of the road. Momentarily, Jimmie thought he saw movement among the grey rocks below the summit. With his hand raised as a shield against the glare he could now make out the shape of a building. So completely did it blend with the rocks that, at first, it had seemed to be part of the mountain.

'Look, Patricia,' he said in English. 'There's a house up there. And I'm sure I saw someone watching us. Now he's gone. No, there he is. He's coming down. There must be a path. But, my God! the mountain's like the side of a house!'

As though he had understood, the corporal said:

'It's Frère Xavier coming down to meet us. See how the path winds. All the water for the Hermitage has to be carried up that path. But he'll be here soon. Go and meet him. I must get on now, but I'll be back this afternoon. Tonight we'll camp with the patrol beneath Séouénane.' He grinned at Patricia. 'Assekrem's a Hermitage, madame. No woman may stay up there after sundown.'

He climbed back into the driving seat and pressed the

starter. With a wave of his hand he drove off and soon the jeep was out of sight over the crest of the hill. Patricia and Jimmie crossed the road and found the beginning of the path that led to the heights. They could see Frère Xavier clearly now, bounding down the mountainside with great strides. In shirt and shorts, he looked like a hiker out for a day's ramble. Vertically, the distance lessened between them. Close above them now, but still a long way away by the path, a voice hailed them. They waved and shouted back a greeting. The path, although zigzagging up the rock face, was steep and both were breathless when they met Frère Xavier less than halfway to the top.

'Gently, madame,' he cried. 'Gently, m'sieu. It is still far to go. We must climb slowly. I'm Frère Xavier.'

He was a big man, round-faced and smiling. His skin was tanned by the wind and sun. He stood above them, smiling and wiping the lenses of his spectacles with a large coloured handkerchief.

'So you are English,' he said when they had introduced themselves. 'Good. Good. We don't often have English visitors. And the corporal's fetching you this afternoon? He is a good fellow. But, come along. Frère Jean-Pierre's waiting for you. Watch your step now. The path's very uneven. It's a long climb.'

He talked as he thrust his huge body up the hill with long, easy strides, stopping every now and then to encourage the visitors.

'Good. Good. Don't try to climb too fast. Just follow me. It's a steep path. It's the same one Père Charles made more than forty years ago. But it's difficult to follow in the footsteps of a man like him. As Frère Jean-Pierre says, it is, perhaps, our most difficult task. But you must be hungry and thirsty. Never mind. Lunch will be soon. Nothing elaborate, you understand. Just some soup and a *couscous*. I do the cooking. We're almost there now. Careful, madame. The rocks are very smooth.'

He pointed to a series of steps cut into the rock. They led to a wide ledge just below the summit. Lying along it was the stone building they had glimpsed from the road. A little dark man, like a friendly Mephistopheles, dressed in the habit of the order, stood smiling in the doorway. Seated on a rock a little distance away, his head bent so that his face was partly obscured, a man wearing Tuareg robes but not veiled, observed the newcomers closely. He remained seated as they scrambled up on to the platform of rock and, paying him no attention, went forward to meet the man in the doorway.

'They're English,' Frère Xavier cried, as he introduced them to Frère Claude.

'You have come a long way, then, to visit us.' The quiet voice, deep and melodious, came from behind them.

They turned, surprised, and found themselves looking into the eyes, at once laughing and sympathetic, of the man they had thought was a Tuareg. As she saw his face now Patricia experienced a deep emotion. She stared, unable to take her eyes away. The other met her gaze steadily, an expression of half-humorous enquiry lifting one eyebrow. It was a face such as had haunted her childhood, the childhood of a faith she had lost. She recognised it at once and knew, immediately, that she could never again forget. Confused images flashed into her mind and she tried to define her emotion, describe to herself the features of the man who still held her gaze. She observed the strength of the chin with its carefully trimmed beard; the mouth that was full but in no way sensual and, she knew instinctively, always kind. The eyes were blue, deep, warm and set wide above the contours of the cheekbones and the long, straight nose. Strength and endurance, yes. But these were only part of the whole, as the endurance of the rocks amongst which he lived were only a part of their strength. She scarcely heard Frère Xavier as he said:

'This is Frère Jean-Pierre, our leader. He has just returned from a journey among the Tuareg.'

Frère Jean-Pierre rose to his feet and unwound the turban from his head.

'Welcome, madame,' he said. 'Welcome, m'sieu, to Assekrem. Let us move out of the sun. Frère Xavier will have lunch for us soon. Perhaps you are tired?'

Patricia shook her head. Beside her, Jimmie, whom she had almost forgotten, replied for both of them. Frère Jean-Pierre indicated the stone building with a slight gesture of his hand.

'This is where we live,' he said. 'The Hermitage is higher up, on the edge of the plateau. It is exactly as it was when Père Charles was alive. Permit me to lead.'

They followed him up the rough path leading to the plateau. On every side the dark peaks of the Hoggar rose majestic and barren. Near the edge of the plateau a humble stone building kept watch over the mountains and valleys. The wind was cold and restless, tempering the midday sun. Away in the distance, down in the next valley, they could make out the jeep and a group of men and camels, scarcely more than specks against the faint green of the pasturage. Further away the colours faded indistinctly to a whitish-brown and were lost in the haze and against the darker slopes of rock. Frère Jean-Pierre led the way round to the far end of the building and pushed open a low door, standing aside for them to enter. The interior was dark and cool after the glare outside. Frère Jean-Pierre motioned them towards a doorway at the far end of the passage. Their eyes were becoming accustomed to the dim light now and they found themselves in a small, low-ceilinged room. There were Tuareg rugs on the floor and walls and, at one end of the room, shelves of books and an immense block of granite from the mountains covered with inscriptions in Tifinar', the alphabet of the Tamahak language. Photographs and a framed letter in the hand-writing of Père de Foucauld hung on one of the walls, near an old-fashioned recording thermometer. A barograph seemed to complete the room, austere yet peaceful, and full of a quiet assurance.

'These were his possessions,' Frère Jean-Pierre said, quietly. 'We come here often. Many of the books, of course, have been published since his death. These dictionaries, for instance, of the Tamahak language are photographed copies of his manuscript. His meteorological instruments are still working, but, nowadays, we have modern equipment installed by the Annexe. Our services to the government in recording the weather help to support us.'

'It must be a hard life,' Jimmie said. 'And cold. To have to carry all your water up the mountain!'

Frère Jean-Pierre smiled.

'In that way, perhaps, it is hard.' He shrugged. 'There are precedents. Would you like to see the chapel?'

He led the way, back along the passage and opened the door on the right. Entering, he knelt down facing the simple crucifix. Patricia hesitated in the doorway, her eyes taking in the little chapel, peaceful and subdued in the quiet light with its host of memories. Then she entered and, genuflecting, made the sign of the cross. Jimmie followed. He stood awkwardly with a bowed head beside his wife. Patricia cast a swift glance at Frère Jean-Pierre but he, lost in meditation, appeared to have forgotten their presence. After a moment he rose and, making the sign of the cross, ushered them out of the chapel. In the passage again he stopped in front of a framed photograph.

'That is Dassîn-oult-Ihemma and her cousin Mousa ag-Amastan,' he said. 'Mousa ag-Amastan was Amenokal, the king, in the time of Père Charles. His cousin, Dassîn, was famed both for her beauty and as a poetess. They were his friends and confidants. Perhaps they could have saved him. It's difficult to argue about such things without presumption.'

'We've seen where he was killed,' Patricia said. 'And his grave. I'm glad it wasn't the Tuareg who killed him. But it seems so senseless that a good man should be murdered in that way. Must fate always be so irresponsible?'

'Do you believe in fate?' Frère Jean-Pierre asked, gently, but with a touch of irony in his voice.

He turned and walked to the door, holding it open for them. Outside, the glare was very bright, momentarily dazzling their eyes.

'Have I time to take a walk over the plateau?' Jimmie asked. 'I'd like to take a few snapshots of the mountains.'

'There's still about twenty minutes before lunch will be ready,' Frère Jean-Pierre affirmed. He looked enquiringly at Patricia.

'I think I'd like to stay here,' she said. 'May I?'

Frère Jean-Pierre smiled at her.

'Whatever you wish,' he said. 'If you will excuse me, I must speak with Frère Claude.'

Patricia watched him as he went lightly down the rough path. Jimmie had wandered off across the rocks and was already lost to sight behind the Hermitage. The cool stillness of the passage closed around her once more. She stood for a moment uncertain of what she wanted. Then, with a sudden resolve, pushed open the door to the chapel and went inside. A feeling of peace came to her as she knelt in the silence, in the subdued light. She was not praying. It was so long since she had been inside a place of worship she did not know how to begin. Nor could she have explained to herself what it was that drew her so strongly now. She had fought her battle with the religion of her upbringing long ago and, believing she had won, turned her back on it. Marriage and her life with Jimmie had seemed sufficient. Only the absence of a child had dispossessed her a little of her happiness. Now, more than anything, she wanted to empty herself; to let the calm and reassurance of the little chapel flow into her and fill her. She felt a confidence that was founded on humility, not pride, in attempting an act of self-negation. She knelt, her eyes open, seeing nothing. Time ceased to exist. Only when, finally, she rose and crossed herself did she see Frère Jean-Pierre in the doorway, watching her. He stood aside to let her pass.

'It is so peaceful,' she said, when they were out in the passage.

'Yes,' he replied.

She turned towards him a face anguished and supplicating.

'What am I to do?' she asked.

'About . . .?'

'About my life, about everything.'

'Do you expect an answer?'

'No. I don't know. I thought it no longer meant anything, being a Catholic. It's never mattered before that my husband wasn't of my faith. Because I'd lost it.'

'Why did you come here?'

'I'm not sure. It's true I'd read something about Père de

Foucauld. Right from the start we'd intended to come here. But like tourists who don't want to miss anything. Then, in the desert, after the sweat and toil of getting through the sand, I'd lie awake at night and watch the stars. It frightened me, that immense canopy of the night. It seemed that nothing was left to hold on to, that nothing mattered. In the daytime it's different but, even so, I can't escape completely.'

'Have you spoken to your husband?'

'Jimmie? No. What could I say? I love him. I don't regret anything. But, for him, life is straightforward, uncomplicated. Cause is followed always by effect. Perhaps all men are like this. Perhaps they are born with an assurance, a belief in their destinies. Even in moments of despair they're safeguarded by belief in something. I don't mean necessarily in God. More than anything by a faith in the future, an ability to believe in a future.'

'Have you no children?'

'It's children I want. We've been married three years now.'

'And your husband? Doesn't he want children?'

'Yes. Yes, he does. But not now, not until we're settled again. Until he finds work. It was he who wanted children when . . . But I . . . didn't want to be tied by them. Not when we were first married.'

Frère Jean-Pierre regarded her closely.

'There's something else,' he said after a moment. 'Something else that's troubling you. Perhaps more deeply. Would you like to talk about it? Confession is the way of salvation. Or so our church teaches. I am a priest, also.'

She hung her head.

'It's been so long, father. I've forgotten the words.'

'Do the words matter? It's not the form that shapes the spirit, but the spirit which gives truth to the word. The Tuareg have a saying: "the palm of the hand does not eclipse the sun." It is one of their many proverbs Père Charles records in his writings. I interpret it as "whatever our sins, they cannot extinguish love." While love endures so also must hope. Perhaps this is what faith means. Do not despair, my child.

133

Remember that it is easier for God to absolve us than for us to absolve ourselves. Because we magnify our sins. And that is also a sin. Go in peace.'

He made the sign of the cross over her bowed head. The door opened and Frère Xavier appeared. Light flooded into the dark passage. It caught Frère Jean-Pierre's head, irradiating his features so that they glowed softly. He smiled at Patricia.

'Go,' he repeated quietly. 'The meal is ready. I will follow. Go with God.'

She went out into the sunlight. Frère Xavier looked enquiringly at his superior, then closed the door gently. Frère Jean-Pierre went into the chapel and knelt.

'Well, and what did you think of Frère Jean-Pierre?' the corporal asked, as he drove them down from the col to where his patrol was bivouacked.

'He looks like a saint,' Jimmie said.

'He's that all right,' the corporal agreed. 'It just does one good to be near him. I suppose, day after tomorrow, you'll be on your way north? Take my advice and get across to the *Tanezrouft* route. Don't go as far as El Golea. Turn south-west at In Salah and take the route to Aoulef and Adrar. Between El Golea and Algiers the country's stiff with rebels. It's just not safe, not according to the radio. Go via Adrar. That's what I'd do in your place.'

Jimmie glanced at Patricia. She did not appear to have been listening. She sat with her head bowed, lost in thought. When she did at last raise her head it was to look backward over her shoulder towards Assekrem. There was a faraway look in her eyes, a look of sadness, as though she had lost something infinitely precious. Jimmie followed the direction of her gaze, then turned his own away quickly, not wishing to intrude. He felt suddenly inadequate, conscious of a gulf between them he could never cross.

'Will you show me on my map the route we must follow?' he said to the corporal. 'If we take your advice it should be possible to cross into Morocco somewhere near Colomb

Bechar. There's sure to be some sort of a road that'll take us to Meknes. Then we'll be on the main highway to Rabat and Tangier. And that again should be safer than striking north from Colomb Bechar to Oran. If the rebels have virtually cut the road south from Algiers it's ten to one they'll try to do the same to the other main route. If they haven't done so already.'

The corporal nodded.

'Better safe than sorry,' he said. 'That's my motto.'

CHAPTER ELEVEN

DRAGGING HER left leg slightly, Abakout limped across the camp. The afternoon was hot and there was humidity in the atmosphere as though rain, miraculously, might fall. She cursed the pain in her leg, grumbling to herself as she went against the ravages of age and the rheumatism which, each year, tightened more closely around her joints. At the edge of the camp she stopped and stood for a moment, as though undecided as to her next movement; but her sharp eyes flicked over the camp, missing nothing. The tents were quiet and deserted looking, cowering beneath the heat trapped between the earth and the haze-obscured sun. Muttering aloud, Abakout turned in the direction of the new tent pitched a little away from the camp where Tebbilel and her husband were living. Arrived at the entrance, she paused and looked quickly behind her. Satisfied no one was about, she pulled aside the tent-flap and peered inside. Narrowing her eyes against the gloom of the interior, she could make out the shape of Tebbilel lying sprawled asleep on some skins at the far side of the tent. Reassured, although she knew already that Ehem would not be back until evening, Akabout entered and sat down quietly to wait. She was in no hurry and began to study the sleeping girl dispassionately, leaning forward in the feeble light to perceive more easily the pale beauty of her naked body. Tebbilel lay on her back, her face in shadow. One slender arm trailed away into obscurity behind her head, the other lay across her body, its fingers touching her breast which rose and fell gently with the barely audible rhythm of her breathing.

As Abakout's eyes accustomed themselves to the diffused light inside the tent, the pale skin of the sleeper seemed to glow as though from an inner radiance. The old woman gazed with envy at the flat, firm belly, at the slender thighs tapering to narrow ankles and small, shapely feet. The limbs were not relaxed, but rigidly asleep; so that the girl's ribs showed faintly beneath the skin and the curve of her sex, delicate and shaven, seemed to thrust upwards as though towards an invisible caress. She's waiting to be taken, Abakout thought. She sniffed. Hingou had been a fool to refuse such beauty. And a fool deserved to die always. She cleared her throat loudly. Immediately, the girl started awake, her pale, frightened face rising out of the shadows as she drew herself to her knees and crouched, peering into the gloom. Abakout kept absolutely still. In her dark clothing she knew the girl could not see her where she sat hugging the shadows of the tent wall. Then she saw a glitter of metal in Tebbilel's hand. The girl was crouching like a beautiful and dangerous animal, her breasts flowing from her body downward to their small conical points, which quivered as though scenting danger. In her hand she clutched a long knife. At last, Abakout spoke.

'Was it thus, Tebbilel oult-Abba, that you stole upon Hingouagg-Ahnet and placed the knife in his side?'

At the sound of the old woman's voice Tebbilel rose and swung round towards her, teeth bared, lithe and deadly in her movements. Abakout cowered away, suddenly afraid.

'Don't kill me,' she whined. 'It is I, Abakout. I mean you no harm. Let me talk to you.'

She watched fearfully the poised hand which grasped the knife. The muscles of the girl's arm were distended and tremors rippled down its length. Sweat stood out on her body, forming tiny rivulets which trickled from the armpit down her side, from the throat and shoulders into the hollow between her lifted breasts. The odour of her body filled the tent, heavy and female, like that of a frightened animal. Her belly contracted and a shudder of revulsion seized her limbs. Her thighs and legs trembled and the knife wavered. The arm

137

that held it returned slowly to her side. Abakout breathed a sigh of relief. Yet, in spite of her fear, she had been filled with admiration, as well as envy and hatred, for the girl's savage beauty, for her strength and her nakedness. To be a man in the face of such fury! To subdue it, drive it back into the cage of the loins and then to possess it, snarling and raging against the prison of the flesh! And this, Hingou had refused. Yes, he had deserved to die.

Tebbilel, still trembling, looked at her dully. A nerve in her groin twitched spasmodically.

'What do you want?' she asked.

The danger over, Abakout regained her courage. She reached out and stroked the inside of the girl's thigh with her fingers. Tebbilel shuddered, but made no move. A note of insolence returned to the old woman's voice.

'Put away that knife, Tebbilel. It can have no purpose now. You have achieved your desires and soon your husband will return. Aie, I remember well the blind anger of the flesh. Age is cruel, for the body does not forget easily.'

'What do you want?' Tebbilel repeated. But she flung the knife into the far corner of the tent and dressed herself. She felt exhausted and the rough cotton garments clung to her sweat-soaked skin.

Abakout's eyes, quick and evil, watched her curiously; then darted to the bed of sand with its dishevelled covering of skins and the deep depression left by the weight of two bodies. A furrow ran to the edge of the flat mound as though an arm, outflung to escape un unbearable ecstasy, had pressed into the soft, warm sand and fingers had clawed its yielding surface.

'The *adebel* speaks of your happiness, Tebbilel oult-Abba. So much happiness for the price of one goat.'

The girl stiffened. She turned slowly and faced the old woman.

'What are you saying?' she whispered, fearfully.

'That I am old and poor. Does your name not mean "she who has everything"?'

'I have paid you well.'

'For the *borbor*, yes. But silence, like the goat, has to be fed.'

'What if I kill you?'

'You won't kill me, Tebbilel oult-Abba. It is too late. Death is no longer your friend.'

'What do you want?'

The old woman rose slowly to her feet. She stood close to the girl and raised a withered arm. Tebbilel shivered as she felt the calloused fingers caressing her neck, then move quickly over her flesh, downwards into the hollow between her breasts.

'The *teraout*,' Abakout whispered, her breath old and evil in the girl's face. 'The pendant of silver.'

Her fingers strayed over Tebbilel's breast and closed suddenly round a nipple, squeezing it cruelly. Sickened, the girl struck out with her fist and the old woman staggered and fell. Tebbilel seized the silver pendant Ehem had given her from where it lay among the heap of skins and flung it at her tormentor. The old woman snatched it up, grovelling on her knees in the sand.

'The Blessing of Allah upon you,' she crooned. 'The Blessing of Allah.'

Tebbilel rushed at her, kicking out with bare feet.

'Take it,' she screamed. 'Take it and go. Filth. Witch. Hyena.'

It was nearly the hour of *aser* when Ehem returned, his robes covered with dust. He kicked off his sandals and, stooping low, entered the tent. It was almost dark but he saw Tebbilel kneeling in the sand close to the entrance, her figure, slight and insubstantial, outlined by the vague glimmer of her white *gandoura*. The freedom he had known in the company of his friends during the hours, heat-heavy and exhausting, they had spent together out in the desert evaporated. They had ridden away before dawn towards the mountains, hoping to pick up the tracks of a mouflon Adelaoui had seen the previous day poised on a promontory of rock, its shaggy head and great, curving horns alert and watchful. The hunt had proved fruitless and Ehem had returned alone, utterly weary, but drawn towards his wife by a power he could neither understand nor wished to admit to himself. Now, as he sensed her presence, even his weariness was taken away from him. His spirit longed to revolt from the spell which overpowered him, but his mind, sapped of its will, gravitated towards her with all the strength and weakness of his body. He reached out to her in the increasing darkness, feeling desire rise and thicken at the very root of his being. Roughly, he raised her up from the floor. She stood, limp and aquiescent, while his hands discovered the image of her his mind always retained and which his eyes could not see. She allowed herself to be led towards the low mound of the *adebel*. The sand, disturbed by her robe, sifted to the floor with a faint, dry hiss. Suddenly, she twisted from his grasp and disappeared into the night which flowed around her like a dark robe from the uncovered entrance of the tent. He heard her voice, close to him, sighing out of the darkness.

'Ehem, my husband, take me away to your people of the north. Let us seek the mountains where the earth is freshened and fulfilled with rain. I am parched, Ehem. My body is parched with this heat. It withers and dies away. My flesh is a pasture, Ehem, where your body, like a white camel, grazes. Take me away, Ehem, my husband.'

The nearness of her body brushed aside the darkness. His hands touched her and he knew she was naked. Then, like a wraith she melted once more into the night.

'Do not withhold yourself from me,' her voice murmured.

Dazed and confused, he reached out for her. His hands closed around her buttocks, soft and yielding. His mouth was dry. His longing for her made him weak and stupid.

'How can I take you away?' he asked, hoarsely. 'For a year we must live here among your father's people. It is the law.'

'Ehem, Ehem,' she murmured. 'My husband.'

Her hands were like the wind shaping the desert with caresses, now gentle, now violent. The smell of sand, rising from her body, intoxicated him. He pressed her back, down into the sand of the *adebel*. But at the last she avoided him.

'Now,' she whispered from the entrance to the tent. 'Saddle two of the camels. The others will follow behind. Now. We will ride to the end of the night. There you will take me.'

Obediently, he followed her out to the tethered camels. She watched him, the night cold stealing up through her body, as Ehem saddled the grey and white camel for her and then his own. Exultation and relief filled her as she brought the *guerbas* to be strapped on the back of one of the other camels. Quickly, she went back and gathered together her possessions, feeling around in the dark on the floor of the tent. Clothed now and ready she gave to Ehem her *tabaount*, the wardrobe bag of ornamented leather used by Tuareg women, to hang from the saddle. As she climbed on to the kneeling beast she laughed silently to herself. Free! her spirit cried. Free of Abakout, of Sekefi, of the past. Free! Free!

They rode silently away into the desert, the string of camels following. Over at the camp, fires gleamed among the tents. The sound of voices and laughter came to them faintly across the increasing distance. No one saw them go.

He has been ill. For two days he was scarcely able to crawl to the radio and attend the fixed-time calls at dawn and dusk. Probably, it was the camel's milk, which carries always the threat of typhoid. Yet he does not believe it was typhoid; unless in a very mild form.

It began with a sudden fainting fit. Takkest had brought him the milk as usual and gone already. The light was fading in the courtyard. Above everything, he remembered on that evening having a tremendous feeling of well-being; a state of mind and body totally at variance with the attack that followed. He had just come from the radio room, having closed down for the day and knew nothing more until he regained consciousness lying face down near the well. It was dark, for the moon had not yet risen. He got to his knees and leaned weakly against the parapet of the well. He felt hot and feverish and had a terrible thirst. Somehow, he managed to get himself to bed where he slept fitfully, tormented by dreams. They were mostly about Lisette and the boy, but once it seemed Takkest was standing by his bed, looking down at him, her pale face beautiful and cruel. He awoke with a start, uncertain if he had been dreaming. It must have been late in the night for a shaft of moonlight fell on to some clothes hanging from a nail in the wall. He was bathed in sweat and trembling. The clothes, to his feverish imagination, had the appearance of a human figure; but the room was empty. He slept again, waking late in the morning. Adhan was standing by the bed. The sun was already hot. After a while he went away, saying nothing. That evening, René reported his illness over the radio, saying he did not need a doctor and would be fit again within a couple of days. This was quite true, for already he felt very much better and was able to take a little food. His intense thirst had abated and he was now sleeping well. He was still weak, of course, and it was sleep more than anything he craved. Fortunately, no further vehicles had been signalled so he was able to nurse back his strength without having anybody but himself to worry about. The oil prospectors and the two Swedes with their ridiculous iceberg had already left before he was taken ill.

Nothing has altered, except that Takkest no longer brought him milk. Perhaps it was as well, for he could not rule out altogether the possibility his illness was connected with it. Nevertheless, he is disappointed and absurdly angry because she does not come. He felt there was some mystery surrounding her. Elralem, when he questioned him, was evasive and declined to say more than that she was the daughter of Akou-n-Aforas. René did not press him further, for he sensed the conversation was not to Elralem's liking. He, having expressed concern about René's health and commended him to the care of Allah, took his leave.

Unexpectedly, Captain Brillet, who commands the territory, arrives. With him is an army doctor, Lieutenant Morel, and two soldiers. They have been making a tour of inspection to the north-west and, hearing over the radio that René was ill, decided to make a detour to In Itaou in case he needed medical attention. Captain Brillet is a small, bird-like man with alert eyes and the reputation of being a martinet, so he is not popular. But his knowledge of the territory and his understanding of the people he is responsible for is second to none. For this he is respected. The doctor is a new arrival, recently transferred from the north, whom René did not know. The captain was surprised, he sensed, to find everything in order and listened to his report with a scowl that, René knew, was intended to conceal his relief that things were no worse. He unbent slightly when René had finished and suggested they take an aperitif when the doctor had made his examination.

In René's room Morel tells him to strip and proceeds to examine him with the thoroughness of a doctor at a recruiting depot. He probes into his medical history and asks whether it is the first time René has been ill during his present tour of duty. Does he find living alone a strain? What are his interests? Has he been recently with any Tuareg women? He listens absently to René's answers, his mind busy with reflexes, his hands, broad and strong, prodding and probing. He lifts René's eyelids and peers intently at the whites, which are slightly discoloured. Bending down, he examines René's penis for signs of infection. Finally, he shakes his head, replacing the stethoscope and pencil-torch in his case, and tells him to dress. René looks at him enquiringly.

'I can't find anything wrong with you,' the doctor says. 'You need rest, that's all. I'll recommend you for sick leave.'

'It's not necessary, doctor,' René tells him. 'I'm due for leave soon in any case. If I hadn't been unable to attend the radio that one morning no one need have known I was ill. As you've seen, I'm fit again already.'

Morel looks at him searchingly.

'Don't underestimate the effect of living here alone, sergeant,' he warns. 'It would be better, after your leave, if you apply for a posting – to the Annexe, perhaps. There's no need to play the hermit here, year after year. And in the end it's a bad thing. Asceticism's all very well, but it's sometimes just a negative approach to life. It's important, I know, to understand the Tuareg, but to exclude everything else from your life is dangerous. Captain Brillet tells me you're an intellectual and, I suspect, a bit of a dreamer also. But it's important to keep things in perspective. You've got to accept that the qualities you admire in the Tuareg way of life must soon be swept away by the machine. It's happening, as you know, up north. To survive, the Tuareg must adjust to the world encroaching so rapidly upon them. The Arabs have done so and Islam is now experiencing an upsurge of power almost without parallel. Simply because it has learned to adjust itself to the demands of present day politics and government.'

René knew he was right. The increasing activity of oil companies in the area was only one visible sign. There were many others. It was not only France that, over the years, had pushed her frontiers in Africa from the Niger and the Atlas mountains to meet at an arbitrary line in the desert, a line that passed inevitably through the black hills south of his kingdom. It was the world itself – the civilised, unseeing world rushing in blinded by its own light – that would put out the sun.

'Thank you, doctor,' René said. 'You're right, of course. I'll try to follow your advice.'

The doctor laughed.

'I doubt it,' he said. 'But that's your affair. Now we'd better go and join the captain.'

The captain frowns at René as he follows the doctor into the mess-room.

'Well?' he snapped. 'I suppose the man's a fraud, eh, Morel?'

Morel smiles. He has a slow, confident smile and René liked him. It was not his fault the world was changing.

'Not quite a fraud,' he says. 'Perhaps someone's slipped him the *borbor*,' he adds wickedly.

'Dammit, Morel!' Captain Brillet's eyes flash. 'I won't have this blasted psychological nonsense. If the man's fit he's fit. Tomorrow we must be on our way. All right, sergeant, I'll give you a signal to send later. Right now I'm thirsty. Sit down. You're not on duty.'

He began to talk about the Sahara and the problems of an

144

administrator. He talked well and without condescension, asking René's opinion on matters affecting his section of the territory. Apropos of nothing, René mentioned the lorryload of ice. The captain's face reddened and his moustache bristled. The doctor flashed René a warning look. He had forgotten Captain Brillet's dislike of tourists – especially those who came to the desert with crack-brained schemes. The two soldiers, scarcely more than boys and awed at having been chosen to accompany the captain, look apprehensive and take gulps of beer to hide their nervousness.

'Listen,' Captain Brillet says, controlling himself with an effort. 'We've just covered over a thousand kilometres in the truck and on camels. Lieutenant Morel has had a threatened outbreak of typhus on his hands. There's a rumour a man called Hingou agg-Ahnet has been murdered and that some petty chief of the Kel Eoui has taken justice into his own hands – not in my territory, thank God! – and when we get back I've got to organise elections to decide who's to be mayor of Tamanrasset. How am I supposed to control my territory with tourists and oil companies and crazy sensation hunters waving their permits and authorities under my nose?'

Like the doctor, he is right, René thought. He knew the captain envied him. He had come up from the ranks. Twenty years ago, perhaps, Captain Brillet also had known the solitude and satisfaction of an outpost; of a life harder, more primitive even than his. René looked at the doctor. Is this the only alternative you can offer me? he asked him silently. Promotion and regret?

Deprived of his customary nocturnal wandering by the presence of Captain Brillet and the doctor, René tossed and turned uneasily on his bed that night, unable to sleep. Something the captain had told him fluttered moth-like at the window of his memory, clamouring to be let in. He lets his thoughts wander freely, hoping they would trap and retrieve it. Instead, they return with an image of Takkest and Amaias talking together on the fringe of a circle of dancers, and he is reminded of the night of the *tazenkharet*. He began to think about the Englishwoman, Patricia; to wonder where she was now and why she had run away from him that night, from the tent in Elralem's camp when ... He checked his train of thought and concentrated once more on the image of Takkest who appeared to be laughing — something he had never seen her do. Did they lie together that night, she and Amaias, out in the desert beyond the camp, or perhaps in her tent? Why did he ask himself this? Was it an association of ideas? Or the suspicion of jealousy? Takkest would surely have lain with someone that night. Adhan? Why not Amaias?

He must have fallen asleep then and dreamed. Later, half-awake, with the dawn not far off, a name clung to his consciousness: Hingou agg-Ahnet. It was the name of a man who had been murdered. Captain Brillet had told him. Suddenly he was wide awake with the discovery that he had known even before he was told. How could he have known? He sat up and fumbled for cigarettes and matches. Had he dreamed it all? About Tebbilel? About Abakout, the witch? And Sekefi's cunning?

The sudden flare of the match lit up the room and flung his shadow against the bare wall, briefly capturing from the photograph beside his bed the features of Lisette and his son. He inhaled deeply, drawing the caporal's dark, acrid smoke down into his lungs, and closed his eyes. It must have been Amaias who told him these things. But when? Was there more to know? Or had Amaias already told him the rest of the story? How could he have done? René ground out his cigarette on the wall behind his head. He closed his eyes once more. Where did reality end and dreams begin? He fell asleep almost immediately.

Early in the morning the captain and the doctor took their leave. The sun rose above the pall of dust hanging limply behind the big, six-wheel-drive army truck. The noise of the engine faded, increasing again as the driver changed gear. Soon it became lost altogether. Beyond the trees the camp was stirring. A camel cried morosely. René felt another link with the world had been severed. Within a few weeks his kingdom would be empty and abandoned, silent except for the shrill laughter of the wind and the crazy Sudanese who will arrive in the same truck that will take him away. Now that Lisette is married there is nowhere for him to go. But he is overdue for leave. There can be no possibility of a further deferment.

As he walks back to the fort he is conscious of being watched. He swings round in his tracks, nervous and alert. A slight figure detaches itself from the shadow of the trees and disappears round the shoulder of a dune. The early light is uncertain and the shadows still heavy. Yet in that instant when she is outlined against the paler shape of the dune he recognises her. It is Takkest.

CHAPTER TWELVE

THE CAMELS were beginning to feel the strain. Every few minutes one or another of them would lower its neck and bare yellow teeth, retching and snarling. The thick saliva dried where it spilled from the corners of their mouths, matting the coarse hair. Yet they kept going, placing their broad feet unerringly at the commencement of each great stride. Swaying to their steady motion, Robert and Carol sat hunched over the pommel-cross of the Tuareg saddles, bare feet outstretched to rest on the necks of their mounts. In dark blue *gandouras*, their faces veiled, they appeared from a distance no different from the tall figure of Amaias striding in front, his broad, desert sandals moving noiselessly over the loose sand surface.

As the sun dropped slowly, slanting shadows spilled westwards from the thrusting dunes and the wind patterns in the sand stood out more sharply. Out of the stillness a sudden, hot wind whipped up and drove a column of dust writhing across the path of the caravan. Just as suddenly the wind died away. The air became still again, more oppressive.

Amaias halted. Behind him the pack camels came to a standstill beside the riding camel he was leading and waited patiently, apathetically, for the command to proceed. But the guide stood for a moment sniffing the air. Then he bent down and, putting his ear to the sand, appeared to be listening. Impassively, he sat down cross-legged, his piercing grey eyes fixed on the sand at his feet. Seemingly without motive he picked up a handful of the fine yellow dust and sniffed at it through the folds of the veil wound across the bridge of his nose. He let the sand trickle back slowly from his fingers, back into the desert.

The others had come up to him now. Robert reined in his camel and, using his feet, pressed down on the neck so that the beast was forced slowly, protestingly to kneel. He swung his leg free from the saddle and slipped to the ground, still holding the rein. Quickly he bound this round the bent foreleg so that the knee couldn't straighten, so that the camel couldn't rise. Then, taking Carol's rein, he made the other camel kneel also. As she dismounted the veil slipped from her nose, revealing her strained, tired features. There were dark circles under the eyes, giving them a curious violet tinge, and her lips were cracked and parched.

'Do you think we'll find water soon?' she asked, trying to keep the edge out of her voice. 'You don't think we're lost, Robert, do you?'

Robert looked at her. His tongue felt swollen and clumsy in his mouth. The thirst wasn't bad yet, but they had got to find water soon. His eyes fixed briefly on the pack camels and took in the empty goatskins, hard and dry from the sun. One *guerba* was maybe a quarter full; perhaps seven or eight litres for the three of them. And Anou-Mellen was how far away? Without water he knew they could never make it.

'We'll find water,' he said with a show of confidence, watching the golden sand trickle through Amaias's fingers back into the desert. 'Amaias is a good guide. He knows what he's doing.'

Amaias did not look up at the mention of his name. He still sat cross-legged, as the Tuareg always sit, unmoving, contemplating the sand at his feet.

'But,' Carol said, urgently, 'we've almost finished the water. What's he doing, just sitting there? Doesn't he know where there's a water-hole? He can't just sit there and let us die of thirst.'

Robert laid a hand on her arm reassuringly. He hadn't thought it would turn out like this. He hadn't thought a lot of things that day at the Guelta Imlaoulaouen when he knew he was going to take her with him. They had made a bargain and he had kept to it. But this wasn't part of the bargain; not this danger he had led her into. Whatever happened, he was responsible for her and he felt guilty as he saw how thin and drawn her face was, how desperately she tried to conceal her fear. He felt a sudden surge of pity for her; pity mingled with affection. They had lived together for so long in an atmosphere of close intimacy that now he could not imagine how he would feel if she were not there. Perhaps I am falling in love with her, he thought. The idea startled him. She wasn't beautiful. With her slim, boyish figure she did not even approximate to his conventional idea of woman. Yet something about her touched him deeply at this moment, as though he was seeing her for the first time as she really was: young and afraid and, no longer protected by her mask of boredom, desperately in need of being loved. A succession of images of the past weeks flashed across his mind; trivial incidents which, at the time, seemed to have no significance. But now, without him wishing it, they began to assume an importance he had not suspected.

'Was it Amaias's fault that the pack camel went over the edge back in the mountains?' he asked, roughly. 'Or that the *guerbas* were split open and the water lost? We've got to trust him, Carol.'

Her eyes flinched from the harshness in his voice. And then he realised how desirable she was; cursed himself for not realising it before when they had shared together the small tent against the night cold of the desert; or when they had sat round the small brushwood fires under the intense moon and the miraculous stars, listening to the love songs that Amaias sang alone by the hobbled camels as though remembering other nights near the tents of his people and the women of the *ahals*, the soft melody of the *imzhad* and the wild love-making. Listening also to the great silence that is the wind whispering across the desert, the soft, ghostly drumming of the wind. Then the world had been filled with the peace and solitude that, perhaps, only the Sahara can give. Then

150

was the time to have held out his hand to her, to enfold her in his own deep silence and in the immeasurable solitude of fulfilled desire. Now, even as his hand strayed towards her and his mind registered the flash of panic in her eyes, he became aware of Amaias standing silently beside him. The guide spoke softly to him in Tamahak.

'What's he saying,' Carol asked, her eyes looking anxiously in turn at the two men who were so alike in their enveloping Tuareg robes, yet so different.

'He says he can smell water,' Robert said, not looking at her.

'I don't believe you,' she cried, angrily. 'You've got to tell me the truth.'

He turned to face her. Amaias stood unmoving, a slight flicker of contempt in his eyes at the emotion her incomprehensible words had conveyed to him.

'It is the truth,' Robert said. 'These people have ways of knowing things we haven't. They tell by the feel, by the smell of the desert. We've got to believe him. In the old days,' he went on hurriedly, as though trying to convince himself, 'they used to send blind men to guide the caravans into the oases. By some infallible instinct they knew where the water was, knew where to dig down into the sand to find it. But all of them, all these people have the gift to some extent. Here, out in the desert, their lives depend upon it. We've got to believe him. Our lives depend upon his being right. And . . .' He let his voice trail away into silence.

'What?' asked Carol, dully. 'There's something else, isn't there?'

He looked at her, trying to remain impassive. The guide stood beside him unmoving, indifferent.

'Carol,' Robert said at length. 'Our camels are tired. We've been riding them almost continuously. They can't go any further. Not without a rest. Amaias must go alone with the pack animals. He'll unload them and take only the empty *guerbas*. We shall have to wait here. It's our only chance.'

The amazement in Carol's eyes turned suddenly to fear. Robert nodded to the guide. Without a word or a glance in their direction Amaias went over to the camels and began to remove their loads, laying them carefully on the sand, pausing a moment incongruously, almost lovingly, as he held Robert's tape recorder, the strange box which had captured and could give him back his own voice. Carol, white-faced, watched him.

'You can't,' she whispered hoarsely. 'You can't let him go like this. He won't come back. I know it. You fool!' – her voice rose in pitch – 'Can't you see I'm right?'

He moved towards her and put his arm gently round her shoulders.

'Carol,' he said quietly. 'Carol.'

But she jerked his arm away and faced him angrily.

'So that's it!' she cried. 'You think when he's gone you can do what I've seen so often in your eyes. Do you think I've enjoyed it, having your eyes on me all these weeks, watching me, never alone, no privacy, nothing, nothing! Do you expect me to respect you?'

Robert was stunned. Had it been so obvious, what he had only just realised himself? Without looking at her he said:

'I'll get the tent up. We must have shade.'

He left her and went over to Amaias. Carol watched him go, watching him as he listened to something the guide was saying. The Tuareg jerked his head towards the north-east and Robert's eyes followed the movement.

The afternoon was still and oppressive. A thick silence hung in the air. The sun, as it moved slowly westward, seemed diffused and opaque. Beside the camels the two men shook hands Tuareg fashion, the palms lightly touching, then quickly withdrawn with a snapping of thumb and forefinger – the salute repeated a dozen times as Carol had seen it done so often since coming to the desert. Alone, beyond the little world of the two men who seemed to understand one another, she felt calmer. Robert was right: it was their only chance. She experienced a sudden hot rush of self-contempt for her outburst, realising she had been unfair. When she examined her feelings she understood that what she had seen in Robert's eyes was only the reflection of her own desires. It was as though some secret part of her was being laid bare and she was aware of it as she had been aware of her naked body that day at the *guelta* by the strange city of rock. Lost in her thoughts she was all but oblivious of Amaias moving away, leading the camels. Without really seeing them she watched until they were lost to sight behind the dunes, moving slowly southward. The sound of tent pegs being driven into the deep, loose sand brought her back to reality. She went to stand behind Robert, suddenly aware of a need to be near him.

As he drove in the last peg and hoisted the small tent ready for the guy ropes to be fixed, Robert straightened up and turned to her, smiling wryly.

'This may not be much use,' he said. 'There'll probably be a sandstorm tonight.'

Carol slipped a guy over a long, light metal peg.

'Is that what Amaias was telling you?'

He nodded.

'Robert.' Her voice was subdued, shy. 'I'm sorry for what I said just now.'

He shrugged.

'It was true,' he said, trying to keep the thickness out of his voice.

'I don't care,' she said, laying her hand on his arm. 'I think I've always wanted it that way. Only I was afraid to admit it. If you didn't want me I think I'd hate you.'

He was silent for a moment. Then he said:

'Amaias left us the last of the water.'

Once more the feeling of self-contempt welled up in her.

'You love these people,' she said. 'You love and trust them.'

'Yes,' he said. 'I trust them and admire them. Perhaps it's a kind of love, too. They've been called jackals, murderers, thieves throughout their history. Probably it's true – but from them I've had only friendship and understanding. Amongst them I feel I'm free of everything I hate and despise in our twentieth-century world. Therefore I admire them and I trust them.'

The sky had become ominous, leaden. In the stillness it seemed as though the world was holding its breath, waiting.

The tent, now secured, looked small and white and frail against the towering, deepening gold of the dunes; beneath the darkening burden of the sky. Robert checked the hobbles of the two riding camels and removed their fragile and valuable saddles. The beasts had settled quietly, though with signs of apprehension, their legs doubled beneath their bellies. They snarled at him furiously from their knowledge of the impending storm, at being disturbed. Satisfied, he turned his attention to his equipment, praying that the dust-proof bags which held the tape recorder and camera would protect them. 'If we ever get out of this,' he thought to himself grimly as he carried the bags over to the tent.

To the north-east the sky gleamed like copper. Westward, the sun hung low in the heavens, a great orange ball. Carol shivered. From a great distance away she could hear, intermittently, a low-pitched moaning noise. Around her the desert was strangely still and hushed. She followed Robert into the gloom of the tent and lay down on her campbed, listening to the distant wind, trembling.

'I'm afraid!' she cried suddenly into the stillness. 'Oh, Robert, I'm afraid!'

'Don't,' he said gently. 'Please, Carol, don't.'

He knelt beside her, and laid his hand on her belly.

'I can't help being afraid,' she whimpered.

He kissed her and she became suddenly quiet, her fingers plucking at the hand caressing her sex through the thin cotton of her *gandoura*.

'Do you think this is love, Robert?' she asked. 'It's always seemed so inadequate before, so ephemeral – what has to happen now, I mean. The love-making, the purely physical thing between our bodies. Is it more than that?'

He disengaged his hand and stroked her hair, allowing his fingers to move downwards over her face, learning her small, not beautiful features; downwards to her breast and then her belly again, his hand lingering in the curve of her thigh.

'I don't know,' he said, hating himself because he did not want to think beyond this moment in which desire for her body eclipsed all that was past, all that might conceivably be future. 'There's a time when you can't name things any more, when it's sufficient to exist and to know that what is inevitable is right.'

He felt her move against him.

'I don't care,' she whispered.

She buried her face in his shoulder, giving up her body to his hands, blindly seeking his with fingers suddenly urgent.

'Please, Robert,' she moaned after a while. 'Please now. Oh please, please!'

He drew her down on to the floor of the tent between the inadequate campbeds and took her. As he entered her he heard the wind rising outside, but it didn't matter. And when she cried out against him that it wasn't the first time, that didn't matter either. There was only this: the striving and the falling and the darkness of their separate solitudes . . .

They must have fallen asleep. Suddenly, the wind was upon them; a low, insistent roar. It rose steadily to a shrill whine, then fell back only to rise again to a higher pitch, more intense, a scream. When they awoke night had already fallen. The air inside the tent was stale and stifling, filled with particles of fine sand. Choked by dust, groping for each other beneath the blanket of dark, they attempted to recapture the earlier magic of their bodies, but the moment had passed. Entry was difficult and slow and once Carol cried out against the cruelty of Robert's penetration. It was as though they had awakened to the realisation of the real world beyond them, the world of desert and thirst and aloneness.

They lay unmoving, wrapped around each other, listening to the wind reviling the tent's obstinate flimsiness; each conscious of the potency and frailty uniting them, until, almost with a sigh, the potency drained out of Robert leaving only the frailty and regret between them. In the darkness the sound of the wind intensified. Soon the storm must break.

'We have to go outside,' Robert said. 'I'll let the tent down and hope it won't blow away. We've got to see this through. We've just got to take it. The camels will be our only protection. When the storm hits keep your eyes and nose and mouth covered. Don't think of anything except that we've got to take it for however long it lasts.'

He felt Carol's fingers seeking his and the fear he sensed in her touch was the replica of his own fear. Then they were outside in the night with the wind tearing at them and the sand stinging their faces and bodies through their clothing. As quickly as he could, Robert dismantled the tent, fighting against the wind, and weighted it down with their overturned campbeds and the pile of stores and equipment. In the suffocating darkness the camels cried piteously, hugging the sand, necks thrust out in front of them.

The storm hit with unimaginable fury, a heavy curtain of driving sand blotting out even the darkness. Beside him, Robert could feel the trembling bundle that was Carol and reached out an arm protectively towards her. The movement seemed to draw all the fury of the storm upon him. Against its onslaught and the agonising pain of the sand on his face he huddled down away from her into his own solitude. Through the scream of the wind the cries of rage from the camels, lower pitched, against whose flanks they crouched, sounded feeble and remote. In spite of their veils, Robert's and Carol's eyes and ears, nostrils and mouths were tortured by fine, stinging particles of sand which lacerated their flesh and penetrated everywhere. Their eyes smarted and watered, then became dry, the eyelids thickly encrusted with dust. Blood began to trickle from their nostrils and a terrible retching thirst inflamed their throats, forcing their swollen tongues out between cracked lips. Yet before long the agony dulled and became that dumb suffering which is humanity's last resort and which raises it to the unswerving endurance of beasts face to face with annihilation. Time ceased and neither Carol nor Robert hoped or cared that the agony was subject to time or that, if they endured it, there must be an end to it because agony is suffered in time, because endurance becomes an end in itself.

Then, miraculously, endurance was no longer necessary and agony the realisation the wind had dropped. It moaned still, dismally, but the driving torture of the sand had ceased.

A pale moon appeared, lighting the scene balefully, coldly. 'It's not over,' Robert thought. 'It's not finished. This is just a lull. Oh Christ! it's not finished.'

He did not move but Carol, who did not know it was only a lull, raised her head and looked out from the protection of her clothing, coughing and retching. The sand, piled like drifted snow, only dry and terrible, against the heap of her body, cascaded from her back into the momentarily stilled desert, sifting down into her clothes, on to her flesh. She raised her head and surveyed through inflamed eyes the desolation in which they crouched.

Robert sensed rather than heard the strangled cry of terror which was all she could manage from her raw throat with the swollen tongue trying to push the sound, the urgent sound of her terror, through stiff, cracked lips. He felt her hand like a claw fastened on his shoulder, her broken nails digging into his flesh. Frightened as he never remembered being frightened before, he raised himself until he could see her face, livid and pale in the moonlight, her eyes unseeing with horror, only the whites paler than the pallor of her skin, staring beyond him, behind him. He knew that behind him there was something and an icy, unreasoning terror gripped him. He did not want to look, but he knew he must. Slowly, unwillingly, he turned and saw it too. It was as though the desert had spewed from its depths a century's death; as though the fury of the storm, lashing the dunes like the waves of a tormented sea, had washed up the human debris of its victims – not forgotten and unrecognisable in a shroud of bones, but clothed and eager in the moment of their deaths – on the shores of a single night.

Robert felt his bowels turn liquid and heard himself muttering meaninglessly, helplessly 'Our Father Which art in Heaven, Our Father Which art in Heaven,' over and over, aware of the nightmare of death behind him and of Carol, her face buried in his lap, silently weeping. Then the scientist in him was battling with his terror; the forces of reason striving to overcome the powers of darkness which had thrown his rational mind into the unreal half-world of Tuareg super-

157

stition, amongst the Kel es Souf and the unreasoning beliefs of primitive thought. For one terrible second he had almost believed this thing could have happened: that, in the holocaust of the storm, the horror could have been enacted silently, ruthlessly, around them during the hours when they had been driven beyond agony.

He let his eyes travel slowly over the scene of carnage, his gaze cold now with the reason of unbelief. Rationally, he began to count the corpses, his mind busy with detail: fifty, a hundred – it did not seem to matter. They lay stark in the fitful moonlight, eyes open and staring. Some were pierced by spears, the broken weapons still protruding from their breasts and bellies; others grasped swords, dead mouths twisted in pain or surprise at their deaths. A severed head regarded him fixedly, blind eyes looking at him with hatred. Half buried in the sand he saw the hilt of a sword and reached out for it. The cold, hard reality of the contact was reassuring. He remembered he was in the midst of the living dunes – dunes whose shapes and contours change, moulded by the wind; which travel across the face of the desert ten, twenty metres in the course of a year, depending upon their height, until their movement is arrested by size and weight, and the coarse, hardy roots of desert vegetation cover their graves. He knew all this, and yet . . .

Grasping the sword, he turned to Carol. At first he thought she had fainted, but when he touched her she trembled.

'Listen,' he said, quietly and distinctly. 'Whatever it is we've seen cannot be explained now. No, don't look. It's still there. But – and you must believe me – it's not malevolent. It's not evil. Terrible, yes. In the way tonight is terrible and what we've seen is only a part of this night. Time's a curious phenomenon and perhaps we've been thrown back upon time in some spiral of history to the aftermath of an event. For centuries there have been internecine wars in this part of the Sahara, between the Tuareg and the Tibboo. What we've seen is a point in time out of time. It isn't real. It's part of the nightmare of the storm. And the storm is returning. We've got to see it through.'

Carol made no answer. The wind was beginning to rise again and sand whipped at them out of the darkness, obscuring the outlines of the dead as the moon faded. Carol crouched beside him, small and alone and afraid. The sword in Robert's hand was cold and substantial and he shivered as he bowed before the returning storm . . .

It seemed he had been travelling through eternity among the dead, the cross-hilted Tuareg sword clutched tightly in his grasp, when he opened his eyes at last. Above him the vaguely outlined figure of Amaias wavered in and out of focus. Painfully, Robert raised himself up, choked with thirst. His eyes hurt and he blinked in the already strong sunlight, but the storm was over. Amaias held a drinking pan in one hand. With the other he was guiding Robert's mouth towards the relief of water.

'*Tamet,*' Robert whispered. '*Tamet.* The woman first.'

Amaias nodded and turned towards Carol. Gently, he raised her up and sprinkled water on her forehead and lips. She was pale, unnaturally pale, except for livid, painful lips. Robert gazed at her with pity. As he watched Amaias bathing her face she opened her eyes and groaned. Immediately, she shrank away from Amaias in terror.

'No,' she croaked through parched lips. 'No, no.'

Robert leaned weakly towards her.

'Carol,' he tried to say, 'it's Amaias. We're saved.'

The words stuck in his throat. With an effort he took the pan of water from the guide and placed it between her lips. She seemed to recognise him and, spilling some of the water, managed to swallow a little. Robert tried to smile at her but couldn't. Then Amaias took the pan from his unsteady hand and forced him to drink. The water tasted of sand, but it was as though he had been given back life, and his thirst began to recede.

The day was already hot and he judged from the sun it would soon be midday. When he began to feel stronger he sat up. Patiently, Amaias was bathing Carol's face again and moistening her lips with water, watching impassively the colour return to her cheeks. Robert looked around him.

Secretive and unbroken, the dunes stretched as far as he could see, their shadows receding as the sun climbed higher and higher. 'It was a dream,' he told himself, 'a bad dream.' Then his fingers touched the cross-hilted sword beside him on the sand and he knew it was no dream.

'I dreamed,' he said to the guide in Tamahak. 'I dreamed the dunes around us were covered with the bodies of warriors. It was a dream, wasn't it, Amaias?'

The guide became motionless, the pan of water halfway to Carol's lips. He looked around quickly, his eyes above the veil two slits in the dark strength of his hidden face.

'The ways of Allah are inscrutable,' he said. 'A dream is but the other side of a stone.'

'It was no dream,' Robert said, and showed him the sword.

Amaias gazed long at the weapon in Robert's hand; at the slots in the blade and at the two Tifinar' symbols below the hilt, the equivalent of the letter 'k', which proclaimed it to be *adadiglen*, a sword no coward would dare wield.

'The ways of Allah are inscrutable,' he repeated. 'There is a legend that tells us in the year of the plant we call *adreilal*, which gives good pasturage to our camels, the year when Agg-Mama, the king, died, a great war was fought in this desert. The legend tells also that the bodies of the dead were buried in the sand. And that when the fury of fighting is upon the heavens and the wind rises against the earth, for a time, the sand gives up its dead. I have never seen it, but this is what I have been told.'

'It is a legend?'

'It is a legend,' Amaias concurred gravely.

'We should not interfere with legends,' Robert said, fingering the sword.

'It is wiser not to,' Amaias agreed.

He watched Robert crawl a few paces away and then, with his hands, scoop out a hole in the sand and place the sword in it. He covered it with sand and smoothed out the surface of the desert, returning to it what belonged to it.

'See,' the guide said suddenly. 'The woman lives. Let us go from here. It is an evil place.'

Still weak, Robert rose to his feet. Some paces away Amaias's camel waited patiently beside the three pack animals, the *guerbas* slung from their sides swollen with the water that is life in the desert. A small mound in the sand close by caught his attention and he lurched over to it. Beneath the drifted sand he discovered his equipment and most of the stores, outwardly unharmed. The tent had disappeared.

Suddenly life and hope took hold of him again. He smiled at Amaias and the impassive veiled face stared back, devoid of emotion except for an almost imperceptible deepening of the grey eyes. The guide looked away and refilled the drinking pan, holding it to Carol's lips. She coughed and choked and then her eyes met Robert's.

'It's all right,' he said. 'We're going home.'

With Amaias's help he loaded the pack animals with the stores and equipment, and placed Carol in the saddle of her camel. She leaned weakly against the pommel and Robert, for fear she might fall, walked beside her, leading his own beast by the halter. Slowly they made their way southwards, their footsteps marking a brief record of the journey, which time and the wind would obliterate. They went with the assurance only water can give in the desert, away from the legends, from the living dunes, towards the world from which they had come – a world which would swallow them up and leave on its frontiers, watching them from the other world of the desert, the lone figure of the Targui, Amaias, his thoughts already turned northwards, forgetting them, intent upon distant mountains and the thin melody of an *imzhad*, distant in time and in space, the melody of the earth drunk with water.

CHAPTER THIRTEEN

THE TOWN, encased in its square of mud walls, looked like a toy set out on the edge of an immense table. To belie this first impression of the traveller approaching from the south, all around it dunes appeared as the distance diminished, their ridges capped with palm-frond mats, the furthest slopes gradual and wind-patterned, those nearest the town abrupt and threatening. It was as if the town were besieged by a fantastic sea; tall waves of sand caught and held in the imagination before they plunged down to engulf the walls. Palm trees, half submerged, raised their plumes like signals of distress above the dry, granular flood. Across the back of a dune, two sets of footprints, four round and two smaller elongated impressions led down towards the as yet unengulfed oasis beyond the town. Under the first palm trees of the criss-cross afternoon shade a camel and its owner, distantly seen, disappeared into the cool, miraculous glades that were haunted by the singing water flowing into them from the *foggarah*. Through the arched south gateway a small saloon car edged into the town and stopped. A handful of Arab children surged round it chanting, '*Donne-moi cadeau, donne-moi cadeau*' and, more specifically, '*Cinq francs, m'sieu. Donne-moi cinq francs.*' On the fringe of the half-uninterested crowd which had collected two bored French soldiers read, hands in pockets, the elsewhere impressive list of place names displayed, rather ostentatiously, on a board attached to the roofrack. They looked at each other, shrugged, and walked away.

Although there was little wind the air was full of dust which hung heavily in the atmosphere, obscuring the vision and making breathing unpleasant: *la cloche* the French called it. The streets were deep in loose sand and the car with its small, unsuitable wheels had sunk almost up to the axles. Each day the sand blew in from the desert and the dunes moved closer. In the town the people were used to it. And at night big lorries rumbled out through the gates, taking the sand back to where it belonged.

The driver of the car, Jimmie, accelerated and let out the clutch. The back wheels spun. The car stayed still. The crowd of urchins, almost on the point of dispersing, lingered hopefully. Jimmie revved up the engine again without success and then switched it off. Inside the car an argument began. After a moment Jimmie got out and took down the spade from the roofrack and stood looking doubtfully at the sand, his face reflecting suppressed anger.

'I told you not to stop here,' Patricia called to him from inside the car.

Jimmie turned a furious face in her direction but said nothing. One of the urchins tugged at his shirt and, having secured an unwilling attention, made signs that the car should be pushed.

'*Cinquante francs, m'sieu?*' he suggested.

Jimmie nodded, resignedly.

'All right,' he said. 'Tell me where the Bureau is.'

'*Le Bureau, m'sieu? Là bas.*' And the child pointed vaguely up the street.

'Is it far?'

'*Pas du tout. Voyez les ethels. C'est là.*'

Jimmie followed the direction of the child's pointing finger. Further along, where the street was lined with dusty tamarind trees, he could just make out through the haze an Arab soldier posted before an arched gateway.

'Good,' he said, 'and the hotel?'

The urchin considered him with narrowed, speculative eyes.

'*L'hôtel, m'sieu? C'est difficile, l'hôtel. Alors, j'irai avec vous en voiture et tout s'accomplit. Je connais bien l'adjudant Bonnier.*'

The hotel was obviously quite close, Jimmie thought. He would be able to get his directions when he reported to the Bureau.

'That won't be necessary,' he said to the small racketeer. 'Now, come on. Push.'

The car moved slowly forward and the back wheels found a grip. Jimmie thrust a fifty franc piece into a grubby palm which appeared over the sill of the open window. The hand disappeared. As the car glided more surely forward a babble of dispute arose in the cloud of dust drifting up from the wheels and reached thinly to the two occupants above the noise of the engine.

'Isn't it incredible,' Patricia said, 'how primary education in the desert manages to impart that unmistakable air of the Paris *gamin*.'

Jimmie grinned, his good humour restored. He had been driving for more than eight hours through deep sand, racing against the threat of a storm. More than anything he wanted to relax. After the formalities at the Bureau he hoped there would be the luxury of a shower, clean clothes and several anisettes before dinner.

'Our young friend back there certainly thought he was on to a good thing,' he said.

In front of the arched gateway, which was similar to the one at the entrance to the town, he stopped. The ground was firm here. An Arab soldier, in khaki burnous with red and gold epaulettes, hitched his leather belt and came over to the car.

'*Labès*,' Jimmie said, greeting him in Arabic – the only word of the language he knew.

The *goumier* looked coldly down at the small Union Jack flying from the bonnet.

'*Labès*,' he replied, noncommittally.

He waited for them to alight, then led the way to an office in a long, low building inside the gateway. He knocked once on the open door and motioned that they should enter. A grey-haired sergeant rose to his feet and regarded them, his hand indicating two chairs in front of his desk.

'*M'sieu, 'dame,*' he said, bowing slightly.

'We've come to report our arrival,' Jimmie said, fumbling with the zip-fastener of his brief-case. He produced their passports and the permits necessary for travel in Algeria. The sergeant took them, thumbed through the passports and read the permits carefully. The Arab *goumier* came forward, selected a rubber stamp and handed it to his superior. The sergeant stamped both passports, scribbled over the stamp, read through the permits once more, then placed them all together in a neat pile on the side of his desk.

'*Voilà,*' he said. '*C'est tout.* You must report before you leave, for the *fiche de controle.*'

'We want to leave tomorrow morning for Aoulef,' Jimmie said.

'For Aoulef? You are not going to Algiers?'

'No. We're making for Morocco. I believe it's safer to go across to Aoulef and then to Adrar and Colomb Bechar than to go to Algiers and drive along the coast road.'

'*C'est une voiture légère, mon adjudant,*' the Arab soldier said, deprecatingly.

'The route to Aoulef is difficult,' the sergeant said. 'There is one lorry each week. No tourists ever go there. For a small automobile it is very difficult.'

'We have the *Contrat d'Assistance,*' Patricia said.

The sergeant smiled.

'Ah, yes madame,' he replied, courteously. 'But that is for either the *ligne du Hoggar* or the *ligne de Tanezrouft*. To cross from the one to the other – that is a different matter.'

'Then we're not permitted to go?'

'I did not say that, madame. I was merely pointing out that the *Contrat d'Assistance* is limited. It provides simply for a single journey by one of the main routes.'

'We could take out another,' Jimmie suggested.

'It will not be necessary. When do you wish to leave?'

'At dawn.'

'Then I'll make out the *fiche* now.'

He drew a block of printed forms towards him.

'What is the make and registration number of your automobile, m'sieu?'

'Austin, E 1998.'

'And you expect to arrive at Aoulef, when?'

'How far is it?' Patricia asked.

'I do not know, madame. I have never been there. Perhaps 200 kilometres. It is far.'

'We should be able to do it in one day,' Jimmie said. 'If we don't get stuck too often.'

'Perhaps. Then I shall put down 18.00 hours tomorrow.'

The sergeant handed them back their passports and a copy of the *fiche*. He rose and extended his hand.

'Where's the hotel?' Jimmie asked.

'Go straight back down the road. It's on your left. There's no sign, but you can't mistake it. It's the only building set back from the road.'

He shook hands with them in turn.

'*M'sieu, 'dame,*' he said. 'I wish you *bon voyage.*'

The hotel, of rambling Sudanese architecture – even so far north into Algeria – was tolerably cool. The bedrooms had been built around three sides of a courtyard, away from the dining-room and bar. A faint patina of sand covered the floor and furniture in the lobby. On the wall near the reception desk a hand-painted poster invited the reader to visit Crepsville for *une grande fête* to be held the following week. Glass-fronted cabinets were filled with souvenirs for sale: leather bags, ornamented daggers, Tuareg sandals and colourful camel and goat-hair blankets. There was nobody about.

'Where do you think Crepsville is?' Patricia asked, idly.

'The poster says 60 kilometres from here,' her husband replied. 'And now I come to think of it, there was a track branching off on the way here with a notice saying CREPS. It's probably something to do with the oil companies. That's obviously meant to be an oil derrick on the poster.'

A head, turbanned, appeared from behind a curtained doorway, looked at them and disappeared. A second later they heard a voice calling out. Distantly, a woman answered.

'*Quoi? Qu'est ce que tu veux?*'

'*Des clients, madame.*'

A brief silence ensued. Then, nearer at hand, an angry muttering and the woman's voice crying '*Poussière, poussière!*' There was a loud crash. A moment later the curtained doorway emitted a small, rotund woman, flushed and breathing hard, a feather duster grasped in her right hand.

'Ah, *pardon, madame*, for keeping you. You wish a room for m'sieu and yourself?'

She bustled round behind the desk and unburdened herself of the duster.

'Yes, please,' Patricia said. 'Just for tonight. We are going to Aoulef tomorrow.'

'*Tiens!* It is far,' the woman said, handing them the police forms to fill in.

The *adjudant* at the Bureau said 200 kilometres,' Jimmie remarked. 'That's not very far.'

'I will ask my son when he comes. He may know. What a pity you will not be here for the fête. It will be amusing.'

'What is Crepsville, madame?' Patricia asked. 'We were reading the poster.'

'Crepsville? It is the town of the CREPS. They are looking for oil. It is very far from here.'

'The poster says 60 kilometres,' Jimmie said.

'*C'est vrai?* I have never been there. It is very far.'

'What a lovely hotel you have, madame,' Patricia said. 'It's so cool and pleasant in here.'

'*Merci, madame.* It is kind of you. We have only been here a few months, my son and his wife and I. The last owner shot a guest. But this terrible wind! The sand is everywhere. What can I do? Look. Here and here.'

She rushed round the lobby, her mouth pursed, blowing clouds of dust off the furniture. Jimmie and Patricia watched patiently, wondering when it would be possible to finalise the matter of their room. The door from the courtyard opened and a mild-looking little man of indeterminate age entered with a quiet '*m'sieu, 'dames*' and went through into the bar.

'That one, he's a CREP,' Madame said *sotto voce*, giving

167

up her battle with the dust. 'His wife is arriving today. That's why he's here.'

'Please, which is our room?' Patricia asked. 'I would like a shower. I'm a little tired.'

'A thousand pardons, madame. I will send the boy to show you at once. Yusef!' she shouted, '*vite, vite*. Oh, these Arabs,' she added, lifting her shoulders in despair, 'they're so lazy. Ah, here he is.'

She handed a key to the turbanned steward.

'*Numéro quatre*,' she said. She turned to Patricia. 'If there's anything you want, madame, do not hesitate to ask. My daughter-in-law will be here soon. She is very beautiful. She comes from Argentina.'

The head of the mild little CREP appeared round the corner of the entrance to the bar.

'*J'ai beaucoup soif, madame*,' it announced, reproachfully and disappeared again.

'*Moment, moment*,' Madame muttered, angrily. 'All day he drinks,' she whispered to the still waiting English couple. 'And when his wife comes – pouf! He can do nothing.'

She bustled off into the bar. As Jimmie and Patricia followed the Arab out into the courtyard her angry voice reached them faintly.

'*Tu bois. Toujours, tu bois. Et votre femme, Monsieur Fievet? Elle vient ici, elle pleurt. C'est comme toujours. Tu bois, elle pleurt. Pourquoi es-tu marié?*'

The bedroom to which Patricia and Jimmie were shown was not large. But it was a pleasant room with wide, comfortable beds and a cool tiled floor. There was no lock on the bathroom door but the water was cold and reviving. A bald-headed man wearing a towel round his immense belly flung open the door, murmured, '*Enchanté, mademoiselle*' and withdrew with a little bow. The sand was still blowing.

Clean, yet already conscious of the fine grit penetrating beneath their clothing, they strolled out to explore the town.

It was nearly six o'clock and the sun was low in the sky, a large, pale disc, its rays diffused by heavy haze. The Arab shops were opening and groups of silent men, their sharply-drawn features coldly sensual, not veiled like the Tuareg, stood about the streets or lingered unmoving in the doorways. Once, and once only, they met a woman hurrying along the sandy street, drawing her veil closely about her already hidden features as she passed them, edging fearfully away. A little naked boy with large, cretinous head and protruding belly, his eyes covered with flies ran out into the road, stopped and urinated with obvious pleasure. Then, laughing, sped away on unsteady, ill-formed legs, his head lolling from side to side as he ran. In the market place camels were being loaded ready for the departure of a caravan. A stench of dung assailed their nostrils and pale green camel flies buzzed round their heads. Above the noise of the market a camel snarled angrily, its neck outstretched in the sand, teeth bared, refusing stubbornly to rise. Every now and again it turned its head to snap at the driver who was beating its haunches monotonously, almost uninterestedly, with a long stick. Distantly, the sound of a bugle announced the hour and, from the flagpole on the roof of the fort, the Tricolor sank slowly. The day was ending. Accentuated by the haze a kind of dusk was falling over the town. Jimmie and Patricia turned and began to wander slowly back towards the hotel, hand in hand, at peace. The faint hum from the town generating plant mingled with the murmur of approaching night. The sky was clearing a little and one star could be seen, ringed with light, as though not quite in focus. Darkness, soft and velvety, came suddenly, masking the rough, red balustrade wall which divided the hotel grounds from the street. The ancient, disused well nearby showed up faintly in the light of an oil lamp set in the window embrasure of a house opposite and then was extinguished as the shutters swung to. The sound of a flute, thin and insubstantial, receded as they pushed open the hotel door that led to the bar. They were enveloped suddenly by harsh electric light, by the unique hubbub of voices that is found only in places where the French forgather in public. The door closed behind them. The night and the desert ceased to exist.

There were about a score of people in the bar, mostly soldiers. In a corner the bald-headed man sat at a table by himself, a glass of beer in his hand, resting his paunch on the low, wet marble top. The little CREP was at the bar with a pretty, dark-haired woman younger than himself. They were throwing dice. Behind the bar, a woman approaching thirty, olive-complexioned and very beautiful, was polishing glasses and watching the dice game. A big, amiable-looking young man with shambling gait and already thinning hair moved between the tables, collecting empty glasses, and joked with the soldiers. As Patricia and Jimmie approached the bar the pretty, dark-haired woman gave a scream.

'I've won,' she cried. 'Madame Charent, I've won. A Pernod, if you please. My husband will pay.'

'Oh, yes, monsieur will pay,' her husband grumbled. 'You win and I pay. And if I win? Who pays then, I ask you?' He raised his voice. 'Monsieur Charent, I appeal to you. There's no justice.'

The big young man, who was delicately balancing a tray of dirty glasses, went round behind the bar and stood beside his beautiful Argentine wife.

'True, Monsieur Fievet,' he said. 'Very true.'

'Oh, Alphonse,' Madame Fievet whimpered, her eyes brimming over. 'You don't love me. And tomorrow I shall be gone.'

She flung her arms round her husband's neck and burst into tears.

'They have been married fifteen years,' Madame Charent said to Patricia. 'They are very much in love.'

She poured out two anisettes and placed them on the bar in front of Jimmie.

'You are going to Algiers?' she asked. 'The road is very dangerous.'

'To Tangier,' Jimmie replied. 'And then to Spain.'

170

'To Spain? I would love to go to Spain. I am from Argentina. But you are English?'

'Alphonse,' Madame Fievet cried. 'You hear? They're English.'

Monsieur Fievet bowed with difficulty from his perch on the bar stool.

'Please,' he said, hiccoughing slightly, 'you will drink with us. This is an occasion. We were allies.'

Monsieur Charent was fiddling with the record player behind the bar. He selected a record and blew a cloud of dust from its surface. A gritty noise came from the loudspeaker, partly drowned by the opening bars of a popular song hit. It sounded odd.

'The motor's running too fast,' Jimmie said.

'True,' Monsieur Charent admitted. 'Very true. It is the frequency of the lighting. It is different.'

'You are so lucky, madame, to be travelling with your husband,' Madame Fievet was saying to Patricia. 'Alphonse and I, we cannot be together. I can visit him here, yes. But to go to Crepsville is not allowed. There is no water. It is all carried by lorries from here.'

'Have you just come from France?' Patricia asked.

'*Mais, non.* I have been to Zinder and back. It has taken three weeks. One travels on the top of an Arab lorry.' She shrugged. 'It is not far.'

'Whatever for?' Patricia asked. 'It must have been a terribly uncomfortable journey.'

Madame Fievet considered her fingernails.

'*Pourqoi?*' She shrugged again. '*Pour faire une petite promenade.* It is better than to stay here. Alphonse has his work. He is a CREP. Tomorrow he must return to Crepsville.' She sighed. 'I shall fly to Bordeaux. I have never been there before.'

'Is it far to Aoulef?' Jimmie asked. 'We're going there tomorrow.'

Monsieur Charent thought for a moment.

'It is far,' he pronounced at last. 'I will ask Monsieur Rouget. He is a transporter. He'll know. Monsieur Rouget,' he called across the room to the bald-headed man. '*La piste pour Aoulef – combien de kilomètres?*'

Monsieur Rouget removed his paunch from the table, stood up and brought his empty glass over to the bar. Jimmie had it refilled.

'*Merci, m'sieu,*' the transporter said. '*A votre santé.*'

'Can you tell me how far it is to Aoulef?' Jimmie asked. 'And what the road's like.'

Monsieur Rouget drank reflectively.

'It is, perhaps, 120 kilometres,' he said finally, regarding his empty glass. 'It is three years now since I have been there.' He waved a fat, expressive hand. 'Things change.'

'At the Bureau, the sergeant seemed to think it was nearer 200 kilometres,' Jimmie said. 'Are you certain?'

'Monsieur Rouget has travelled for many years in the Sahara,' Monsieur Charent said. 'He knows.'

'You are going far, m'sieu?' the bald-headed transporter asked as Jimmie ordered him another beer.

'They are going to Spain,' Madame Charent cried. She threw back her lovely head and danced around her husband, clicking her fingers.

'M'sieu,' a voice said, close to Jimmie's ear. 'Permit me to introduce myself. *Sous-officier* Archat.'

Jimmie turned and was confronted by an earnest, short-sighted soldier with thick, studious spectacles and a fringe of lank, black hair which reached almost to his eyebrows.

'You must pardon my temerity, m'sieu,' the soldier continued, 'but it is very important I should speak with you, since you are going to Spain. You see, I have a theory.'

'How interesting,' Jimmie murmured.

'Yes. It concerns the method by which one is enabled to understand the Spanish language.'

'You speak Spanish?'

'Oh, no, m'sieu. It was compulsory I should study it for the Baccalauréat. I did not pass, m'sieu, but I remember one lesson well: *Donde está su hermana? Señor, no tengo hermana.* Which is very true, because I haven't got a sister. Of course, I have a brother.'

'Does he speak Spanish?'

The soldier shook his head, sadly.

'Had we been permitted to continue with our studies . . . but that is another story. You don't speak Spanish, do you, m'sieu?'

'Yes,' Jimmie lied.

'That's a pity. You would have found my theory very helpful. You didn't mind my speaking to you?'

'Of course not,' Jimmie said. 'Let's have a drink.'

'Thank you, but I must return to my studies. You see, like you, I'm going to Spain one day. Goodnight, m'sieu.'

'He is mad, that one,' Madame Charent said, when he had gone. 'That's so, is it not, Monsieur Charent?'

'True, very true,' the reply came with another stack of glasses.

Madame Charent senior appeared suddenly, a duster in one hand, an empty glass in the other.

'A byrrh, if you please, Madame Charent,' she said to her daughter-in-law. 'Oh, this dust! It is everywhere.'

'He's won! M'sieu has won,' Madame Fievet cried. 'Two Pernods, Madame Charent. M'sieu will pay.'

'Champagne, Madame Charent,' Monsieur Fievet said, magnificently drunk. 'It is an occasion. Not every day do I win.'

'Can we have dinner soon, madame?' Patricia asked.

Madame Charent senior looked at the watch pinned to her silk-swathed bosom.

'*Tiens!*' she said. 'It is ready now. *Messieurs, 'dames, à table*. Dinner is served.'

Monsieur Rouget was aready seated in the small dining-room, a large napkin spreading from his throat down over the expanse of his belly. He looked up from his plate as Patricia and Jimmie entered.

'*Monsieu, 'dame*,' he murmured. '*Bon appétit.*'

It was a good dinner. In the middle of Paris or in the middle of the Sahara, it is all one to the French. Jimmie wondered, as he helped himself liberally to soup from the huge tureen, about the previous owner who had shot a guest and what would happen to all these people who characterised the expatriate communities on the fringes of the desert. He would be sorry when they finally reached Morocco. How long would it be before the Sahara was opened up to the full force of the world's greed for oil? Before improbable places like Crepsville were streamlined into the coldly economic power-producing plants the modern world demanded? When that happened, would this town – and others like it – be finally abandoned and the sand creep back from the desert, no longer hindered by man, to cover and reclaim the walls which had once belonged to it? And would the Fievets be replaced by hard-faced, gum-chewing efficiency? The prospect made him feel sad. It's probably because I'm English and sentimental, he told himself. I see everything through the eyes of a tourist.

The bar was almost deserted when they left the dining-room. Only a single light was burning. Monsieur Charent was busy upending chairs. In a corner the Fievets were weeping silently in each other's arms, a half-empty bottle of champagne on the table in front of them. Monsieur Rouget, the transporter, was seated at the bar, sipping at a glass of beer. He half rose to his feet as they peered in.

'*Monsieu, 'dame,*' he said, and belched loudly.

With murmured goodnights Jimmie and Patricia withdrew. The door to the courtyard closed behind them and the true silence of the Saharan night greeted them. The air was cool and fresh at last. There was no moon, but the stars gave a pale luminosity to the darkness. It was peaceful and reassuring. Jimmie put his arm round Patricia's shoulders. As they walked down the pathway towards their room, a roar of engines broke the stillness as the lorries rumbled out to carry the day's sand back to the desert. Inside their room, the door locked behind them, they undressed in silence. When Patricia finally came to bed Jimmie turned towards her in the dark, his hands seeking her. She lay quite still, as though listening, while he caressed her breasts, feeling herself begin to respond, her muscles contracting involuntarily when his hand rested

174

for an instant on her belly before resuming its journey. She caught it in her own and drew it gently away from between her thighs.

'No,' she said. 'Please don't.

'It's been so long,' he whispered, his voice choked. 'I love you, Pat. I want you.'

She let him have his way, surrendering her body to him while she remained somewhere else, hoping he would not notice, grateful to him for his gentleness, holding him tightly when he cried out, feeling suddenly maternal when at last he was still, the weight of his body crushing her into the mattress. She stroked his hair, conscious of tears behind her eyelids.

'Jimmie,' she said softly.

He tried to raise his head, but she held him close, aware of him still, deep within her, going away from her now, receding. From somewhere in the night the noise of the lorries reached her, growing fainter.

'I think I'm going to have a baby,' she said.

'Pat,' he began, then broke off, realising she was crying. 'Don't. It's all right. Everything's all right.'

'I don't know,' she cried out. 'I can't be sure.'

'You mustn't worry, darling. If it's true, I'm glad. It's what you always wanted. We'll make out.'

'Yes,' she sobbed, hating herself. 'It's what I've always wanted.'

CHAPTER FOURTEEN

IN THE encampment of the Kel Ikenbiben at the Oued Tiberler-larin on the eastern fringe of the Hoggar Tehit was lying on her stomach outside her tent, her unbraided hair falling into the lap of an old black woman kneeling beside her. The air had become cooler and the shadows were lengthening. Clouds were massing in the sky to the north and a capricious wind flung the lighter grains of sand into the air where the setting sun caught them and coloured them with a tired reddish hue. The mountains had already lost their harsher outlines. Soon it would be the hour of *aser*. The breeze ruffled Tehit's clothing. The sand beneath her was warm to her belly, relaxing and soporific. Yet she was restless.

Setera, a slave, regarded the girl impassively while her thick fingers deftly separated the long strands of fine hair and combed them out, using a special knife, broad-bladed and ornamented, that the Tuareg reserve for this purpose. Her gaze was weary, as if sensing the impatience underlying Tehit's submission.

'Ei, keep still, little wasp,' she muttered angrily when Tehit suddenly kicked up her heels and twisted sideways like a young, rebellious camel to slap at a stinging fly. 'If this knife should slip you will have many strings for your *imzhad*.'

Tehit relaxed again. She lay quietly and thought about her *imzhad*. Tonight she would play it at the *ahal* and Isef would sing to her, sad and plaintive love-songs which spoke of her beauty and desirability above the answering love and sadness of her violin. Perhaps she would make him jealous by flirting with other men. I shall be famous like Dassîn oult-Ihemma, she reflected dreamily, and the men will cry out: 'Tehit, little wasp, amuse us with your *imzhad*. Play us the melody of the earth drunk with water.' Everyone would crowd around her, admiring her beauty and her skill. She felt a sharp, agonising tug at her head and the dream was gone.

'Old fool,' she stormed. 'Take care.'

Her anger died as quickly as the pain in her scalp. She settled down contentedly as Setera began to rub melted butter, rancid and oily into her hair. She even smiled up at the old woman and Setera smiled back, gathering up with her rough hands the glistening tresses to begin the long and careful task of plaiting them.

At that moment Taouhimt came out of the tent and squatted down on her heels beside her sister. Tehit's senior by a year, her name in Tamahak signified 'gazelle', just as Tehit meant 'little wasp'. Taouhimt's adolescent body and graceful legs had justified the promise of her name. Her skin was the texture of marble, and pale compared with Tehit's darker, more vivid beauty; for the younger girl took after her mother, whose ancestors had come, generations ago, from among the Sonrhai people who then ruled from Agades to Timbuktu. Taouhimt took after her father. Her features were not beautiful: the eyes were set too far apart, the oval of her face a trifle too accentuated and her nose, like her father's, was too strong, too pronounced to be entirely feminine. Altogether, her features hinted at a nature cold and aloof. Only the sensuality of her mouth softened the impression, and even that could become thin and calculating.

Tehit looked closely and enviously at her sister's body, for the elder girl had taken advantage of the hour when the men were still out with the herds to come naked into the cool of the shadows outside the tent. What Tehit was seeking was some sign of the maturity she believed must be apparent in a girl who has become a woman. It was a year now since Taouhimt had attained the state of *asri* and become eligible to attend the *ahal*. Recently, the family celebration with its presents of beautiful clothes marking the attainment of puberty and entry into the state of *asri* had been held for Tehit. Tonight for the first time she would also be present at an *ahal*.

Setera, on the other hand, frowned at Taouhimt's nakedness disapprovingly. Slave and child of a slave, her mother had been ravished away from the rich and fertile lands of the Hausa south of the desert, and her devotion to these children of a noble tribe was tempered with envy. When, as a girl, she had been taken by their father for concubine she summoned all the knowledge of witchcraft learned from her mother to dominate him, so she would conceive a son who, when he grew up, might be fortunate and be taken by a noble woman as a lover. Setera had been born a slave and would die one, her children likewise. But if her child, a child engendered by her noble master, were male then could the issue of his seed find freedom in the loins and womb of a noble girl. Amongst the Tuareg the descent of the race is always through the woman, and thus the child of a noble girl and a slave is free – the freedom of the third generation – whilst the child of a slavewoman and a nobleman is not. Setera had borne a son and her hopes had risen. Then, scarcely a year old, the boy had died of a fever. Setera, whose name means 'by love', was supplanted in her master's bed by a girl taken in a raid upon the Fulani in the sahil region of Tamesna. Discarded, she grew old and bitter. Now she scowled at Taouhimt and scolded her.

'Such shamelessness is better kept for the tents,' she told her, 'where leopards prowl.'

Tehit doubled up with laughter, for it was well known that Taouhimt had lain with Amaias when he had come with the two heathens to the camp at the commencement of the last moon. It was also rumoured he was riding in again, alone as always, to take part in the *ahal*.

Taouhimt spat on the sand in front of the old woman.

'*Iebikatet*,' she sneered. 'You whose skin is old and used. You're meat for jackals, not leopards.'

Secretly she feared the old slave. Because she was ashamed as well as frightened by what she had said, she rose abruptly and disappeared into the tent. Setera sighed and her hand shook. Tehit touched her knee.

'My sister meant no ill,' the girl said. 'Tomorrow I will recount to you all that passes.'

Setera looked down sadly at the child who was to become a woman.

'Aie, little wasp,' she said, 'your childhood is soon over. Heed an old woman, for when Taouhimt rose to go into the tent her shadow fell across your face. Take care, little one. Take care.'

The tents of the *ahal* had been pitched on the far side of the *oued*, behind a slight rise and so were invisible from the encampment. The *ahal* and the sexual licence it portends is for the unmarried, the divorced and the widowed. As it is seemly amongst the Tuareg for the unattached to be promiscuous, so is it unseemly for wives and mothers and matrons to acknowledge its existence. Yet, as the sound of singing and the notes of the *imzhad*, punctuated by the shrill, exultant trilling of the women, the *terelilit*, carried across the wide, dry river it would find its echo in the yearning towards youth of the married women. Perhaps one, whose husband was absent, more daring than the rest – for adultery is punishable by death – would steal out into the night and, like a shadow, glide across the sands to keep an assignation with a man whose face she would never see, a man of whom she would know nothing beyond the weight of his body and the sudden warmth of his urgent seed, poised briefly between the cold, unyielding desert and a firmament of stars.

Instead of directing his steps towards the tents where the *ahal* was to take place, Isef began walking slowly away from the camp. He was aware of both tension and anticipation, and of a vague disquiet which was the memory of an earlier humiliation that made him feel acutely his youth and inexperience.

179

The clouds which earlier had hung over the mountains to the north were drifting westwards, carrying with them a promise of rain. The night air was clear and chill. The moon had not yet risen but the desert shone palely in the reflected light of stars – *Amanar, Tazzait-n-engoug, Ma-teregreg, Lenkechem*. Isef knew their names by heart. When he was away in the mountains looking after his father's herds they were his sole companions.

He loitered, listening to the silence of the night. Somewhere in the now invisible camp a dog barked briefly. Faintly, as though further away, yet distinctly he could hear the sound of a man's voice singing. Isef paused, turning his head and sniffing at the air. He thought of Tehit, whom he had watched for so many years across the barriers imposed by childhood, and swore to himself that tonight he would possess her. He thought also of Taouhimt, who Amaias had once stolen from him and how, instead of challenging him, he had slunk away into the night and, like a child, had comforted himself with his own hands.

Ashamed of the memory of the seed he had spilled that night into the sterile desert, he turned resolutely in the direction of the tents. Circling the camp, he came to the dry, crumbling banks of the *oued* where rank grasses, sharp and coarse, tore at his ankles as he strode through them down on to deep, loose sand. He was conscious of the blood surging in his veins; and the swing of the long, cross-hilted sword against his thigh kept pace with the rhythm of his pulse. Besides a *takouba* in its leather sheath, he carried, strapped to his forearm, a *tilek*. The arms he considered to be the mark of his estate as a warrior; though, not being a stranger and so excused, he risked censure for carrying them to an *ahal*. For the occasion, he had put on a richly embroidered *rati* of violet-blue and beige stripes and had arranged his darker blue veil with extra care, low over his forehead and across the bridge of his nose, to give the most striking effect. Only his eyes, coldly watchful, were visible.

His sandals made little noise as he came stealthily up out of the river-bed and moved towards the tents. Near the first one he stopped and stood for a moment, listening. Murmured conversation reached his ears and occasionally a tentative, brief melody from an *imzhad*. A man's voice was raised in laughter, followed immediately by excited chattering from the women. In spite of the darkness, Isef could distinguish a circle of figures grouped round the entrance of a tent some distance away. As he walked towards it the chattering ceased and a silence took its place which was almost audible. Out of the stillness a man's voice began a love-song, rising in wild arabesques until it broke, deeply falsetto, dying away in a cadenza, then rising again. Unnoticed, Isef moved forward to stand on the fringe of the group of robed figures.

In the entrance to her sister's tent Tehit sat listening dreamily to the conversation around her, the *imzhad* lying forgotten for the moment in her lap. There was no sign of Isef, but she was happy and proud because Taouhimt had been chosen *tamrart n ahal*, the title bestowed upon the leader of the festivities who would be sole arbitress of any dispute which might arise during their course.

The other women present were congregated around the tent, forming an excited circle on the sand outside. The men stood in small groups, not yet making a serious effort to flirt or indulge themselves in facile gallantry – a gallantry which would subtly change as the stars moved across the sky until the atmosphere became tense and charged with sexuality.

One other *imzhad* was present, belonging to the woman who had played earlier, Agisa, a friend of Taouhimt, ac-companying a man Tehit did not know. Certain of her superior skill, she was content to sit quietly, enjoying the luxury of her new clothes and believing herself to be more desirable than the other women – except, perhaps, for Taouhimt. So she kept her face half-concealed behind a long veil, the *tabarikant*, which had belonged to her mother. Of finely woven wool and imported from Tripolitania, the *tabarikant* was handed down from generation to generation and worn only for special occasions.

After a while, the men began to relax. Singly or in pairs, sometimes in a group, they would approach a woman and talk with her. Simulating indifference, they appraised her beauty with eyes narrowed above never relaxed veils, fingers still conscious of the hilts of the swords and daggers they had put off for the evening.

Tehit was talking to Elemech when she first caught sight of Isef among the group of men surrounding her sister. She recognised him by the sumptuousness of his *rati* and his nervous habit of adjusting his veil every few minutes, as though he were not yet used to it. Elemech had greedy, protruberant eyes and she disliked him. Nevertheless, she set herself out to flirt with him and laugh at his stories, all the time keeping one eye on Isef. Before long, Isef came over and squatted down cross-legged beside her. Tehit pretended to ignore him, devoting her attention to Elemech but with her veil so adjusted that the side of her face nearest to Isef was hidden from the former. At the same time she contrived to let her right hand lie open, palm upward on the sand beside Isef in such a way Elemech could not see it. Isef understood and, with his forefinger, traced a circle in the middle of the open palm telling her he desired her. Elemech, observing the expression on Tehit's face, mistook its meaning. His eyes glinted. Unseen by him, Tehit's hand fumbled for that of Isef and quickly traced a line diagonally across the palm from the base of the thumb towards the little finger. This said 'No'. Then, with just sufficient hesitation, she traced another line in the opposite direction signifying 'Later when we are alone.'

Just then there came a cry from across the circle of faces barely visible in the light of a newly risen moon.

'Tehit. *Ehl aner s imzhad.*'

The cry was taken up by others.

'Play for us, Tehit.'

'Who will sing?' somebody asked.

'Akemmi. Akemmi will sing. He is talking so earnestly with Taouhimt. He will sing about Taouhimt.'

Tehit picked up her *imzhad* from her lap, Isef and Elemech momentarily forgotten. She tuned the instrument by adjusting the loop of hair encircling the neck and the single cord, then drew the short, deeply-arched bow softly across the string. Dissatisfied still, she altered the angle of the bridge until the tension of the string was right. She moistened the bow-string with her tongue and played a short introduction, pausing on a dominant. From the darkness Akemmi's voice rose, harsh and resonant, against the answering notes of the violin. He sang a phrase quietly, trying out his voice, then stopped and cleared his throat. A chattering from the women broke out excitedly above the plaintive, waiting dominant. Then Akemmi sang and from the women came the piercing *terelilit*, swelling and rising in pitch, filling the pauses:

> 'I have lain down to sleep
> between two dunes
> whose beauty is less
> than the breasts of Taouhimt.
> I have searched for the stars
> her eyes have extinguished.
> Aie, Taouhimt,
> when your beauty
> blossomed into a woman
> a gazelle stood before me.'

As she played and listened Tehit was aware of a man standing close behind her. It was not Isef, who had moved back to give her room. The presence behind her in the darkness was too strong. Her hands, usually so sure of themselves, faltered as she followed the flight of Akemmi's voice.

The song faded. Talking broke out again, but to Tehit it sounded far away, beyond her. She felt she were suddenly alone, isolated from her sister and her friends, with only the sense of this presence behind her to give her reality. A voice deep and soft, almost a growl, reached her ears.

'Tehit,' it said. '*Ehl aner s azel oua m medouten.*'

From around her, voices cried out:

'Tehit, Tehit. *Azel. Azel.* Play us the melody of the earth drunk with water.'

Tehit was frightened, yet strangely calm. Her fingers, as

183

she again adjusted the pitch of her *imzhad*, were sure and untrembling. The first notes she played were clear and plangent like water. She almost felt them enter her. The *imzhad* resting lightly against her body, touched a resonance deep within herself. Then the melody leapt away joyfully, cascading its notes into the night. Tehit's fingers followed, checking it and urging it on, the earth saturated and fulfilled, quickening with the life that springs forth in the brief flowering of the desert after rain.

Abruptly, it ended. The ensuing stillness was heavy and ominous, like the stillness before a storm. Tehit peered up at the figures standing around her. Where were Isef and Taouhimt? She rose to her feet, laying her *imzhad* aside in the sand. Nobody paid her any attention. As she walked away she noticed the overcast sky, the moon ringed with a promise of rain. The ground beneath her feet became uneven and she stumbled, uncertain of where she was going. Some distance from the tents she stopped and looked round. She thought she could see a shadow sprawling across the slope of a dune, a darkness deeper than the night.

'Isef?' she whispered.

The shadow moved towards her, materialising silently into a figure taller, darker than Isef. She recognised him immediately, as she had recognised his voice calling for her to play to him. She spoke his name once, with a kind of wonder.

'Amaias!'

When he touched her his hands were gentle. She felt the sand cool against her back, his body hard and muscular against her breasts and belly. Nor did she make any protest or think again of Isef. She merely pressed upwards against his weight, pulling up the skirt of her *gandoura* and spreading her thighs as wide as she could to make it easier for him. Amaias lowered his face towards her and she lay quietly in his arms, their nostrils touching, inhaling each other's breath in the manner of the Tuareg, who do not kiss with the mouth. She drew in her breath sharply with mingled fear and anticipation when she touched and then took hold of Amaias's penis to guide him.

'It is a lance worthy of a great warrior,' she whispered into his ear. 'Do not keep me waiting, Amaias. Show me how you wield it. What could resist a blow from such a weapon?'

Her involuntary cry of pain at his first thrust changed to one of wonder. The awakening of her body was like the resonance of her *imzhad* vibrating to the caress of the bow, a melody that grew and throbbed within her as it had grown beneath her fingers in the circle of listening figures outside her sister's tent, as the earth is swollen and drunk with water after the rain. It ceased abruptly: just as her fingers had sought and found and held the last trembling note of the melody; just as the rain dies suddenly away and the silence which follows is quiet and deep. It ceased and the silence contained her.

Isef saw them almost before Amaias, his instincts scenting danger, rose from the sand to meet him. The younger man advanced slowly, sword in one hand, *tilek* in the other. Amaias, without hurrying, withdrew his own weapons from their sheaths where he had carelessly thrown them. He stepped over Tehit and took up his position a few paces away. Neither man spoke. Each accepted the moment, whatever its outcome. Tehit also. A man had taken her and now she belonged to him. He would fight over her. If he were killed, so also would she die. She lay and waited, her acquiescence neither fear nor indifference, as Amaias stepped over her and reached into the darkness for his weapons.

Isef rushed forward suddenly, striking at his opponent's head. He felt the shock in his arm and heard the ring of metals as his sword, parried by that of Amaias, was deflected harmlessly towards the sand. Almost at once he recovered and swung the *takouba* back as Amaias struck at him. Both fought with their feet planted firmly in the sand, giving no ground, each seeking for a chance to close under the other's guard and strike home with the dagger. Amaias, older, more experienced, fought calmly; pitting his cunning against the impetuous anger of the younger man.

It was over quickly. The sword in Amaias' hand shuddered

and twisted in his grasp, taking almost the full force of Isef's on the flat of the blade. It snapped off near the hilt. Isef raised his sword to strike again. He saw Amaias crouched motionless as he brought his arm swiftly down for the death-blow. Then there was pain burning into his flesh. He fell without a cry, the sword slipping from his fingers, his body half-supported by the blade of the *tilek* in his side which Amaias still grasped.

As Tehit rose to her feet Amaias withdrew his dagger and Isef's body collapsed grotesquely, rolled over on the sand and came to rest face upwards. His veil had fallen away exposing his face, pale and young and still expressive as though death had not quite caught up with him. A thread of blood ran from one corner of his mouth down over his chin into the folds of indigo cloth. Tehit stared at him as she would a stranger. She felt no pity. He had desired her and he had died: that was all. She watched Amaias clean the blade of his dagger on a fold of Isef's embroidered *gandoura* and then return it to its sheath. Retrieving the broken blade of his *takouba* he strode away into the night without a word or glance at Tehit.

She watched his dark figure merge silently with the desert and disappear, making no attempt to detain him. Neither did it occur to her that she should go with him. She straightened her clothing, brushing away the sand, and stood a moment longer looking down at Isef. The night was very still. Standing there above the dead man, feeling the life pulsing through her own body, she knew she would conceive. She turned at last and began to walk away, back to the camp where the evening meal was being prepared, for it was almost the hour of *azouzeg*. The tents of the *ahal* were silent and deserted when she went in search of her discarded *imzhad* and she wondered how Taouhimt had fared. With whom had she lain? Tehit tried to reconstruct in her mind the intricate confusion of her senses in that moment when Amaias had seemed totally within her power, but she found that he eluded her. Tomorrow she would ask Setera to help her: there were ways and means of bringing Amaias back. She wondered also why Isef had disappeared after his declaration, instead of remaining near her to sing the songs she had dreamed about, so long ago it seemed, when Setera was combing her hair. The palm on which he had traced the circle of his desire itched, and she scratched it abstractedly. If she had gone with Isef, would it have been the same? The same, sudden pain? The same surging torrent of pleasure like the flooding of a dry *oued* in the mountains? She only knew that if Amaias did not ask for her in marriage she would not be allowed to bring up a bastard among her people. The realisation her child would be strangled at birth if Amaias did not marry her made her shudder. She would have to go away. 'This that has been done to me belongs to me alone,' she told herself. 'I shall call the child Irzar, for he will bring me happiness.'

Before she reached her tent the first drops of rain fell. The desert received them gratefully.

CHAPTER FIFTEEN

'THERE HAVE been several instances of bodies being preserved in the sand,' the old commandant said to Robert. 'After all, climatic conditions are very favourable. It happened in the case of Père de Foucauld, for example. When his body was recovered years later from its grave in the Oued Tamanrasset for proper burial it was as though he had died that same day. Have no fear, Monsieur Lestrange, what you have told me is quite feasible. I've heard the Tuareg speak of it amongst themselves, but you're the first European who claims to have seen it.' He turned to address Carol. 'You're very brave, mademoiselle, to have undertaken such a journey. And Monsieur Lestrange is very lucky if I'm not mistaken, eh?'

Carol blushed. She had not yet accustomed herself to the fact that her relationship with Robert was taken for granted by the entire community of Anou-Mellen. Fortunately, at the hotel there had been no embarrassment for her over the question of rooms because she and Robert preferred to sleep on the flat roof where it was cooler. The old commandant's eyes twinkled as he lifted a tall square bottle from the table. It was almost empty and his expression changed to one of regret. He sighed.

'Come,' he said. 'There's still a little anis left. Let us drink a toast.'

He poured three generous tots and added water.

'To you, mademoiselle,' he said with an air of gallantry, raising his glass to Carol.

'Tell me,' he said to Robert, when they had drunk. 'Is it easy to buy anis in the Hoggar? I've heard it is so. Here it is very difficult.'

'It's easy enough in the hotel bar,' Robert said, 'but you can't buy it in the town. And, of course, it's expensive to buy it by the bottle from the bar.'

The old man gave Robert a melancholy stare.

'Life is becoming very difficult these days,' he said sadly.

He was silent for a moment, lost in thought. Suddenly he chuckled. He turned his old, blue eyes on Carol.

'You don't paint, do you, mademoiselle?' he asked.

Carol looked at him in surprise.

'Why, no,' she said.

The old commandant chuckled again.

'It's just that I'm reminded of something which happened a long time ago. But it's a story that won't interest you.'

'Please,' Carol said. 'I'd like to hear it.'

He looked at her gratefully.

'Then you must excuse me one moment,' he said, rising to his feet. 'There is something I must show you. I'll bring a lamp also. It'll be dark soon.'

He disappeared into the house, his broad sandals flapping on the dry mud floors. Robert reached out his hand to Carol. She took it hesitantly.

'Happy?' he asked.

She nodded uncertainly. For a moment neither spoke.

'Robert,' Carol said suddenly, the words coming in a rush. 'I've been thinking. About us.'

He squeezed her hand.

'What about us?' He grinned confidently. 'In a week, perhaps less, we'll be back in Paris. With all of the summer in front of us. The museum owes me leave. Once I've edited the recordings and written up my notes we can go away somewhere. Switzerland, or Denmark. Somewhere cool. We can laze away the days and go sightseeing like ordinary people. And make love in big cool beds. I won't even have to begin to think about coming back here before September. I may have to give a few lectures, that's all.'

Carol bit her lip.

'That's what I meant – you'll want to come back.'

'But, *chérie*, of course! It's my job. Next winter I plan to start off here and travel west through Tamesna to Timbuktu. And then north through the Adrar-n-Iforas to Tamanrasset. I'm hoping I'll be able to twist the museum's financial arm and get an adequate allocation of funds when they realise how much I've achieved this trip.'

She struggled to free her hand.

'You won't need me any more,' she said.

'Carol, I love you. What I've achieved is due to you. I don't just mean because of the money. It's so much more than that. You've added a new dimension to my life. I hadn't realised how alone I was. It's no longer enough just to live for myself.'

'I don't understand why you want to come back here, why it's so necessary to you.'

'I told you – it's my job. My livelihood. And because there's so much more to learn, to understand – before all this is swept away. Once France relinquishes Algeria and her African colonies – and she must do so: remember Dien-Bien-Phu – a whole way of life will disappear. The Tuareg will have to adapt or die. Their way of life suited our romantic and sentimental paternalism. It won't suit Ben Bela or whoever emerges from the present struggle as Algeria's ruler. This morning, near the mosque – the same building Heinrich Barth sketched over a hundred years ago, in spite of being constructed almost entirely of dried mud – I was nearly run down by a Tuareg driving a Peugeot. His eyes above the veil were hidden behind sun-glasses. As though he were a Kel es Souf emerging into the twentieth century!'

'Why would it be a bad thing if everything changed?' Carol said sulkily. 'I'm sick of this filthy place, of the squalor and heat. Do you expect me to come with you next time? That would be boring. I'm bored now.'

Robert's expression hardened.

'Don't you understand anything? About how I feel about the desert, about the Tuareg? About you? Perhaps you're bored with me.'

'I didn't say that.'

'But you meant it.'

'No, Robert. That's not true! It's unfair of you to say things like that. You're twisting everything, making out I'm in the wrong.'

'Aren't you?'

Carol remained silent. The light was fading. She could no longer make out Robert's features. Over her head stars began to show through the sky. Distantly, from the old part of the town the monotony of a drum sifted across the intervening stillness. It reminded her of the desert, of the strange sibilance of the restless sand at night. Suddenly she wanted to get up and go to Robert, to touch him, reassure herself. The sound of the old commandant returning kept her in her chair. There's still time, she told herself. Everything will be all right. But she wondered if time was on their side.

The lamp in the old commandant's hand flickered, its light bringing Robert's face into sudden sharp relief. Carol studied it anxiously, but it was devoid of expression.

'Voilà,' the old commandant said. 'You must forgive me, mademoiselle, for taking so long.'

The road leading north from Colomb Bechar was wide but the surface had been badly corrugated by heavy lorries from Oran and Algiers. The small, cream-coloured saloon clattered over the rough, undulating highway, leaving behind the factories and mines of this fringe-world of the Sahara the railway has penetrated. Patricia drove, with Jimmie sitting watchfully beside her, a small automatic pistol in his lap. The fighting had spread rapidly westwards towards the Moroccan border and, near Ain Sefra, a bus had been machine-gunned and a woman and child killed. Several ambushes had been reported in the narrow passes through the Atlas mountains on the road to Oran.

But there was a back way into Morocco, Jimmie had discovered, which crosses desolate, sparsely populated country lacking the barren splendour of the Sahara. The road leads, finally, to Ksar-es-souk and joins the magnificent highway which climbs over the snow-clad Atlas, through the Col du Zad to Meknes and Tangier.

A few kilometres north of Colomb Bechar the road forked and Patricia swung the wheel to the left. The surface became better, now they had left the highway. The country was quiet and peaceful. Not far from the road some Berber peasants were driving cattle. The sky began to lose its harsh, metallic glare and white clouds were piling up in the west. Only the landscape was ugly: gaunt and brown. On the horizon ice glittered in the sky as the first peaks of the High Atlas appeared through the haze. Jimmie relaxed and began to whistle: soon they would be across the frontier and into Morocco. Patricia turned to look at him. The road entered a narrow pass between boulder-strewn hills.

'We'll be in Spain soon,' Patricia said, her voice strangely choked. 'There's something I've got to tell you, Jimmie. About In Itaou. About René.'

'The sergeant? Go on, but for heaven's sake keep your eyes on the road or we shan't get as far as Morocco!'

Patricia just managed to avoid a large stone which lay almost in the middle of the road. The back of the car slithered sideways as she fought to control the skid, but the nearside front wheel passed directly over the landmine.

Sekefi agg-Ali dismounted and led his camel to the water-hole of Tesa-n-adou. He lay down on the sand and, reaching down with his arm, scooped up the brackish water with his drinking bowl. After the camel had drunk he slaked his own thirst and then set about replenishing his goatskin. Daylight was almost gone, but he did not intend to make camp yet. Thoughtfully, he examined the ground near the water-hole. The sand had been disturbed recently by a large caravan going south, but he soon found what he was looking for. For three days he had been following the tracks of the eight camels, always drawing a little closer to his quarry, not hurrying, but gaining persistently on them daily. It was not difficult, for one of the camels had gone lame. Always there was the telltale, uneven impression in the sand made by an injured foreleg. By the fresh imprints near the water-hole he estimated he could overtake them before dark and was startled to realise how close he had come. The broken *tanezrouft* with its undulating basins of sand and ridges of rock favoured his progress. In flat, open desert he would have been visible to those he was pursuing. Even so, stealth and caution were necessary: to stumble suddenly upon their camp would lose him the advantage of surprise. Had Tebbilel expected she would be followed? Or did she imagine he would let her escape so easily? By her sudden departure, inexplicable to everyone except himself, she had played into his hands. Abba ou-Sidi, in his distress, had not suspected any ulterior motive behind Sekefi's offer to go after them and appeal to Tebbilel to return to her father. And if none of them returned? The desert was big, but not big enough to separate two hearts. No one would look for them in the lands east of the Tassili-n-Ajjer. Cautiously, he led his camel, following the direction they had taken; moving soundlessly into the deepening night.

The small fire was dying, but the night was warm and Ehem did not bother to put on any more of the dead wood he had collected. He had made camp soon after dark at the side of a sandy basin sheltered from the wind by low hills of rock. He would have preferred to go on further, for the place made him uneasy, but Tebbilel had pleaded fatigue and he was worried about the camel that had gone lame. They had already eaten the meal Tebbilel had prepared and now lay awake on their bed of skins covered with the saddle blankets. Beyond the faint glow of the fire Ehem could make out the restless shapes of the camels against dark rocks. He raised himself on his elbows, half decided to go over and reassure himself they were all right. Then he felt Tebbilel's hand on his arm restraining him.

'Ehem,' she whispered. 'What is it disturbs you?'

'The camels are restless,' he said, straining his eyes against the darkness.

'It is only the wind. Tomorrow, when we find pasturage, they will be quiet. I, too, am restless, Ehem.'

She pressed herself against him, commanding him with her body. He felt her power rise up within him, subduing his uneasiness. He began to caress her and she settled into his embrace, her fatigue forgotten, conscious only of desire. Suddenly, one of the camels cried and struggled to its feet. Ehem thrust Tebbilel away from him.

'It is the lame one,' he said. 'Let me go. I must attend to it.'

Tebbilel rubbed her aroused body against him, then relaxed and lay submissive by his side.

'Go,' she said. 'Go, but return quickly.' She laid her face against his arm. 'Quickly, my husband.'

He rose and went over to the camels, moving among them, quietening them with his hands and voice. He stooped to feel the leg of the injured beast and, as he did so, a shape moved forward out of the darkness behind him. Ehem barely felt the pain in his back as the *tilek* entered and pierced his heart. He fell forward without a sound.

Tebbilel took no notice of the sudden commotion the camels made. She lay, relaxed and waiting, thinking only of the moment when Ehem would return to her. Soon she saw him, a dark figure, silhouetted in the dying glow of the fire. She reached out her arms towards him, her body impatient with anticipation.

'Ehem,' she murmured. 'Ehem.'

There was news now over the radio of increased rebel activity in the north. The road from Ain Sefra to Oran has been closed to civilian traffic following the ambush of a bus in the mountain passes. Near Colomb Bechar, on the road leading into Morocco, a landmine has exploded under a car killing the occupants, two British tourists. A rift was appearing between France and Algeria. The struggle is no longer a simple issue with the FLN: Algeria herself is divided and loyalties become increasingly difficult to maintain. America is exerting dangerous pressure in North Africa. The French government is again on the brink of collapse. France needs a strong man. Perhaps General de Gaulle will return from retirement. Only the army seems capable of action now.

The broadcast is a special bulletin from Algiers. René spins the tuning dial, sickened by this sudden encroachment of the world outside, but he can find only voices declaiming, accusing, justifying. The atmosphere is devoid of music. He felt restless, unable to settle. The world beyond the desert was suddenly closer, like a threat. He switched off the radio and prepared for bed, hoping he would sleep.

The next morning Adhan, accompanied by Elralem, comes into the fort. They standing watching René as he tops up a set of batteries he has been recharging, talking quietly together, not demanding his attention, as though their presence is accidental. His task finished, René turns to them, offering cigarettes. Elralem refused, but Adhan takes both. (René has learned never to proffer a whole pack of cigarettes for the Tuareg assume, quite naturally, that the gift is not limited to one and take possession of as many as can be grasped without exhibiting greed or discourtesy.) Adhan places one cigarette in his mouth – a gesture of friendship, since it necessitates the lowering of his veil – and the other in the hidden pocket of his *gandoura*. The three men squat on their heels. René strikes a match and holds it out to Adhan. Elralem draws vague figures in the sand at his feet with a piece of stick.

'*Salem aleikoum*,' he says, for they have not yet greeted each other.

'*Leikoum esselam*,' René replied gravely. '*Ma-t-oulid?*'

'Irmar,' Elralem announces, the formalities over, 'tomorrow we shall be gone. It is our wish that tonight you shall be with us. There is a rumour' – and he glances at Adhan – 'of an *ahal*.'

Adhan shifts uncomfortably on his heels and stares sullenly at the sand.

'Be that as it may,' the old man continues, 'for I am too

old for such things, it is fitting you should be with us. Besides,'
he adds slyly, 'Takkest commands it.'

René looks at him sharply, but Elralem's gaze is withdrawn,
intent upon the figurations flowing from the piece of stick in
his hand. So Takkest commands it, René repeated to himself.
Takkest, whom he does not want to desire, pale and beautiful
as many Tuareg women are, with skin smooth and finely
grained as alabaster. René has slept with Tuareg women
before – a man cannot live alone without recourse to a
woman, he believed – but always he has known a feeling of
aversion engendered by a body washed only with sand, by
the pungent odour of the rancid butter with which they dress
their long, gleaming hair.

'Takkest,' he says. It is a thought spoken out loud. He needs
to have a woman – and Takkest is very beautiful.

'Takkest,' he repeats the name and Adhan smiles.

'It means the "hour of *aser*",' Adhan says softly. 'The hour
when day joins the night.'

During that afternoon René sleeps fitfully, waking to a
harsh crackle of morse from the radio which he has left
switched on so as not to miss the evening call. There is a
message for him. Two vehicles are expected to arrive on
Thursday. He looks up at the calendar hung above the radio
set. A pencilled square tells him today is Sunday. There are
four days yet before they will arrive. He switches off the radio
and lights a cigarette. His eyes are still heavy with sleep. He
knows he has dreamed, but the dream is forgotten. All that
remains is a pleasurable feeling of lassitude and it reminds
him of the night to come.

'Takkest,' he murmurs. 'The hour of *aser*, the hour when
day joins with night.'

The significance strikes him suddenly.

'The hour of the Kel es Souf,' he says out loud.

The *ahal* is a poor affair, the skill of the *imzhad* player
indifferent; and when Adhan attempts a poem in praise of
Takkest his voice, hoarse and unmusical, breaks on the first

mordent. He clears his throat and begins again. Once more his voice falters. Unabashed, he tries a third time amid laughter and excited chattering, singing the phrase over and over and clearing his throat while the *imzhad* waits patiently on the sustained dominant.

René has been drinking and desire begins to mount up inside him, coiling and writhing in his belly as the fumes of alcohol reach slowly to his brain. Takkest appears not to notice him – as if she were avoiding him.

Then the *ahal* is over and René begins to walk back to the fort, angry and humiliated. As he reaches the darkness of the trees outside his kingdom Takkest is suddenly there in front of him, gliding like a shadow out of the night. She is smiling.

The sand was cold beneath them. René did not expect her to be a virgin, for the Tuareg have no word for this in their language. It surprised and strangely pleased him. He felt no aversion. Her body, naked and pale in the uncertain moonlight, was warm and intoxicating, her hair heavy and silken in his hands as he loosed on her yielding, demanding flesh a passion for too long pent up. Then, as suddenly as she appeared, she was gone.

They are gone. Only a disturbance of the sand shows where the tents were pitched. The day wears on. Habit induces in him a routine, but it no longer interests him. As the sun again sinks below the line of sky and the desert turns gold and rose-coloured, and finally indigo, he steals out on to the sand and stands listening, his eyes searching the darkening wasteland. He knows she is out there somewhere, beyond the rim of the horizon. And yet he could feel her near him. Far away, so distant as to be imagination, he hears the faint drumming of the night begin. Or is it the wind?

The two vehicles which had been signalled arrived on time. One was a small, unsuitable family saloon with advertisements plastered all over its sides, the other a tough, four-wheel-drive truck. The occupants, Germans, greeted René with overbearing enthusiasm. There were two men and a woman. She is pretty but older than she appeared at first sight. Her husband who drives the small automobile is short and middle-aged with a heavy paunch. He is aggressive and rude in his manner. With ostentation he proffered a pack of cigarettes and the other, a young man, blond and tall and arrogant, clicked his camera as René was about to take one. The clumsy stupdity of their publicity stunt nauseates him. Later, over glasses of beer they shout at him in atrocious French, boasting of the epic journey they are making across Africa; and try to prove to him that France will lose Algeria because she does not know how to rule. René lets the noise slide over his head and brought more beer from the refrigerator. The pot-bellied German is sick: he is too old for the heroic role in which he has cast himself. His wife examines René with speculative eyes, then turns to the blond Adonis with a scarcely veiled look of sexual complicity. René longed for the night to come when they would be gone, when he could wander out of his kingdom into the pale desert and watch the last light fade, hear once more the ghostly drumming begin. He knew one night soon she would come to him, steal out of the heavy shadows at the hour when day joins with night, the hour of the Kel es Souf.

Now it is night once more and a faint breeze stirred against his body. The desert has become withdrawn, impenetrable. The darkness fastens closely around its shallow contours. A star falls, tracing a line of sparks westwards like a pointing finger. Perhaps it was a sign, but René is unable to interpret it. Tonight he had wandered further than is his habit. In front of him the first kilometre marker of the trans-Saharan route loomed suddenly. The lights of the fort were distantly pale, but comforting. For a second he thought he could hear the sound of an engine away to the south and his ears strain against the silence. There is nothing. No traffic has been signalled.

The wind freshened and he shivers. Cold steals up out of the sand, chill against his bare feet. Yet he does not want to go back to the fort. It is too soon. As he stands there hesitating, out of the night and close beside him a shape looms, silent and ghostly. Then another and another. He felt a tremor of fear. But it is only a string of unattended camels which filed slowly past like a spectral caravan, moving southwards with unerring instinct towards the pastures of the Sahil. He laughed quietly at his fear, but his heart was thumping loudly.

'Takkest,' he whispered to the night. 'Takkest.'

He sees her pale form glide out of the shadows and steal softly to his side. Her body smells of sand. A pungent, rancid odour clings to her braided, glistening hair. She smiles. With a cry he went towards her, his arms outstretched. But it is only the shadow of the kilometre marker, thrown by the rising moon, that he is embracing on the cold sand. And even this eluded him . . .

POSTSCRIPT

THEY TELL me the well at In Itaou is full of sand now, like the mouths of the dead. The love-birds, too, are gone. With each cycle of sandstorms the walls of the fort would have surrendered a little more to the weight of the encroaching desert. Even the crazy Sudanese guardian will have passed on into the oblivion of his briefly recorded passage, like a message traced momentarily with a stick in the sand. If his message was obliterated leisurely by the wind it is the most he could have hoped for. The erasures of men are more brutal.

Our universe continues to change – and remains the same. For the Tuareg, the illimitable confines of the desert – where, season by nomadic season, they follow the dictates of scant pasturage and the obsession of the warrior, who knows only how to kill – are the finite boundaries of the world. From Agades to In Salah – from Anou-Mellen to In Itaou, or any of the other fictitious places which exist elsewhere in the Sahara under different names – they will pursue their obsessive migratory purpose. That they now contrive to do this wearing dark glasses and driving Peugeots is merely one of those practical jokes of which the Kel es Souf are fond.

I do not know what happened finally between Robert and Carol. Or to Tebbilel. Perhaps she has returned to her people, now that the old woman, Abakout, is dead. Her father would welcome her and Sekefi agg-Ali was an ambitious man. Can one ever conceive of endings that are final? Amaias I see occasionally. He is still a guide, but growing old now. He talks about a son he fathered on a girl of the Kel Ikenbiben ten or twelve years ago and has the crazy idea of sending him north to Algiers – or even to France – to school if he can borrow the money. His years in prison for killing a man in a fight at the Oued Tiberlerlarin have affected his mind.

As for the sergeant at In Itaou, René . . . Well, he remains too close to my own divided psyche for comfort. Perhaps we know too much about each other – or think we do. Perhaps, like the Kel es Souf, we are people of illusion.